A Remarkable Stillness

Jonathan Rush

Published: 2023 by The Book Reality Experience
An imprint of Leschenault Press
Leschenault, Western Australia.

ISBN: 9781923020313 – Paperback
ISBN: 9781923020320 – eBook

Cover Design by Brittany Wilson | Brittwilsonart.com from original imagery provided by the author.

This book is inspired by the true love story of

Win and Teddy Bisset

and is dedicated to them and their daughter,

Laura

For Julia, Lennie, Jeremy and Edward

A Remarkable Stillness

Though lovers be lost, love shall not;

And death shall have no dominion

Dylan Thomas

1.

Win

I love the piano.

I first love the piano because of Miss Ida Roberts. A childish love at first followed by adolescent fumbling. And then the piano eventually returns my love because of Sol, the Great Solomon, Solomon Cutner - the world's greatest pianist. An adult emotion as intense as two young lovers entwined in passion. Like Teddy and me.

Oh, dearest Teddy, *mon âme*. But I'm running ahead of myself. Teddy enters much later into my life.

My father, Pop, notices first I might have an ear for music. One Saturday afternoon he chuckles when he catches me on the swing hanging from the roof over our shady veranda - one of my favourite places at weekends - pendulum-like I am gently daydreaming about a boy I remember from Sunday school. Even though the Jarrah timber floorboards are dark brown, they are so well-polished that I can clearly see the reflection of my shoes, like black swans gliding in to land on a still, evening river.

I hear my mother and her sister in the sitting room playing in tandem on our old battered, family piano, their laughter almost swamps the sound of the cicadas singing in the oven-hot garden. I cock my ear and start to hum along to the tune, gently waving both hands like a conductor.

Pop interrupts, 'Do you like music, Win?'

Do I like music? I've never thought about music as something to be liked or disliked. I struggle to answer. To buy time, I gaze down at the book Pop has in one of his hands, his thumb marking his place. He's always reading. He's a bookworm my mother says. I know him as a gentle man of few words. My mother more than makes up for him.

Our awkward silence is broken by one of the chooks in our back yard who clucks loudly and impatiently.

Pop and I giggle.

He brushes his typically Scottish sandy hair back, his blue eyes pressing me for a serious answer. 'Well, Win?'

'I'm not sure, Pop.'

My introduction to music had begun not long ago with my Methodist Sunday school choir. But my mother got wind of the fact I had a crush on one of the boys. A common baker's boy, he drove a delivery cart for his father – definitely not *the right sort* for me. Even though the minister, Nicholas Richards, is a family friend, my time at Sunday school is swiftly terminated. I take some solace by writing moodily to my German penfriend, Wolfgang, in Dresden.

The day has been baking hot and, in the evening, it is still too warm to sleep inside. On my camp bed on the veranda, I overhear my parent's anxious voices floating out from the kitchen.

They are talking about me.

Again.

'Do you think Win would like piano lessons?' says Pop.

'Can we afford it?' my mother replies as softly as she can - so I hear every word.

'Look, she needs to find something she's good at. She's not like Lloyd…'

I know my parents worry that I risk being overshadowed by my younger brother. They are right. Even aged ten, Lloyd shows great promise: Arithmetic, English and Art. Top of the class. Good at football. Good at everything. What's more, he's a good-looking young boy.

Sometimes I can't help hating my brother.

2

Me? People say I've got Pop's lovely bright eyes, but I don't think I'm particularly striking. As I moodily brush my dark, wavy hair, the hand mirror shows an average-looking, young teenage girl. A few pimples. Not pretty, not plain. Not fat, not thin, not *anything*. I know I'm intelligent but not a particularly good student.

I hear my mother scream in frustration. Average is not her favourite word. But there it is, writ large all over my school report coupled with: *Could do better.* My mother fumes as she reads my teachers' words.

My mother: the Mater. It was Pop who starts calling her by the Latin tag. He explains to Lloyd and me that it's short for *Materfamilias* - the mother of the family.

My mother laughs but even I, a gauche thirteen-year-old girl, can tell she enjoys the backhanded compliment that it is she who is really in charge of the family.

Bright and brave is the Mater, always determined to prove anything a man can do, a woman can do just as well.

Or better.

She hits the headlines as the first woman to fly, daringly, in a small, rickety biplane, from the west to east coasts of our enormous continent. She hears that Pop is going to fly with a pilot called Kingsford Smith.

'I'm coming too,' she demands, impatiently brushing off Pop's attempts at refusal.

Lloyd and I are bundled off (as usual) to our grandparents to allow Pop and the Mater to fly away.

To everyone's surprise I do well enough at school to win a scholarship to Perth Modern, a top state academy. Not good enough for the Mater though – she decides that she would rather send me to a private school. So, I am sent to the Methodist Ladies College.

'We're Methodists,' she says firmly, explaining her choice.

'Haven't you got any friends?' the Mater snaps at me one weekend, irritated to catch me moping around the house by myself. She has a point. Yes, I did get along with two or three other girls at my new school. But not well enough to call anyone my best friend.

I don't take long to notice that some of the other pupils are picked up from school in bright, big cars and whisked off to homes much larger than ours in places with expensive names like Peppermint Grove and Mosman Park. Although I know we are not poor, for us money is tight. Pop works for something in the city centre called the ABC. Not a special school for children finding it hard to read, but a radio station.

Our family bungalow is in a sandy, windswept seaside suburb called Cottesloe, not far from my school on the other side of the railway line.

Money is scraped together for private lessons. Pop asks the Mater why I can't be taught the piano at school. She sniffs that she finds the school's music teacher, 'Average.'

She interviews a Miss Ida Roberts who the Mater tells Pop comes highly recommended.

Now it is time for me to be inspected by my proposed teacher.

Miss Roberts looks at me sternly, her hands in her lap, back ramrod straight, all her cardigan buttons done up, sitting on a wide stool in front of a piano. So shiny is its wood, I can see my scared, wide-eyed face looking back at me.

'Could you please hum a tune for me - anything you like?' Miss Roberts' lips smile but her eyes are hard, summing me up.

I panic at first but then I remember a Sunday school hymn: *All things bright and beautiful.* My voice quavers.

'Again,' Miss Roberts says, her voice kinder. But her eyes remain as hard as granite.

4

This time she conducts me and I obediently follow her lead, my eyes on her hand, my voice steady now, rising and falling. Miss Roberts puts her hand down. The room is still.

But then I surprise her and the Mater by suddenly, without invitation, singing the words. In tune. Miss Roberts' eyebrows rise. She swivels around, her sensible shoes squeaking on the floor, to face the keyboard and pats the stool. 'Here, come and sit down next to me, my dear.'

She takes my hands and lifts them upright against hers, palms pressing palms. She measures my fingers against hers. A smile flits across her face as she registers how long mine are.

'Now push your fingers one by one against mine,' she orders.

I press each one hard in turn. We are both surprised that even my two little fingers are quite strong. Miss Roberts smiles again, her eyes softer now.

Miss Roberts suddenly releases my hands - they drop quickly onto the keyboard. I gasp as static electricity hits my fingertips. Shocked I jerk back. I sense the Mater judging me. I gather myself and spread the fingers of both my hands wide on the smooth, cool keys. I press each finger firmly down on the notes, one after the other and laugh with pleasure at the ten different sounds. At that instant I know, just know, I have found my best friend.

Miss Roberts turns round and nods at my mother.

'Winfred?'

Silence! My head is swimming in happy expectation.

Then again, 'Winfred?'

'Yes. Sorry, Miss Roberts.'

'Let's begin, shall we?'

Behind me I know the Mater smiles.

Definitely, not Average.

2.

Sol

I hate the piano. Inside, my stomach churns as I weep for something I once loved.

I remember *the Monster*, Miss Verne, talking to Sir Henry Wood at my first orchestral concert at London's leading venue, The Queen's Hall. I play a Mozart concerto. The audience is stunned, ecstatic. They clap for five minutes when I stand up and bow, bobbing up and down in my little boy's sailor suit.

It is 1911 and I am eight years old. 'I told you he was another Mozart,' Verne says afterwards, talking over my head as if I am not present.

Wood nods. 'His phrasing is quite exceptional.' I remember him saying.

A special piano is built for me by the German company, Blüthner, with narrow keys for my small hands and high pedals for my feet. Such is my precocious fame that a year later I give a private recital to our King and Queen. My appearance at Buckingham Palace generates huge interest.

After another sell-out concert, I am presented with a little tricycle. I pedal around the stage, giggling in excitement. The audience stand and cheer, sharing my glee. It's the last time I have fun for many years.

By now, four years later almost aged twelve, I am an experienced concert pianist. I will become the best in the world Verne tells me, provided I continue to work hard.

I often look back to how my young boy's love turned to teenage misery. Even though we were poor, my musical parents had a small upright piano in our home in the crowded Spitalfields area of London's East End. I was the seventh and youngest son of my father who in turn was the seventh son of my Polish grandparents.

My mother teaches me to read music when I am five. Father is too busy slaving away as a master tailor. At my Free School I am soon picking out tunes. My talent catches the headmaster's eye.

I overhear mother whispering excitedly to my father in Yiddish that I must have tuition.

I am enrolled with Miss Jacobs in the more genteel area of Canonbury, North London. My parents scrape together her charge of 14 shillings and sixpence for each lesson. It takes me an hour to walk to her house. But my parents are dissatisfied with Miss Jacobs. With the support of my headmaster, they turn to the Jewish Education Aid Society for help.

I am taken to Miss Mathilde Verne's piano school in her large West End home. It feels about as far away as the moon from our Spitalfields ghetto. Yes, the Monster says she will accept me. Her fees are high but the charity says they will stump up the money. I find out later that my parents sign a five-year contract with Verne, giving her total control of me until I turn thirteen. My parents will not get a penny from her.

I move into a small bedroom at Verne's house. I quickly become her star pupil. I am locked in a room and forced to practise up to four hours a day.

By myself.

Practise, practise, the Monster demands.

I perform fifteen concerts a year in the major halls around the country. By the time I am twelve I have a repertoire of the same number of concertos. I perform ten of them in one Promenade season. I am told that because of the Great War, it is difficult to obtain foreign performers and I am needed to help Sir Henry Wood fill the gap.

Verne is making a lot of money as my concerts sell out. She insists I wear clothes which make me appear younger than I am. I feel like a performing monkey.

Verne, the Monster; I hate her.

Wood smiles kindly as he conducts me at Promenade concerts - I recognise sympathy and traces of guilt in his eyes as he sees that I am exhausted.

I witness how Verne's school prospers. Parents queue up to have their children taught by her. Society people, celebrities and aristocrats. Verne's fees rocket but still the demand rises for the person who teaches the famous child prodigy.

Although my orthodox Jewish parents have reservations about mixing with heathens, I start school lessons at the King Alfred School in Hampstead - mornings only. The school provides me with welcome relief and the other boys and girls call me a genius, but I have no spare time to make friends.

One summer's evening during my precious rest time, I am trudging back to the Monster's school, my leaden feet scraping along the Old Brompton Road. I see a large, polished motor car waiting outside Verne's front door, its engine purring. I shrug my shoulders - as her clients get richer, the cars get bigger. I enter the entrance hall of my prison and climb the stairs.

I open the door of the first-floor drawing room and see Verne is teaching a pretty girl, sitting next to her on the stool.

The girl looks up. 'Hello,' she says, smiling happily at me.

I blush and look down at my shoes. Apart from my sisters, who I hardly see, I have had no practice with speaking to girls.

Verne stands up and puts her arm around my shoulders and orders, 'Solomon, this is Lady Elizabeth Bowes-Lyon. Say hello.'

I mutter a greeting, avoiding her face.

The girl giggles at my name.

'I've never met a Solomon before.'

She pauses. 'What do your friends call you?'

Friends? I don't have any.

Verne interrupts. 'Solomon has to practice very hard. He has little time for play.'

The girl's face registers sympathy. 'You're famous, aren't you?'

I nod.

'Miss Verne, may I have a glass of water please,' she asks politely although it sounds more like a command in an accent unknown in the East End.

The Monster leaves us alone.

'Oh, come on, let's have some fun,' the girl says, plucking my shoulder and skipping out of the room.

I follow.

She hops onto the banisters with practised ease and slides downwards, her buckled shoes slapping onto the tiled ground floor as she lands.

She looks up and sees my hesitation.

'Come on Scaredy Cat,' she shouts.

I slide down to join her.

I realise I'm having fun.

I'm laughing.

I'm playing.

The Monster appears on the landing and shrieks down, 'Solomon! What are you doing?'

Her face a mix of fury and fear.

A year ago, when I was eleven, I summoned up enough courage to protest at the long hours I'm forced to practise.

Verne screamed at me, 'This is how Clara Schumann taught me. And this is how I shall damn well teach you!'

The Monster got my parents to support her. 'Sol, do as she says. She has made you famous. And she is very powerful. Everyone knows her in the music world. You mustn't antagonise her. Besides it is not long to go before her contract finishes.'

Now, I lie in my bed and pray for release from my misery. Too drained to sleep, my head is ready to burst as it spins in a nightmarish vortex of pianos and hundreds of Verne's screaming faces. My hands shake and my legs twitch.

Oh how I hate Verne. Now I hate Clara Schumann too.

I doze off eventually and dream of Elizabeth Bowes-Lyon.

I realise that the music the Monster now orders me to play is demanding, even for an adult. Sir Henry Wood tells Verne I can't continue playing. After one concert I feel groggy. My eyelids droop and I'm on the point of fainting.

'The boy's exhausted. He needs rest,' Wood says.

But Verne does not agree and takes me back to the prison.

'Don't worry Solomon. You've got the flu. You'll feel better tomorrow,' she says.

I collapse onto my bed and snatch a couple of hour's fitful sleep. I'm scared that I am finished, washed up. I shall be thirteen in a few weeks and my contract will finish. The Monster blithely assumes I will continue to work with her.

How wrong she is.

The next morning the monster raps on the door. 'Solomon, get up. You're late.'

I dress and stumble downstairs, ignoring breakfast in the dining room. Unkempt and unwashed I leave Miss Verne's house forever. I walk home. I shall never mention the Monster's name again.

As if in a dream, I head off in what I know is an easterly direction along the Old Brompton Road. I walk along busy streets, sobbing. A few kind mothers turn from their children for a second to ask me, 'What's the matter dear?' I shrug them off and eventually find myself trudging through Green Park. I pause outside Buckingham Palace and clench the black railings. I gaze up through white-knuckled fists and see the heavy-curtained window of the drawing room where I played when I was nine years old.

I sigh despondently and look around, unsure which way to go.

'Oi, move along young man,' a policeman's gruff voice orders with a rough hand on my shoulder.

'Hello, what's this then?' he asks not unkindly as he spots my tear-stained cheeks.

'I'm lost,' I stammer.

'Where's home?'

'Spitalfields.'

He inspects my features. 'Ah yes, my son. *Vy* am I not surprised?' he chuckles, mocking my East End, Jewish accent.

Nonetheless his face is friendly as he points the direction I should take. 'Follow that road down to Big Ben and turn left at the Thames. Keep going until you're just past St Paul's.'

He pats my back and I nod my grateful thanks. St Paul's Cathedral I know well. Not far from home. Two hours after my escape from the Monster I knock on my parents' door.

'Solly,' my mother screams at the sight of my face.

In a corner I see the old family piano. I shiver in hatred. A doctor is called and he recommends complete rest. I recover slowly.

My contract with the Monster has expired, so I am free to play for myself. I am thirteen now and intelligent enough to think for myself. Despite everything I am determined to continue playing as much as possible.

A big mistake.

My brother, Jack, accompanies me to my concerts. Verne's agent agrees to work for me directly and has no difficulty in arranging recitals around the country, even though the Monster writes to many concert halls warning them not to book me.

I give nearly forty concerts in 1916 and continue in 1917. Audiences still flock to see me, but I know that I am no longer a prodigy, rather a young teenage boy struggling to play like an adult.

Verne returns in nightmares and I collapse once more.

I am pale and thin and cannot sleep. I am exhausted and hold my head in my hands, weeping. My mother has to dress me. I recover enough to stand and walk unaided. I learn later that the doctor said I had suffered a nervous breakdown.

I mope around but refuse to touch our piano. I try to help my father with his tailoring but can't concentrate. Even menial shopping errands for my mother defeat me.

Hanukkah coincides with the Christmas holiday. It is a disaster. I normally gobble up my mother's delicious doughnuts and potato salad. Now I chew them as if they are gravel. My elder siblings scrutinise me as if I'm an animal in a zoo. I sob when I cannot answer even the simplest of questions. The doctor examines me again and prescribes me pills to make me sleep.

My father takes me to see Sir Henry Wood who takes pity on me.

He coughs diplomatically. 'Perhaps your son was, er, *persuaded* to play too much, Mr Cutner?'

Do I catch a glimpse of, in both my father and Wood's eyes, a flash of complicit shame?

'Like many prodigies, Solomon is finding the transition to adult playing difficult,' Wood continues after a moment's silence.

'He needs to rediscover his love for the piano,' he tells my father. 'Otherwise, his great talent will be wasted.'

Wood strokes his well-manicured beard thoughtfully. 'Yes, I think I've got it. I know someone who might be able to help.'

He stands up and puts his hands on my shoulders. 'You'll have to forget the way Miss Verne taught you, my boy. He is Russian and was a student at the Leschetizky School in Vienna.'

I look blank and feel embarrassed later when I'm told Leschetizky was the greatest and most famous piano teacher of all time.

3

Win

I have a boyfriend. And the Mater approves. His name is Grahame Deans and he comes from the *right sort* of family, she says.

I meet him and his mother at the Mater's Cottesloe tennis club, where I'd started taking lessons. I pick it up quickly and am soon in demand for mixed doubles from the boys. Grahame and I click from the start. I giggle to myself when it is Love All. He's a good-looking lad and I adore him with all the intensity of a first teenage crush.

But Miss Ida Roberts most certainly does not share the Mater's opinion about Grahame. 'Your mother tells me you have a boyfriend,' she sniffs, looking over her spectacles at me. 'I presume that's why you are not practising enough.'

I know I am her best pupil and she has high hopes for me, which makes her doubly critical if she spots the slightest drop in my standards. She's a stickler for hard work is Miss Roberts.

But it's the start of the long summer holidays and Grahame's father has a motor launch, *The Victory;* she's a beautiful, fast boat with swept-back lines, a gleaming white hull and a glistening varnished cabin.

These are Huckleberry Finn-halcyon days.

Together with Grahame's Christchurch school mates, we cruise around the Swan River, sometimes taking trips over to the other side and down the Canning River into Bull Creek. Nearer to home we drop anchor and don swimming goggles and flippers. Grahame shows me how to shove a small gidgey – a trident harpoon - down catfish holes. At my first go I do not press hard enough and a wounded catfish, as long as my arm, catapults out of its hole, gargoyle mouth furiously agape with streaming tendrils and poisonous spikes sticking out. It nearly grazes me.

We swim ashore and sell our catch to the fish 'n' chip shop. Grahame winks and tells me the owner sells them as tasty Tailor fish at about five times what he pays us.

Choosing a fair-weather day, we venture out in *The Victory* on the undulating limpid sea to Rottnest Island - a glistening limestone jewel, about ten miles off the coast.

The island is peaceful with dozens of beautiful little coves and beaches. We hire bikes and cycle around, stopping where the fancy takes us. Swimming, splashing and flirting between white rocks and in sparkling blue waters, screaming at the sight of a giant ray scudding over the waves and big goannas disturbed in their holes. The small, almost tame, Quokkas scoff our picnic leftovers.

I experience the sensual joy of my first kiss. A proper kiss and a boy's arms wrapped around me tightly and feeling his excitement.

And me wanting to respond and go further.

But the Mater's blunt words of warning explode in my ears. 'Do not, I repeat, do not forget your decorum. Never, ever have sexual intercourse until you are married.'

She'd wag an admonitory finger in my face. 'Unwanted pregnancies are shameful. Remember the girl is disgraced, while the boy gets off scot-free.'

We head home, the afternoon sea breeze has whipped up waves and it is blowing behind us, pushing *The Victory* up and over the frothy crests. I hold Grahame's hand and watch Rottnest as it slips behind us, a shimmering streak against the ruddy evening sun. Grahame lets go of the wheel to hug me tightly. The launch veers off course and tilts alarmingly, surfing at an angle down a big wave to the sound of jeers and cat-calling from our shipmates. He kisses me hastily and puts two hands back on the wheel. Will I ever be as happy as this again I wonder?

The Mater sees that Grahame is distracting my attention away from my lessons. She warns me not to let my piano slip. 'Win, Miss Roberts tells me you could be very good. Not everyone is lucky enough to be born with the talent to be good at everything' - I know she is thinking of my brother - 'we have to concentrate on what the cards have dealt us.'

She sees my doubtful face. 'Win, Grahame is a nice young man. Trust me, there will be others. But your piano will be forever.'

Pop has replaced our old honky-tonk piano with one of Germany's best, an upright Rönisch. I step up my practice. Miss Roberts confirms my decline has been arrested. The Mater is satisfied.

Grahame tells me towards the end of the holidays, 'I'm losing you to that bloody piano, aren't I Win?'

I shrug my shoulders in dumb reluctant agreement.

Every now and then I correspond with Wolfgang in Dresden, but really, I'm writing partly to Grahame.

I practise and practise. My fingers get stronger and even more nimble. All the pieces I play for Miss Roberts must be learnt off by heart - she's a stickler and mistakes are rewarded with sharp intakes of breath. One day, Miss Roberts corrects my playing of Debussy's *Clair de Lune* while sitting next to me, 'No Win, like this,' she says, pushing my hands aside.

I heed her correction and replay my piece. As I play, it dawns on me that my version is better than hers. This has not happened before. Finished, I place my hands on my lap and silently reflect on the repercussions. Am I being disloyal to think I'm now better than Miss Roberts?

'Yes, yes, good, that's right Win,' Miss Roberts nods her head in approval. But sideways on I glimpse something unfamiliar in her expression. Yes, in her eyes there is now not just a teacher's pride but also the faint sad recognition that I am now the better pianist.

I realise from here on there will be a tacit unwritten agreement that her role shall be less of a tutor and more of a coach. Am I too arrogant to think of myself as a swimmer going to the Olympic Games, who is already very good, but needs a coach to train rather than to teach?

To my surprise this tacit change in Miss Roberts' status invigorates me. Freed from being merely her pupil, I have the motivation to practise even harder. The Rönisch needs regular retuning. My prowess soars. I realise I am good.

Very good.

Oh God, how I love the pianoforte. Grahame is but a pleasant memory filed away for future reference.

One day the Mater comes to hear Beethoven's *Moonlight Sonata*.

She and Miss Roberts sit together on one side of the room observing me. This is not just a mother coming to check on her daughter's progress, rather a rigorous inspection by two tough women.

I address the keyboard.

The room is silent.

I start.

I finish and bow my head.

To my ears, Beethoven had never been played so well by me.

Silence.

I stare down at the keyboard. Why are they so quiet?

I swivel around.

Miss Roberts looks at me calmly. 'Well played Win. That was very good,' she says matter-of-factly, as if playing all three parts of the *Moonlight Sonata* from *memory* happened routinely.

The Mater looks at me. 'Win, that was,' she hesitates, 'excellent.' She smiles and nods her head in confirmation of her verdict.

'Excellent, excellent,' I scream silently. The Mater has never before used that word to describe anything I've ever done.

Another incredible thing happens. Miss Roberts's smiles. Yes, she actually smiles. Not for long, but smile she does.

'I think you're ready to take the national examinations, my dear,' says Miss Roberts.

It is 1935 and I am 17.

4.

Sol

Imagine a middle-aged Russian man and a young teenage English boy walking in a leisurely manner through Kensington Gardens, a large park in the centre of London.

The two exchange few words, content to enjoy the summer sun as it flickers down through the tree-lined path, casting amusing, dappled shadows on the crunchy, gravel footpath beneath their shoes. Promenading, or even ambling, would be a more accurate description of their slow, relaxed progress. Now and then the Russian tips his hat in response to a polite, 'Good afternoon,' from a passing jovial father, proudly escorting his wife and children.

Their reverie is interrupted by a faint, cheering crowd.

The Russian says, 'The state opening of parliament, Solomon. They must be shouting for the king and queen.'

He turns to me and sighs. 'You English are lucky. We murdered ours.'

He inclines his head quizzically, 'Of course, you played for yours, didn't you?'

I nod, smiling politely, and say they were very nice. I don't mention the Monster was with me and played as well.

The Russian, Simon Rumshisky, and I continue our gentle walk. He looks at his feet and begins to exaggerate the action of walking by placing the heels and then the toes of his shoes firmly down, in the manner of someone who is preparing to say something meaningful. He pats me on the arm to draw my attention to a sprinting athlete training in the distance and remarks, 'It is rightly said that one must learn to walk before one can run.'

He sees that I am mildly disappointed - even at fifteen I had expected something more profound.

Simon gently strokes his beard. 'One might do even worse than learning to walk properly before learning to play the piano.'

He leads me to a bench next to the large Round Pond. 'Come Solomon, let us sit down and compare the principles of walking and pianoforte playing.'

Cupping his chin in a hand, he says, 'Solomon, I want to introduce you to the application of kinesiology to the playing of the pianoforte.' He chuckles at the confusion playing on my face.

'I promise that this will become clearer as we progress.'

He weighs his words carefully. 'In the act of walking one does not point the toes but rather curls them up and grips the ground with sufficient strength to support the whole weight of the body.'

He smiles affectionately at me. 'Are you following me, young man?'

What on earth is he talking about I ask myself. I do not wish to seem rude, so I nod my head slightly.

'Now apply this principle to the arms, hands and fingers in pianoforte playing and find that the fingers curl on to the keynotes from the knuckles down and, whilst bearing the weight of the arms and hands, produce various quantities of sound according to the varying degrees of strength used.

'In walking one uses the minimum of effort to gain the maximum of distance. And so it should be with pianoforte playing. Therefore, we may discard the unnecessary parts of the body from the very beginning and send them into a complete state of relaxation, or lack of tension. Bear in mind that lack of tension produces comfort and that the kinder we can treat our piano, the better quality of sound we are going to have.'

Rumshisky finishes his, what shall I call it, lecture? He looks expectantly for my reaction.

I am nonplussed – lost for words. What am I supposed to say?

He then astonishes me by taking his shoes and socks off, stretching his legs out as far as he can from the bench. He rests his legs on his heels and wiggles his toes, pretending to play along to a tune which he hums.

'Come on Solomon join in.'

I show embarrassed teenage reluctance but expose my pink feet to the world as well.

'*Parfait,* Solomon, your toes play very well!'

We both laugh loudly as somebody's inquisitive poodle, startled by the sight of twenty human toes, scuttles away, yapping, back to its owner.

'Now let's play a Mozart concerto. You hum.'

This is silly but great fun. I giggle as our toes wrestle with the glorious sound.

More seriously he says, 'Solomon, look how I'm keeping my arms and hands relaxed while my brain concentrates on my toes. You can also see how very strong our toes are going to have to be to play properly, can't you?'

And so begins Dr Simon Rumshisky's rehabilitation of a grievously damaged, former child prodigy.

I am told to imagine walking along a giant keyboard jumping from note to note and another time to place the piano's hammers and strings on the outside and the keynotes inside the piano. We sketch levers, seesaws and hands to illustrate in detail the internal machine of the pianoforte and the mechanics of fingers and knuckles. I learn to play with the inside of my fingertips not on the outside and my elbows are tucked into

21

my ribs. My finger strength increases even more through lengthy and exhausting, painful exercises. Simon, as I now call my friend and mentor, teaches me to use my increasing strength not to play the keyboard but to aim right through it.

'Remember, we drop our wrist to its lowest extent, relying on finger strength to do the playing, and only raising our wrist in order to drop it again for relaxation.'

And then, 'The same control is applied on leaving the note as it is on approaching it.'

I am intrigued by his method. My head is clear and I realise I am enjoying the mental and physical challenge. A month passes before Simon considers that I have grasped enough of his theory and practice.

'Solomon, think of a beautiful note like a rocket, soaring upwards until it reaches its climax where it separates into thousands of lovely stars.'

I close my eyes and see hundreds of fireworks exploding across a black sky. I see and touch their bright beauty.

My love for the pianoforte has returned, deeper and more intense than ever before. The Monster is banished, never to be spoken of again.

I bow my head. 'Thank you, Simon.'

'There there, my boy,' he says, patting my shoulder, as I sob quietly, my joy unrestrained.

Simon gently guides me for almost three years. After a lesson one day, we exchange a look. There is no need to say anything. We both know there is nothing more he can teach me - I have been rehabilitated by the world's best.

'Take a holiday, Solomon. I shall write to a friend of mine in Paris. I'm sure he'll agree to – how should I say – polish your playing.'

I leave for Paris in the knowledge I have been taught by the world's greatest living teacher of the pianoforte but with the excitement of a highly trained athlete who has heard the bell signalling the last lap.

Even though I am eighteen, my mother insists on accompanying me to Paris. In one of Paris' smarter *arrondissements*, we follow a *concierge* who leads us to the front door of a large apartment.

We are welcomed in by a young man whose face we immediately recognise. He is as famous in France as a pianist as I am in England. His name is Lazare Lévy.

I sit quietly as my mother and our host engage in preliminary pleasantries. I observe Lévy: he has a beaky nose, high forehead, bright eyes and very frizzy hair.

'Simon Rumshisky tells me you are very talented, Solomon. Like you I was young when I started playing. I had an English teacher in Brussels who helped me at the beginning. She taught me English too.'

Lévy takes my hands and smiles. 'Well, look at these broad hands and thick fingers. And look how long your third and fourth fingers are. You've got every other pianist beaten before you even start.'

He waves vaguely at the photographs on his piano, showing the various triumphs of his career. 'I showed promise and entered the *Paris Conservatoire* when I was twelve.'

He leans forward, hands on his thighs. 'I made my adult debut only when I was twenty.'

Explicit in his face is criticism that my concert career, which started aged eight, was far too early. My mother looks down, avoiding Lévy's eyes.

'I would be delighted to help you, Solomon.'

I nod.

Lévy smiles. 'Excellent. I'll take you, if I may, and show you some lodgings which I think you will find agreeable. The landlady is, in fact, the daughter of my concierge.'

My mother agrees a rent. I find out later that Lévy has made a big contribution. And he charges me not one *sou* for his lessons.

Once Lévy is certain I have my bearings, I am allowed to wander around at will. Even though it is a couple of years after the Great War's Armistice, the French capital is still celebrating victory in a mood of feverish gaiety. Dashing French officers, resplendent in blue and red uniforms, fill the bistros, brasseries and cafés and stroll with their female companions, eyes in eyes and hands in hands as they flirt down the Champs Elysée.

Lévy introduces me to his social circle - musicians, composers and artists. Some are famous too, like Saint Saens and Marcel Dupré, the Notre Dame organist. It seems they have all heard of London's *wunderkind* and welcome me as a friend.

Oh, how I envy Lévy's easy, languid enjoyment of the piano as he plays a funny variation of *Für Elise* and his friends sing along to his renditions of popular songs. They all smoke and drink a fizzy wine. The sitting room is a bubbling, hazy mecca for the *bon ton* of the artistic Parisian world. Nobody seems to care much when I surreptitiously sample my first champagne and cigarettes.

I arrive in Paris as a young man. At Lévy's *soirées,* women kiss me on the cheeks and call me *chéri*. I have my first sexual encounter – a tipsy woman kisses me on the lips and I taste her tongue. This is heady stuff for an eighteen-year-old, whose life has been completely dominated by music for so long.

More conventional tuition now begins with Lévy and Dupré, those two giants of the world of music. I take time off to go regularly to Longchamps with my landlady who has a passion for betting on horses. I quickly share her enthusiasm and win money on her tips. I sip champagne with her and smoke cigars. What a swell I've become!

I love Paris but know it will not be forever. Another two years pass while I shout every day what a lucky fellow I am. But I realise I will soon have to leave and take my chances to prove myself.

After a lesson with Lévy, I play a Chopin *Ballade* for him. He listens intently, registering every note.

Then quiet. My nerves are on edge. I sense a critical moment. I hear a clock ticking. *Notre Dame* bells ring in the distance, registering a quarter past the hour.

'That is not how I would play it,' Levy says softly.

'What should I change?'

Lévy smiles proudly, shaking his head in approval. 'Nothing; don't alter a note. That is your interpretation. Stick to it. As many people will like it as if it was mine.'

A moment for reflection.

Then he takes both my hands in his. 'Solomon, it is valuable - priceless even - because it is what *you* think of the music and not someone else's interpretation that you have been taught to repeat like a parrot.'

He stands up and kisses me on both cheeks. 'My friend, you are ready. Music lovers will welcome you back and delight in your talent.'

My London adult début is in the Wigmore Hall in 1921. My recital is a triumph. My mentors and benefactors Rumshisky, Lévy and Dupré join in the standing ovation. I do not invite Mathilde Verne.

5.

Win

'*YES*,' I yell as I excitedly push myself to-and-fro on the veranda swing. A fresh copy of *The West Australian* lies fluttering at my feet as I swoosh by.

My brother, Lloyd, trots out from the kitchen, wiping breakfast from his lips. 'Are you alright Sis?'

He picks up the newspaper and reads that I have, '*gained the distinction of securing the highest marks in Australasia in the 1935 examinations held by the Royal Schools of Music, London. Miss Marshall was also awarded the Royal Schools scholarship for the piano, tenable for two years at the London College also the Royal Schools of Music (Sydney) prize.*'

'Bloody Hell,' my fourteen-year-old man-of-the-world brother gasps and looks hastily around, but our parents are out of earshot, still eating breakfast.

'I'm going to London and I shall play in the Queen's Hall in front of the King and Queen,' I say grandly, trying not to smirk.

'And, you never know, I might invite you, provided you behave.'

Lloyd grins and shows his delight in the only way boys are capable of towards their older sisters; he punches my arm.

'Have you told Pop and the Mater yet?'

'Not yet. Anyway, the Mater will say I'm too young. But I'm allowed to wait two years. I'll be getting on for twenty then.'

Of course, I am not old enough. But I take the exam again the following year in 1936 and come first once more. I am just five points short of a perfect score.

Even Miss Robert's can't believe my result. 'Ridiculous,' she sniffs proudly.

But the Mater forces me to wait until I am twenty-one before I can go. God, how we argue! But she is adamant.

'Win, get on with life, the three years will pass quickly.'

She is right. My reputation as Australia's best young pianist enables the Mater and Pop to find plenty of work for me. I play as an accompanist on ABC wireless broadcasts for overseas artists during their Australian tours. I'm in demand also for local ensembles attempting ambitious piano concertos. I begin to save money for London.

The Mater insists I learn to drive. Pop – who hardly drives - occasionally lets me chauffeur him to work and I drive the Mater to the shops.

Pop lets me try a cigarette and a glass or two of wine, while I play at home during the Mater and Pop's parties. Oh, what a thoroughly modern young woman am I!

I keep up my tennis at the club. How satisfying it is to eye up the white ball bouncing towards me on the green grass and whack it back as hard as possible, humming to myself, 'I'm going to London.'

I see Grahame with his new girlfriend regularly at the club. He grins ruefully. 'How's that bloody piano, Win?' I can see in the mirror that I'm now an attractive young woman – the teenage awkwardness and pimples are long gone. But the club's young men know that inviting me out for a date is pointless – 'That Win, she's going off to Pommyland to become a piano player,' I overhear them say, as if I am mad.

Across the road from the tennis club is a large, sprawling Spanish-looking house. I know it belongs to somebody called de Bernales who made his fortune from gold mines.

I also know Pop definitely does not like him. 'I'm beginning to think Claude de Bernales is a tax-dodging crook. He's persuaded thousands of people from overseas to invest in his land on the promise of gold in the ground. It turned out to be fool's gold.'

'Poor Helen,' the Mater says about Mrs de Bernales.

Of course the Mater knows her. She knows everybody.

'I think you're being a bit harsh, John. I've heard from Helen in London. She seems confident that Claude will clear his name. In any case I shall write to Helen asking her to keep an eye open for Win when our daughter is over there.'

Pop is silent.

So the Mater is already planning to keep tabs on me when I'm studying in London, is she?

The Mater imposes another condition when my twenty-first birthday approaches - a chaperone. She hears that Alice, the daughter of a distant acquaintance, is going to England to visit her aunt. Her family passes the Mater's due diligence tests and, glad of companionship, the young lady, ten years older than me, accepts the responsibility of shielding me from sinful temptation.

As we say our goodbyes at Fremantle, the Mater presses a small package into my hand. I open it later in our cabin and find a bottle with a blue label of her favourite perfume, Guerlain's *Jicky*. She's written a card:

"The best in Australia deserves the best in the world."

I smile at that. It would have taken the Mater a lot to have written something so complimentary about me.

Alice and I join a small group of pensive fellow-youngsters gathered at the ship's stern, waving last goodbyes to friends and family. Some are going to visit relatives, some to study and others to travel. Our emotions, exhilaration and apprehension, are as mixed as the turbulent white water whipped up by the thundering propellers below us. Some of the girls wipe a tear or two away and a couple of young men clear their throats. Many of us have never left Western Australia before, let alone the whole continent. Now we are heading *Home* – the centre of the British Empire and Anglophonic culture. Although I'd always found it odd, I know my parents, and most of my generation, including me, still called England, *Home*. Not surprising, perhaps, that the colonial term still had currency, when most of us had British grandparents, or even parents. Our sun-tanned arms and legs contrast with the white faces of the ship's English crew. Returning to our cabins, we suppress giggles at the strange North Country English accents of some of the ship's stewards.

As for Alice, she is a lovely person, but she quickly forgets her duties as she is swept up by the delirious thrill of a shipboard romance. In fact, I have to protect her from the eager advances of her *beau*, which on occasions threaten to get out of hand.

Most passengers settle into the pleasant routine of a long voyage: deck quoits, fancy dress dances, hearty constitutional walks and reading. My practice twice a day on the ship's piano in the main lounge soon attracts appreciative listeners. I can tell from rumpled sheets and blankets that Alice takes full advantage of my absence from our cabin.

We sail peacefully on through the steaming tropics of Ceylon and the Suez Canal before we reach the kinder climate of the blue Mediterranean and onwards to England's white cliffs. My excitement grows. The Queen's Hall beckons.

***

My introduction to London is not encouraging.

'I'm sorry Miss Marshall. I can't help.'

The woman who works in the cultural attaché's office in London's Australia House smiles primly. She looks down her refined Melbourne nose at me when she finds out I am from Perth.

'Really?' she drawls, her more English-than-the-English accent betraying wonderment that anything of artistic worth could emanate from such a provincial backwater. She drums her well-manicured nails on her desk, fiddling with the pearls around her neck with her other hand.

'You should really have checked first. The English Autumn academic term starts in October.'

She coughs genteelly, hand over mouth, trying and failing to cover her patronising amusement. 'All college places are usually decided by at least July.'

I chew my lip.

More kindly she adds, 'Why don't you try and get a job for a year? While you're working, I would be very happy to identify to whom you should apply.'

'But my scholarship funding will expire if I don't get a place soon,' I reply lamely.

She sighs and tries to smile sympathetically as I leave.

Oh God, I see myself already drafting the telegram home. 'Need more money to tide me over. No college places. Need a job.' What will Pop say? I inwardly shrink from the Mater's frown of disapproval.

I walk, head bowed, down the broad pavement of The Strand when I hear a woman yell, 'Cooee. Cooee, Win!' from the other side of the avenue. Only an Australian would shout like that.

Somebody told me that in life one first meets 100 people, and then spends the rest of the time meeting them all over again. And so it seems, as Mercia de Mamiel - who could forget a name like that - the young soprano star of Perth music society, scampers excitedly across the road, dodging red buses and taxis.

She hugs me but takes a step back when she notices my red-eyed face. 'Why Win, what is it? What's the matter?'

I can't reply. I'm on the edge of weeping.

'Come on, let's grab a coffee,' she orders, tugging my arm into a small Italian cafe.

Mercia dazzles the owner with her good Italian and two cups arrive *subitissimo*.

'How funny, bumping into each other like this. Two young Perth musical talents in the middle of London.

'The last time we met was when you accompanied me and Nino Marotta on the wireless. We sang well. And *you* played beautifully. It was obvious why you'd won the national competition.

'Do you remember the broadcast?'

I nod, light a cigarette and sip my coffee, trying to recover my decorum, conscious that Mercia is keenly observing me.

'I thought you left Perth to study in Italy with him?' I ask keen to delay her questions.

'I did, Win, but I didn't really enjoy it. That ghastly Mussolini has taken over the country. Those fascists are awful. I left and I'm now studying at the Royal College of Music.'

'Lucky you,' I say enviously.

'What's wrong Win?'

I explain my predicament – I'm too late to be accepted by a college for at least another year.

Mercia sits back in her chair and thinks aloud, 'Have you thought about a private tutor?'

'My scholarship is for a Royal School.'

'Ah, but if the tutor is associated with one of the schools?'

I shrug my shoulders helplessly.

'My agent,' she smiles, 'Yes, I have an agent, *dahling*. He gets me bookings during term holidays.'

'So?' I say rudely.

'One of his clients is Solomon. You know, the pianist,' she explains patiently.

'Of course I've heard of him, Mercia,' I say dismissively.

'Well, why not get Solomon to teach you?'

I laugh. 'What, one of the world's greatest pianists teach me?'

'Why not?' she smiles and draws on her cigarette.

'Your money's as good as anyone else's.'

Mercia sees I am unconvinced. She says, 'You know, Win, unlike you, I never won a national competition. And you won twice.'

Mercia adds sadly. 'I've learnt that I'm a good, very good singer. But I'm never going to be Australia's next Dame Nellie Melba. I'm cursed with enough talent to recognise greatness in others but,' her voice trembles, 'cruelly aware that I will never be able join them.'

Mercia pauses. 'I hope to get good roles, but I shall never play a leading lady at La Scala. It took me some time to get used to that.'

She sips her coffee and flashes a brittle smile at me. 'But you, my dear, have a chance of reaching right to the top. Nino told me you were one of the best accompanists he'd had.'

She gently touches my arm. 'Promise me that you will go and see Solomon.'

My cynicism dissolves in the face of her honesty and kindness. 'Of course. Of course, I will.'

'Then I'll ask my agent to arrange it for you.'

6.

Teddy

My mother is dying. I can tell from her breathing, which has become rapid, rasping and shallow as the doctor warned me it would. I leave my bed and go into her musty, dark bedroom.

As I tenderly take her elderly, arthritic hand, I ponder the mordant symmetry that my mother, who gave the painful gift of life to her son, in this very bed, is now being shepherded to her death by her only child.

My mother clenches my hand and her eyes open momentarily in a wild-eyed, sightless stare. She sighs and stops breathing. Her hand gradually becomes as tender and supple as a baby's and the wrinkles on her forehead's muslin-thin skin are self-soothing themselves away.

I gently close her eyelids and kiss her still-warm forehead. A tear falls from my eyes and mixes with her sweat. I wipe it off with my handkerchief, leaving a faint, viscous smear.

'*Adieu Mama*,' I whisper.

I am alone in our Paris house.

The doctor comes. He feels her pulse and pronounces my mother officially deceased. He will inform the necessary authorities. She was a good woman he says and recommends a competent undertaker. Nodding at the rings on my mother's fingers he advises me, 'You should take them my boy. They have a habit of disappearing *en route* to the undertakers.'

'May I attend her funeral,' he asks?

'Of course,' I reply. 'It will be in Normandy. Her family come from St-Denis-sur-Sarthon,' I add. He nods but I know he has never heard of my mother's village and now has no intention of coming to her burial.

The doctor lets himself out of the front door, momentarily allowing the muffled sounds of the busy street to float upstairs into my mother's bedroom,

I leave my mother behind, go downstairs into the living room and pour myself a cognac. My trembling hand spills my drink. Cursing, I manage to telephone my mother's Lacroix family in St Denis and make tentative arrangements for her funeral.

Sipping my drink in solitude, I sit back in a chair and gently weep. I contemplate that I am an only child with no siblings to share my grief. To recover my composure, I tap a cigarette on the case of a slim, silver holder - a gift from my father. I am not a keen smoker but I need one now. I exhale and watch the smoke drift slowly upwards and consider what my future holds.

Out of habit I check my wallet for cash and notice among the franc notes my driving licence. On a whim, I fish out the pink card. Even though the photo is not flattering, I'm told it shows a young man with an open, pleasant face. I remember my mother was proud of it. Taken three years ago, when I was twenty-one, it shows a dark-haired young man with his brilliantined hair brushed down heavily to accentuate a side-parting. He has a self-conscious glimmer of a smile, uncomfortable in the dark jacket and tie his mother insists he wear.

My family name, Bisset, has been hand-written by a clerk with a thick-penned, calligraphic flourish in stark contrast to my type-written Christian name, Edouard, and address: Paris 9th Arrondisment, 2 Rue de Maubeuge.

It is natural that after the death of the last parent, an offspring's thoughts turn to family memories.

I am no different.

My reminiscences become tinged with the uncomfortable realisation that the next funeral of my small family will be mine.

I shake my head free of self-centred despondency and return to the thoughts of my happy holidays in St Denis when my parents and I used to swap the stifling Paris summer heat for the dark cool woods and streams of Normandy.

Fishing in rivers and learning to shoot wild boar with my mother's family. I pride myself on becoming a good shot and comfortable with guns and ammunition. One of my relatives has a souvenir from WWI - a German Luger pistol. I become a crack shot with this too.

I also accompany my father on trips to England. My banker father is Scottish but his siblings live in London. My father died five years ago. I'm brought up bilingually, equally proud to be French and Scottish. The English capital is different from Paris. More exciting in its novelty. The girls seem more intriguing too. I have had a couple of liaisons in Paris but these have fizzled out.

Although neither of them is grand, I realise I am now a man of property - two houses, one in Paris, one in Normandy.

It is July 1939 and I must make a decision. War is looming with Germany again, but Paris holds nothing for me now. Normandy or London beckons.

I know my father's siblings in London would welcome me. My mother's family in St Denis would certainly offer me a job in their business. But I sense, as a bilingual Frenchman, I may be of more use in wartime London rather than in Normandy, where I would be just another unremarkable member of the provincial *petite bourgeoisie*.

I stub my cigarette out.

I choose London.

7.

Sol

Oy vey! Oy gewalt!

Such melodrama and vulgarity in the way she plays. I can't resist the temptation to have some fun. I jump up and slap a wall. She's astonished.

'I'm just making way for your elbows,' I chortle.

Nervously she starts again. But under the melodrama I detect talent lurking. I study the young Australian carefully. She does play with enthusiasm and she clearly loves the music. And she *is* playing from memory.

'Thank you, Winifred.'

'Winfred,' she corrects me.

I raise my eyebrows. I'm not used to being spoken to sharply by potential students, particularly women. Perhaps I deserve it for poking fun at her?

'Tell me, why did you choose Franck's *Symphonic Variations*?'

'I wanted to show you that I am capable of expressing myself across a wide range.'

Well, you certainly did that, I smile inwardly.

'But without orchestral accompaniment this piece is difficult.'

Her face registers deep disappointment that I am on the brink of saying 'No' to her request for me to teach her.

'I tell you what *Winfred*,' I say cheerfully, 'come back here tomorrow and I will hear you again.'

'What shall I play?'

'Why not the second movement of the *Moonlight Sonata*? Two o'clock after lunch?'

Relieved, her face cheers up. 'Thank you.'

A parting shot from me, 'And this time Winfred concentrate solely on what you believe Beethoven is saying, without too many exaggerated hand and elbow movements.'

I notice at the second audition that she has indeed absorbed my advice.

She plays well - her version is passable, almost good.

But is she too old at twenty-one? I would have to break and remould her. Would she accept that?

I smile. 'That was much better.'

Her face is radiant. I feel her joyous relief. It would be unkind to refuse her but I'm not yet certain. On the other hand, I do need the money. Concerns about an impending war means many of my overseas concerts have been cancelled. Although I already have three students, I still have time for another.

'Come on, Winfred, it's a nice day. I fancy a walk in the park. Would you like to accompany me?'

It's a short walk to Kensington Gardens and a stroll towards the Round Pond. I smile. Yes, by chance, the same bench by the Round Pound is free.

August has been warm and dry; the green grass is going a patchy brown. I have anticipated an afternoon stroll and am suitably attired – I enjoy good clothes. After my appearance at the New York World Fair concert in June, I have some money in my pockets to indulge my tastes. I take my new blazer off and fold it carefully over my cream-coloured slacks. I loosen my silk cravat and adjust my spotless Panama hat to shield my eyes, content that I look ready for a flutter on the horses at the Epsom Derby.

Sunlight flickers on and off. The gentle breeze creates ripples on the water. A beautiful white swan glides elegantly towards us followed by her paddling brown cygnet. Disappointed that we have no bread to throw, they pass by.

'Do you mind if I smoke, Winfred?'

'Not at all.'

She watches me go through the masculine ritual of rolling and lighting a Havana cigar.

Then she chuckles. A full-throated uninhibited sound with her glinting eyes crinkling in amusement.

'You remind me of my father. He smokes the occasional cigar at Christmas. My mother, who usually gets her own way, does not approve.'

This girl has personality — she might be fun to teach.

Appreciating my Havana, I sink into a reverie for a few moments. I catch the faint sound of tennis balls wafting across from Kensington Palace gardens and absent-mindedly play a backhand shot across my lap, admonishing myself as ash falls on my trousers.

'I play tennis too,' Win says.

'Oh yes, how good are you?'

'Pretty good. I was always being asked by the boys at the tennis club to be their partner.'

She mimics my backhand. 'How good are *you*?'

I'm enjoying her banter. 'Not bad. I play regularly with my friend, Gerald.'

I puff reflectively. 'He plays the piano too. Very well but not quite good enough. He's reconciled sadly to the fact that he'll never be a soloist. But he makes a good living from being an accompanist.'

'I have a friend like that. She's training to be an opera singer. She's good, very good but she says she'll always have supporting roles.'

'Ah, never the *prima donna*,' I say, trying to be sympathetic.

I am more interested in tennis than her friend. 'I warn you, if we have a game, I always play to win.'

She returns my shot. 'So do I.'

Yes, this young woman definitely could be good to teach.

'Do you know I sat here in this self-same spot more than twenty years ago, Winfred, with someone called Dr Simon Rumshisky.'

Uncertain how to respond, she nods with a slight movement.

'He was taught at the Leschetizky School in Vienna. That was the world's most famous piano academy,' I explain.

She is becoming nervous, unsure as to the direction of my conversation.

'Don't worry Winfred, I was as ignorant as you when I first met Simon.' I blow some smoke out and laugh. 'When we sat here, Simon took his socks and shoes off and got me to do the same.' I stop when I observe her nervous surprise.

'Fear not Winfred, I won't ask you to take off your shoes and stockings.' I draw deeply on my cigar. 'He wanted to show me the similarity between the function of toes and fingers.' I chortle again. 'Oh my, it was *so* funny.'

I use my cigar to point to the ripples on the pond's surface. 'Look how perfect those little waves are. Most people think the water is being pushed along by the wind. In fact, the water is merely going up and down. It is only the wave which moves along, travelling through the water.

'Winfred, fix your eyes on a spot of water. See how it appears to rise and fall seamlessly but, in fact, at the top and bottom of its movement for a second, a split second, it is still. Perfectly still, which enables the discerning viewer – in this case you and me – to appreciate better what has just been and anticipate what is coming.

'Nature is often like that. Now listen to the song of those birds in that tree over there. At the end of each note, there is a moment of silence, it might only be a split second, but listen intently and you will find it, gently inviting your ear forward, while softly releasing the last note.'

I observe Winfred out of the corner of my eye: she is a striking, handsome young woman with a determined face and bright eyes.

I detect strong character and courage – she'll need both.

'Alright Winfred, I will take you on as a student.'

No more a grown-up adult, Winfred gasps and puts her hand to her mouth.

'Thank you, Solomon. I can't tell how much this means to me,' she gushes.

I wag my finger at her to get her concentration. 'I have three conditions. You must, I repeat must, learn and completely understand my technique. Don't underestimate how long that might take. It could be six months. Second, you stay for two years. Third, you have your own piano. That last condition should be easy: The music shop, Cramer's, not far from here in High Street Kensington, is happy to allow my students to practice on their pianos for the princely sum of one shilling per hour.'

I see she is still deliriously happy.

'Now when can you start? I suggest the week after next.'

'Could we make it three weeks please?' she replies apprehensively.

'Why?'

'I have promised to visit a penfriend.'

'Where does she live?' I ask, expecting her to say somewhere like Scotland or Cornwall.

'It's a *he* actually. He lives in Dresden.'

I scream silently, Germany! Is she mad?

'Winfred, you do realise what's happening there? You've heard of Adolph Hitler?'

'Yes, I've seen the photos with his arm sticking out. I think he looks silly,' she giggles. 'But Wolfgang tells me it's perfectly safe for tourists.'

Oh my God! I realise, of course, that she is not Jewish. She's a naive young Australian girl who probably hardly reads a newspaper. She hasn't heard the stories about Jews being beaten up and their shops smashed. But I can tell from her face that she has decided.

I say resignedly. 'Alright Winfred. Let's say early September? But take care.'

'Thank you. I will be careful.'

It is August 1939.

8.

Win

I tell Alice after Gibraltar and not long before we dock in London, that I plan to visit my penfriend, Wolfgang, in Dresden before settling down to my studies. She jumps at the chance to come along. Why not, it sounds so simple and fun for two young Australian women who'd never travelled abroad before. The world is our oyster.

Of course, *I* arrange everything: buy a little second-hand car, ferry crossing tickets, maps, foreign currency and visas. Thanks Pop, I say to myself, even though you probably didn't intend the money you'd given me to be spent on travel in France and Germany.

France is a blur of quick stops at *relais routiers*, too much red wine and hazy *Gauloises*. We press on. I can't wait to meet Wolfgang. He seems so nice in his letters and he's keen to meet me too.

The German border police and customs officials take a long time checking our tourist visas, but we think that might be normal. There are a lot of red flags with swastikas and we glimpse photos of Hitler through the windows of the border offices. We agree he looks ridiculous in a uniform with his arm raised in that silly salute.

Which is why we now find ourselves in front of a nasty, little man in the Heidelberg police station.

'*Fraülein,* insulting our *Führer* is a very bad crime in Germany.'

His German accent is so thick it would be comical under any other circumstances. He looks menacing in his thick black leather coat, angrily leaning over the table towards Alice and me. Our passports are on the desk in front of him.

'Are you a policeman?' I ask, my voice steady, not betraying my fear. The Mater has succeeded in training me to be tough.

'No - *Gestapo*,' he snaps.

Pushing his podgy chest out proudly, he adds, 'More important than police.'

'What are you doing here in our country?' *Gestapo*-man presses.

'We are driving to Dresden,' I reply.

'Why?' he scowls.

'I have a penfriend there.' Why, oh why did I do it? I think to myself furiously. Why turn that silly photo of Hitler around to face the wall in our hotel room? It seemed funny when we arrived yesterday afternoon. Someone must have reported us.

I had parked our little English car, a Standard 8, outside an inn with a sign of a red ox swinging gently in the breeze in Heidelberg's old town. The beauty of the view as we crossed over the Rhine had put Alice and me in a cheerful mood - we imagined a decent meal and a glass of local wine on a sunny terrace overlooking the river. We had shrugged off some hostile looks by a small group of brown-uniformed youths by the hotel entrance. One of them had scowled at our car's Union Jack bonnet emblem.

'Spell penfriend,' the officer barks, looking up the unfamiliar words in an English-German dictionary.

'*Ach so, Brieffreund*,' he mutters. 'The name of your penfriend?'

'Wolfgang Schmidt. Here,' I hand over a crumpled airmail letter, the sender's name and address on the reverse, the thin paper rustling in my shaking hand as it dawns on me that we really are in serious trouble.

Alice sobs in fear.

Gestapo-man leaves the room, Wolfgang's letter in his hand, his leather coat creaking ominously.

I kick Alice's ankles and order her to shut up. 'Don't you see, he enjoys making people cry,' I hiss.

We hear a telephone ringing in another office and our captor answering it. We hear him shout *'Heil Hitler'* as he finishes his call and returns after ten minutes. It feels like a lifetime.

He hands back our passports and says, his voice dripping in disappointment, 'You may go.' On the way out he warns, 'You should leave Germany by September.'

'Don't worry mate, we're getting out as soon as we can,' I mutter silently.

We find my little car has had its tyres let down and the petrol gauge registers empty.

Before we lose all faith in Germany, some students help us to pump up the wheels and put in some fuel.

We drive back to Calais as quickly as possible, looking fearfully at the German soldiers near the French border.

Back in London, Alice and I part. She books a passage on the first boat back to Australia.

***

The Times, Win, that's the best place to look for flat-share advertisements. You know, by the *right* sort of people,' Sol tells me.

Everyone says, *the right sort of people.*

There are plenty of vacancies. Many have left the capital as war might be coming. I respond to one in South Kensington – cheaper than fashionable Chelsea and not too far from The Royal College of Music.

Which is how I come to be interviewed by Marjorie - *do I detect a trace of an Aussie accent?* - and her flatmate, Katie. They are nice girls, bemused by my account of the harsh regime of piano lessons and practice which I observe and the evening concerts I attend. They have heard of Solomon and are suitably impressed. They quickly realise my primary need is for a bed and I will be out of the flat for long periods of time.

'No boyfriend, Win?'

'No, I don't have time.'

This flat is ideal for me. The B&B I'm in at the moment is proving expensive and uncomfortable. What would the Mater do? I look at my watch and feign concern.

'Are we keeping you, Win?' Marjorie asks.

'It's just I have another viewing organised in half an hour,' I fib.

There's a speedy exchange of looks and slight nods of agreement.

Katie stands up and offers her hand. 'Welcome to 33 Lexham Gardens, Win.'

'Thank you,' I gush.

'Good on you, Win,' Marjorie says - definitely an Aussie accent this time.

Turns out she was partly raised in Melbourne, but her father's job had brought the family back to England.

Sol nods his approval when I tell him where I'm living. But I notice an unhappy frown on his face when I add, 'It's not far from the Cromwell Road, an easy twenty minutes' walk from here.'

He sees my puzzlement. 'I used to know someone who lived off the, er, Cromwell Road. But it was a long time ago. It's of no concern.'

9.

Sol

'Can you draw, Winfred?' This is her first lesson. She's taken aback by my question and frowns, puzzled. 'I mean sketch with a pencil.'

She hesitates. 'Yes, I was one of the better ones in my school art class.'

I see she has a large notebook on her lap.

'Good,' I smile encouragingly and hand her a pencil and rubber eraser. 'Why don't you sit down at that desk over there and draw your left hand with its index finger curled and poised, about to play.'

I light a cigarette, read my copy of *The Times* and sip my coffee while she draws. I see that, although war was officially declared on 3rd September and we are now about a month later, nothing appears to be happening yet. Although there is a small naval battle at the River Plate in Uruguay - I have to check where that is in an atlas - all is quiet in Europe. Even in Poland, which capitulated in a matter of days after the German and Soviet invasion. This hiatus has been dubbed the Phoney War. The Germans call it *Sitzkrieg*.

We are all keen *to do our bit*. I become an air raid warden. My job is to walk the blacked-out streets and remind people to close their curtains tightly to stop any light guiding the German bombers. In fact, it becomes a good excuse for pleasant, nocturnal ramblings around the Kensington streets.

My new Australian student volunteers as an ambulance driver. But it's a waste of time. Sitting around, doing nothing for hours, waiting vainly for a call which never comes, compels her to make her excuses and return to her musical studies.

There is gossip at the college that Germany and its arm-jerking leader doesn't really want a war and that he will withdraw from Poland. I'm not so sure. Winfred has told me about her nasty German episode and mentioned she saw army vehicles and soldiers near the French border. But, for now, we agree lessons will continue, not just for her but also for my other three pupils.

Win shows me her drawing. It's quite good. I get her to write sequentially, 1, 2, 3 and 4 above the knuckle, the two joints and the fingertip.

'Now Winfred, from your sketch we can follow the working of the fingers. From point 1, the finger is dropped onto the note, strength is added from points 2 and 3, and the finger should be firmly enough held to allow a direct blow on point 1 to be hit without causing the joint 3 to collapse.'

So far, so easy, I can see Win thinking.

'Of course, we all know that the finger stops at the keyboard but remember the penetration goes through, right through.

'We then pass on to the next note but our preceding finger doesn't leap up as though stung.'

She grimaces, realising that I am criticising her style.

'No, the same control is applied in leaving the note as it is on approaching the next one, thus providing a beautifully rounded finish.'

Winfred is frowning. No doubt remembering and trying to discard the teaching of Miss Ida Roberts, her first teacher.

I watch Winfred's face and continue when I judge she's ready. 'When we pass from one note to another, it's the note that we're leaving behind us that counts.

'This is very important. It's not easy, I know.' I give her some more time to digest what I'm trying to impart. I drag on my cigarette and wait.

'Remember what I told you about our old friend, the walking movement? It is the back foot that takes all the stress and strain. The front foot is well on its way before the back foot is finally released.'

I feel advance sympathy for her because I know what I will say after I invite her to sit at my piano and play. Sure enough, after only a of couple minutes, I am forced to stand up and slam a side table with a fist. 'No, no!'

'That first note is awful. Your fingers are too weak. Your wrists are too rigid. Your approach is wrong and your follow-through a disgrace!'

Winfred looks forlorn, her eyes swell.

'Excuse me,' she says as she looks down and blows her nose. She turns her head up and looks straight at me, her face strained but determined.

That's my girl. You're not a quitter.

But there's is no point in sugar-coating my criticism. I reflect that if only I had got Win a few years ago, I would not now have to break her in like a half-trained colt.

'Winfred, I'm afraid part of the remedy is a painful necessity. If you wish to continue with me, you will have to strengthen your fingers. Yes, I know your Miss Roberts probably thought they were strong enough. But I'm afraid they are not.'

I get her to push her stool back, stand up and look inside my piano under the sloping cover.

'The best illustration of how the fingers should work are found in here.'

I repeatedly press some keys in slow succession and tell her to look at her sketch again. 'All the points from 1 to 4 are the lever; 2 is the hammer; and 3 is the felt.

'Watch how the levers push the hammers up until the felts hit the strings in exactly the same way, every time. And that is what you must replicate.'

I motion for her to sit again.

'Try placing the finger in such a way that the fingertip is resting on the note, the bone of the first joint makes a perfect vertical line and the rest of the finger falls naturally into place.'

She bites her lip. It dawns on her that weeks of finger-numbing exercises lie ahead. She doesn't realise it could be months.

'At our lesson next week, we will continue with what I have started to instruct you. I shall ask you to take notes so you can refer to them and fully understand my method.'

I dismiss her with the instruction to exercise her fingers five hours a day. They will ache painfully to begin with but that's the price she has to pay.

10.

Win

Sol is irritable. I guess he's just had a difficult lesson. Was his student as bad as me I wonder.

There's no wasting time with the niceties of small talk. He gestures me to sit at his desk while he puffs on his cigar, pacing slowly around the room, deliberately exaggerating his foot movements. Heel and toe, heel and toe.

'Now take this down word for word, Win. I'll tell you when to underline. Forget about the grammar, if needs be.

'You won't find this in any textbook, so pay attention,' he adds curtly.

God, he can be so rude sometimes.

He clears his throat and dictates, starting with the word 'Heading':

The Analogy of Walking to Piano Playing

In walking, toes curl on to ground and fingers curl on to piano from knuckles down and bear the weight of arms and hands.

In walking both back and front foot are on ground together before back foot is lifted to go in front, otherwise one would be hopping.

In legato playing the same principle applies to the fingers, otherwise one is playing staccato.

Heading: Structure of Piano and Piano Playing

When keynotes are pushed down, the hammers are correspondingly pushed up to hit the strings, like a see-saw.

Heading: Physical Principles

Keep arms to side of body.

Try to play on inside of fingertips.

Wrist relaxed and dropped.

Action of finger comes from knuckle.

Strength of finger comes from middle joint.

Bone of first joint should make a perfect vertical line when fingertip placed on keynote.

The same control is applied to leaving a note as it is to approaching the next one.

For example, the walking movement - it is the back foot that takes all the stress. The front foot is well on its way before the back foot is released.

In playing we drop our wrist to its lowest extent relying on the finger's strength to do the playing. The wrist is raised only in order to drop it again for relation. This action must give emphasis to the note on which we drop the wrist.'

Solomon stops and demands, 'Did you get all that?'

I nod.

'Good. This is your textbook. You will make other notes. But these are the first and most important. Memorise them.'

Yes, the pages of my notebook gradually fill up, but I continually refer to my original lecture to refresh my memory of Sol's first principles.

Some weeks later I lift my notebook out of my large carrier bag. With a smile at Sol, I let him read its introduction which I have recently written.

Being the trials and tribulations of one Winfred Marshall
of 33 Lexham Gardens, W8
who tried to follow in the
footsteps of one Solomon, and asked,
not for so many wives, but enough lives, to carry her through,
till she could eschew, the wisdom and lore right at her door.
He who I praise, is just counting the days,
when his pupil just plays,
just what he just says.
Anyway –
Here's happy days.

Sol checks at first but then bursts out laughing. 'That is very funny, Win.'

He pats me affectionately on my shoulder. 'You know, you're the only one of my students who dares to tease me.'

11.

Teddy

An undulating blue fog of tobacco smoke floats above the excited din of a room crammed full of chatting, laughing and shrieking young men and women. I'm at a crowded party hosted by four girls in a flat – 33 Lexham Gardens, Kensington to be precise.

All the men, well, we're boys really, are in uniform. Just one window is open, keeping the December chill at bay. The room is heating up. Cool drinks are being downed at a speedy rate on top of empty stomachs. This is not just a Christmas party. It is more of a farewell to *our boys* who will be shortly leaving for France. War may have been declared in early September after Germany invaded Poland but since then nothing much has happened on land. Week followed week and month followed month of training, but no action. Was there a war on or not? The French have dubbed this inactivity, *Drôle de guerre*.

The party's mood is one of overwhelming confidence. Our trip to France will be a holiday. I hear coarse jokes about French letters followed by raucous men's laughter and tipsy girls' giggles.

Men off to battle, too much alcohol and looming Christmas jollities make a heady cocktail for young women - I can see eyelids fluttering and flirtatious glances zooming around the room. Quite a few are directed at me. Lipstick becomes brighter and cleavages more obvious. There's no denying it, despite the girls' outward appearance of respectability, there is a strong under-current of sex seeping into every corner of the room. The boys pick up on it and testosterone fuels their excitement. Ties are loosened and faces become shiny with sweat.

Most of the men are officers in smart, smooth uniforms with gleaming Sam Browne belts but here and there are other ranks like me, a mere Lance Corporal, clad in rough serge. Now and then I catch a glance thrown my way, curious that a lower rank is present –then it catches my Field Security Police shoulder badges and looks away warily, whispering a word of caution to friends – our branch of the military police already has a reputation for being staffed by well-connected oddballs who have scant regard for rank.

Like a thrashing salmon heading upstream, I bump my way through the crowd to fetch drinks for one of my new colleagues, Paul, and his girlfriend Marjorie, who is one of our hosts. I lose count of the number of times I hear, 'Jerry's bitten off more than he can chew, old boy. We'll be home by next Christmas.'

In the tiny kitchen which serves as the bar, I squeeze next to a striking brunette talking to someone politely but showing no particular interest. I catch his words designed to impress, 'I'm in the Blues.'

She looks blank. 'That's a cavalry regiment, darling,' he says, languidly.

'We guard the King,' he adds, hoping to impress again but failing to disguise his patronising tone.

I reflect that I don't know what the Blues are either.

He sighs, slurring his words badly, 'We don't have horses anymore but tanks.'

He takes a long swig of his beer and licks his lips. 'We'll be in the thick of any fighting.'

'Oh,' she says with obvious disinterest, 'I thought there wasn't going to be any fighting.'

She has an accent which I don't recognise. I feel a momentarily twinge of empathy. I am used to being teased about my French accent. I don't mind. I've already found out English women find it very attractive.

I am forced to reach between them to find a gin bottle. Using me as an excuse, the girl extricates herself and smiles briefly at me as she passes by. I catch her eyes and the hint of a perfume that I vaguely recognise.

The young officer swears under his breath while I fix my drinks. He catches my eye and shrugs his shoulders, wiping cigarette ash off his smart uniform. 'Wasted my time with that one.'

I ignore him. He's had too much to drink.

Miffed that I hadn't responded, he sneers. 'Police are we, *Corporal?*'

'Yes, that's right.'

'I suppose you'll just be on traffic duty?' he jibes.

'I expect so,' I mutter before jumping into the melee once more and pushing my way back to our group.

'Sorry I was a bit long. There was a drunk in the way. He was pestering that girl over there.' I point with my chin as I hand the drinks round. The brunette notices I'm talking about her and smiles distantly.

Paul says, 'That's Win, Teddy. She's one of our hosts.'

Marjorie laughs. 'He's wasting his time with her.'

Why, my face wonders.

'She's in love with the piano,' she replies.

'What do you mean?' I ask.

'She wants to be a concert pianist. We all like Win but don't see much of her.'

Marjorie sighs at a hopeless case. 'She has private lessons, practises for much of the day and goes to concerts two or three times a week in the evenings. By herself, would you believe.'

'She has an accent I didn't recognise.'

'Ah, monsieur Teddy, elle est Australienne.'

My face registers interest - I've never met anyone from Australia before.

'Alright Teddy, I'll introduce Win to you later,' Marjorie says. 'But first, tell me, what is it you and Paul are training for exactly?'

I raise my eyebrows and look enquiringly at Paul.

She prods a finger into my chest. 'No, don't you dare make that face. That's just how Paul looks when I ask him the same question.'

Like me, Paul speaks fluent French. Which is why we are training for the Field Security Police in Aldershot, the town which proudly claims to be the home of the British Army. We trainees are an unusual bunch. One of us, called Malcolm Muggeridge, a bit strange himself, describes us hilariously as a bunch of Baghdad carpet sellers, tourist agents, and unfrocked priests. He has a point.

We learn quickly. First the fun part, pistol shooting and riding motorbikes. Then counter espionage and interrogation techniques. We soon realise that we may also be expected to gather intelligence on enemy forces – the eyes and ears of our army in advance of our own front lines. Dressed in civilian clothes, if necessary. Paul whispers in my ear during a lecture, 'Christ, we could be shot as spies.'

The party is in its closing stages. People shout thanks and wave goodbye as the room clears. The brunette joins our group.

'Hello,' she says and shakes my hand. She has a firm grip and a steady gaze radiating from beautiful, bright eyes - I am immediately struck by her.

'I hear you are learning the piano?' I ask. I can tell from her reply she's making polite conversation. I could have been anybody.

'Yes, that's right. I'm having private lessons at the Royal College of Music.'

'Oh, who's your teacher?'

'Solomon,' she replies wearily, knowing how the conversation will develop. She repeats the name as I register surprise.

'He must be very wise.' My joke falls flat. I'm embarrassed - she's heard it hundreds of times before. 'Is he a good teacher?' I ask.

'Yes, he is very good - brilliant. Strict but underneath he's…' she searches for the words. 'Quite a darling.'

I find myself drawn to this Australian. She's attractive and intelligent – definitely not a flirt. I'm relieved when she decides to continue speaking to me.

'What part of France do you come from?'

'Paris. But my mother was from Normandy and my father Scottish.'

'Oh yes? My father's family came from Scotland,' she responds.

I detect a scintilla of interest in her voice.

'I'd like to visit Scotland one day,' I say, worried that I sound predictable.

'Me too. I hear Edinburgh is beautiful. Perhaps when I finish my piano lessons?'

'You must be very good to have come all the way over to London to study?'

Someone hands her a lit cigarette. I glimpse a Polish badge on a shoulder which is trying to edge into our conversation.

'Thank you, Jan,' she says, blowing smoke sideways. I note she does not encourage Polish Jan to join us. Mind you, she's not exactly encouraging me either.

She nods. 'I found out quickly that I was not as good as I thought I was.'

Paul is tugging at my shoulder. 'Teddy, we can't miss the train.'

I shrug him off. 'I'm off to France soon. Is there anything you'd like?'

'France?' Then she smiles mischievously. 'Yes, as a matter of fact there is. Wait here a second.'

She returns with her calling card. Embossed on the front is, *Miss Winfred Marshall* with her Lexham Gardens address. On the back, she has written in blue ink,

Jicky par Guerlain - Champs Elysees, Paris

'It's my favourite perfume. I've run out,' she says, congratulating herself at being *so clever* to remember something from France she needed. Her eyes crinkle in amusement and I realise she's throwing down a challenge – woman to man.

I grin. 'I'll see what I can do.'

'Here, let me give you some money.'

'No, that won't be necessary,' I reply over my shoulder, clutching her card as Paul shoves me along.

I catch a broad, eye-crinkling smile whose memory stays in my mind over the coming months.

12.

Win

'Hello Win, I'm Lorne. I've been looking forward to meeting you.'

Even before I've sat down properly, he puts me on the spot. 'Do you think you could write some articles about what life is really like for Aussies living in London?'

We're sitting in a cramped office at 85 Fleet Street. He has to raise his voice over the rat-a-tat of his secretary's typewriter.

She types very quickly and noisily.

Almost as if it's on purpose.

The phone, which is sitting on a pile of dog-eared newspapers, rings regularly.

Each time she answers it, '*Sydney Daily Telegraph/Australian Women's Weekly.*'

Depending on the caller she either passes the phone to Lorne or offers to takes a message because, 'Mr Campbell is in a meeting.'

Between calls, he says, 'I know your father well, Win. He's a great journalist. And if you can write half as well as him, I'm sure you will be too.'

Before I have a chance to answer him, he says, 'You're studying the piano, I hear. I imagine the extra cash from writing would come in useful?'

Lorne's right. I need the money. I'm finding it hard to make ends meet. Pop had hinted heavily that Lorne might have work for me.

'I'm rushed off my feet writing about the War, or lack of it, and the progress of conscription back in Australia.'

Even though I've had hardly any chance to speak, I evidently pass muster because he stubs his cigarette out with nicotine-stained fingers and stands up. He puts on a creased tweed jacket with arm patches - his shiny, well-worn trousers could do with a press as well.

'Let's grab a bite to eat, Win,' he says, seizing his hat.

His secretary raises her eyebrows wearily. 'What time will you be back, Lorne?'

'Shouldn't be more than a couple of hours.'

Her eyebrows signal faint disbelief.

Lorne smiles conspiratorially, ushers me to the door and down the narrow flight of stairs into the busy street.

I follow him over to the other side, weaving our way through a slow-moving queue of cars, black taxis and red buses held up by building works further down Fleet Street.

I follow Lorne into an alleyway, past Ye Old Cheshire Cheese pub and then it's just a hop, skip and a jump into a street called Wine Court.

We enter a door marked Press Club.

In the bar Lorne grabs a small table and our hard wooden chairs scrape across floorboards stained black by centuries of shoe leather since the Great Fire of London.

'The usual Mr Campbell?' the bartender asks.

Lorne nods and asks, 'Would you like a drink, Win?'

'It's a bit early for me,' I manage to hide any disapproval in my voice. 'A glass of water would be fine.'

We eat some pea soup and bread. Both taste awful but our wartime palates have grown accustomed to poor food. I imagine Lorne's neat whisky probably masks the taste.

He eyes me over the top of his glass. 'I don't know what your father said about me exactly, Win.' He takes a sip from his glass and adds sympathetically, 'I have to say I don't need help with the *Telegraph*.'

'Oh,' I whisper, disappointment writ clear on my face. 'But you said you needed help with articles about London life,' I add weakly.

'Yes, that's right. I could do with some help with *The Australian Women's Weekly*, not the *Telegraph*.'

But I want to write for a newspaper.

Lorne is frequently distracted as people stop by our table. Sometimes a quick hello. Sometimes a quick gossip about the news.

He turns to me. 'This is the best place in London to find out what's really going on, Win.'

He lights a cigarette and draws in deeply. 'Churchill seems to be making a lot of speeches and his stock is rising by the day. If he ends up taking over, it may be a bit of a double-edged sword. He has a habit of taking Australia for granted. And this Phoney War can't go on forever.'

The club is slowly filling up as more men drift in.

I notice I'm the only woman in the bar.

'Are there no female journalists, Lorne?'

'There are, Win. But all these men,' he waves his cigarette around, 'work on newspapers. Women usually work for magazines.'

'You mean like *The Australian Women's Weekly*?'

He smiles. 'Yes, correct. A very good publication. And profitable. Packer sees to that.'

'Packer,' I ask, not familiar with the name.

'Frank Packer. He's the owner. And he's appointed a woman as its editor.' He looks at me seriously. 'Win, don't make the mistake of thinking the '*Weekly*'s not as good as a newspaper. In fact, it's one of Australia's most influential publications. Getting printed in the '*Weekly* would be quite an achievement.'

'Oh,' I repeat myself but with less disappointment on my face this time.

That sounds better.

I'm smiling, now.

'I didn't mean to sound ungrateful, Lorne.'

'No worries,' he grins. 'You're a woman. You've got a much better idea than me what will appeal to the *Weekly's* readers. You choose a topic; write about 300 words – let's start small, shall we? Anything you like: rationing, how people are coping, social events, that sort of thing. When you've finished, bring it over to my office. I'll give it the once-over before I post it off to Sydney.'

He orders a couple of coffees. I feel the need to celebrate and surprise him (and myself) by accepting a glass of brandy.

Lorne swallows a mouthful, sighs and asks about my parents. 'We exchange Christmas cards now, but that's about it. It's a pity.'

He sips his whisky. 'I miss chatting with your dad. I enjoy the *craic. Craic's* Irish for banter,' he adds, seeing the confusion on my face at the unfamiliar word. 'I always thought your dad should have gone into politics. He has a feel for the underdog. He would have made a great Labor MP.'

Yes, I know Pop and the Mater vote Labor. But I never mention it. Most of my old school friends' parents support the Liberal Party.

'Many of his mates became politicians and have done well. Our prime minister's the classic example,' Lorne says.

'Ah yes. He pops in for a cup of tea when he's not in Canberra.'

'You know your dad was a better journalist and writer than John Curtin?' Lorne adds.

I shake my head. I know Pop and our prime minister had once been colleagues and became very good friends, but he'd never talked much about it.

'Pop's always reading. My mother calls him a bookworm.'

'She's right, Win. I've never met anyone so well-read.' He smiles, remembering some episode shared with Pop. 'He was a quiet man, alright. But, hell, he could have a furious pen.'

'G'day Lorne, who's this?' an inquisitive Aussie twang interrupts, looking down at me.

Lorne tips his head in my direction. 'This is Win Marshall. She's just started writing for the '*Weekly*.'

'Congratulations Win,' says the voice, now sounding impressed before manoeuvring through the thickening throng.

I decline another brandy and leave Lorne standing at the bar, swapping stories and leads with his friends.

Outside I scream silently. 'I'm a journalist!'

Oh yes? You've got to write something first!

***

'Congratulations Win, here's your first article in a national publication. And I hardly changed a thing,' Lorne says, handing over a copy of the *Australian Women's Weekly*.

My hands shake as I read:

April 13, 1940

She plays hostess to Australians

From WIN MARSHALL, Our Perth Writer Visiting London

Go along any afternoon you are in London to 21b Cadogan Gardens, and ask for Lady Frances Ryder's rooms, and if you hail from any part of the Empire, you are bound to meet somebody you know there.

Sitting around a table you might see an Australian Air Force boy talking to a Canadian soldier; a South African art student comparing notes with a New Zealand university graduate; Lady Frances herself encouraging some shy newcomer to make himself at home - Miss MacDonald of the Isles carrying on half a dozen conversations at once, while pouring out the tea.

Lady Ryder told me that her mail amounted to something like 32,000 letters received and answered during the year.

Behind this organisation of friendliness and hospitality lies a charming story. During the last war, Lady Frances used to accompany her mother, the Countess of Harrowby, to the hospitals to talk to wounded overseas officers to cheer and help them any way they could.

One day in 1920, Lady Frances received a pathetic note from a South African saying that his friend was in Guy's Hospital and was absolutely alone. When Lady Frances met the wounded soldier, she was horrified to find there were 120 more men, all from the Dominions, in the same position at the same hospital, and 400 at Edinburgh.

Lady Frances has always been interested in Empire visitors and is working hard on her new scheme. She has the names of 430 of her friends whose homes are situated near flying centres, and they are making arrangements for the airmen - who will certainly include many R.A.A.F. representatives - to spend their leave with them.

I sit down in Lorne's office and read my article again.

He grins at my girlish, wide-eyed delight. 'You remind me of when I read my first piece.

'Seriously Win, you've now been published in the '*Weekly*. It may be a small beer but it has your name next to it. It will stand you in good stead if you ever want to work for them or someone else in the future. You never know,' he adds.

13.

Teddy

The sergeant grabs me by the neck and shoves me forward. 'He's a fuckin' German spy, Sir! A fifth columnist.'

'He tried to drive through our check point. He's riding a Norton 500, no less. Imagine that… Fuckin' Jerry spies using our best motorbikes. He's lucky we didn't shoot him on the spot.'

'I'm English,' I manage to gasp.

'Says he's one of ours but he's got no ID card,' snorts the sergeant.

'Just listen to his accent, Sir. He's a fuckin' Frog traitor.'

The British Army major looks doubtful as his ear picks up my faint French accent.

It's early May 1940, not long after the German attack replaced the Phoney War with *Blitzkrieg*. The major and the sergeant are unshaven, their uniforms caked with dust. The major has a bandage around his forehead, dark red with dried blood. Under both men's eyes are dark bags of exhaustion. They ooze fear. Defeat and near-panic retreat do that to soldiers.

'Look, Sir, I'm Field Security. My CO is Captain Buckmaster, 50th Division, Lille HQ.' I'm desperate now.

The major frowns. I can tell the name Buckmaster rings a bell.

'Alright, what were you doing?'

'I was reconnoitring German advance positions.'

'Oh yes? And where are they?' the officer tests me.

'Only a couple of miles away. Advancing slowly towards you.' I see a crumpled map on a table. 'Let me show you.'

The officer nods and the sergeant reluctantly lets me go.

'Here and here,' I stab the map, my hands trembling. 'I got close enough to see their battalion HQ... here,' I stammer. 'It looks like they're trying to encircle Lille.'

'How did you get close enough to see that?'

'I hid my bike and crawled through the bushes.'

'Any tanks?'

'Not seen, but the woods are too thick. I did see armoured half-tracks.' I pause, and then add, 'Sir, they looked fresh and ready to attack.'

The officer looks at me again. 'You saw all this, but you got away?'

'Yes. I stayed under cover for the rest of the day and crawled back to my bike at night. They'd got within a couple of hundred yards of my bike and fired at me when I started it. But it was too dark.'

Half-satisfied he sends a messenger to Lille. There is no functioning radio. It takes an hour before the dispatch rider returns with a hand-written note from Buckmaster confirming my story. I glimpse Buckmaster's order. 'Do not shoot him.'

The officer smiles and shakes my hand. 'Good luck, Corporal.' He shakes his head. 'Oh, and Bisset.'

'Yes Sir?'

He forces a weary smile. 'For God's sake stop wandering around in civvies - you'll get yourself shot.'

Jesus Christ, don't worry, I swear to myself that I'll never work again in civilian clothes in this bloody war.

The major hands me a handwritten note which gets me through the edgy Military Police check points.

Back in Lille I find Buckmaster pacing around his office, ripping papers up and throwing them on a fire. He looks exhausted. All around us is the noise of people packing up quickly. Voices, on the cusp of panic, shout orders. Heavy army boots stamp rapidly up and down corridors.

'We're leaving, Bisset. Heading for the coast. In rather a hurry, I'm afraid. A place called Dunkirk.'

'But not you,' he adds. Before I can ask a question, he gestures me to sit down. 'I've recommended you for another job, but your new CO would like to meet you before he decides. I suggest you give your report when he arrives.'

I join him in sipping a welcome cup of tea, wondering uneasily what's in store for me.

'Your father was in banking, I understand?' Buckmaster says in French, eyeing me over the top of his cup. 'Morgan bank was it not? Scottish, wasn't he?'

Surprised, I nod.

'I think I might have met him. I worked in banking in Paris for six years. It was quite a small world.'

There is an uneasy silence, not untypical between a British army officer and a lower rank placed in an awkward social situation.

'Decent chap, your father...' Buckmaster says, half to himself.

I nod.

'You're a lucky fellow. Mine turned out to be a bit of a bounder. I did well at Eton and won a place at Oxford. But I couldn't take it up. No money, you see, my father went bankrupt.'

I nod again. I'd heard of Oxford but what was Eton? I fill another awkward pause. 'Eton, Sir?'

Buckmaster sees my slightly perplexed face. 'Ah, you've never heard of Eton? It's England's top boys' school. Near Windsor Castle. We lived not far from there in a place called Gerrards Cross.' He adds more bitterly. 'We lost our home too.'

I take another sip of tea, unsure what to say to sympathise with the social misdemeanours of Buckmaster's father.

'Eton and Oxford run the country, more or less,' he says half-seriously. 'A bit like a *Grande École* in France,' he explains.

Now in English, he asks, 'How good do you think my French is? Honestly?'

'Excellent Sir.'

'But still with an English accent? I mean I couldn't pass off as a Frenchman, could I?'

'No Sir.'

Through the commotion of an army preparing to retreat, I hear the brisk metallic heel and toe sound of officers' shoes before the door opens swiftly.

'Sorry I'm late, Buckmaster. A few things needed taking care of.'

'I can imagine.'

I stand up and salute a captain well into his forties. Like everyone he looks exhausted. Breezily following behind, puffing on a cigar, is a very tall, barrel-chested lieutenant.

'Bisset, this is Captain Whetmore.'

'I hear you speak French like a native?' the captain asks in his passable French, looking me up and down in my dirty civvies.

'Yes sir. I'm half French and was brought up here.'

Like a human Tower of Pisa, his companion, the tall lieutenant, now leans forward, exhales smoke and introduces himself. 'De Guélis.'

His pronunciation signals immediately he is French. He extends his hand. Mine feels crushed.

He continues in French. 'I'm a liaison officer with the French Army. It is refreshing to meet another Frenchman in the British Army.'

Apart from his larger-than-life demeanour, I am startled by his pure, pure French. I chuckle inwardly. So beautiful was the giant's French that a Norman peasant would have difficulty understanding it. I guess from his name and accent that he must have aristocratic lineage.

De Guélis oozes self-confidence and presence. I can see the other two officers, despite the difference in rank, treat him as an equal.

Buckmaster asks me to give my reconnaissance report. All three wince when I say that the Germans will encircle Lille, well before expectations.

'Putain de merde,' De Guélis swears and then coarsely in English, 'Fucking Germans. I hate what they are doing to my France.'

Bloody hell, his English accent is better than mine. Only the slightest word here and there betrays some French influence.

Whetmore asks me further questions in French about my education and where I lived in Paris. I confirm that I can use a typewriter. He looks at de Guélis who nods, satisfied with my answers.

'Alright, you'll do. I want you to be my secretary.' He smiles at my startled face. 'Don't worry, Bisset, I'm the British liaison officer with the *Bureau de Centralisation de Renseignment* - French Army Intelligence. There's only me. A native French speaker could be very useful to make sure there are no misunderstandings between allies.'

He studies my face. 'You might also overhear things! You know what I mean, old chap?'

I nod obediently.

'Marvellous! Welcome on board Bisset. Come on, we have to dash.

'Good luck,' he adds hurriedly to the other two as I chase after him.

I catch a glimpse of de Guélis waving his cigar through a blue cloud. '*Bonne chance.*'

I'm ordered to change back into uniform, pack my things and accompany Captain Edwin Whetmore to the French Intelligence HQ in Lille. We don't stay long. The Germans get closer, so the next day we travel rapidly to Paris.

Our offices are in the Army Headquarters in Paris's government quarter. I see for myself the near panic in the faces of senior officers and civil servants. There are muttered insults thrown at my uniform as news of the British Army's hasty retreat to Dunkirk spreads – deserters and cowards are the more polite ones.

I have to wait a few days until Whetmore gives me a couple of hours off in the evening to visit my home in Rue de Maubeuge.

'Don't dawdle, Bisset. You never know, we might have to leave in a hurry again.'

It takes me less than ten minutes to walk from the French Army headquarters to the nearest *Métro* station. The streets in the government quarter are quiet. The occasional black chauffeur-driven car with a senior civil servant in the back whizzes past. Now and then a camouflaged army staff car with a pennant on its mudguards drives along with a general and his aide-de-camp in the back. I catch white, strained faces peering down at reports.

The *Métro* is packed with people but all going in one direction - south. I hear accents from Belgium and northern France. I'm heading in the opposite direction and share a carriage with only a handful of people.

One of them, an elderly man approaches me. Despite swaying from the hand straps, I can tell from his upright bearing he has a military background. 'Good afternoon, Corporal,' he says in English. 'I recognised your uniform. I served as a staff officer in the last war and liaised closely with the British,' he explains.

His sharp old eyes look at me. 'Could you please tell me what information you have on the war situation?'

I make a quick decision. Shall I tell him what I know, or should I fob him off? I decide the former. Rumours are flying around. This old warrior deserves the truth.

He is startled when I report in French in a formal military fashion. 'Sir, I regret to inform you that the French and British armies are in full retreat. The Germans are advancing rapidly. The French Army valiantly defended Lille to help the British evacuate from Dunkirk to England. They surrendered three days ago.'

'And how do you know this?' he demands, astonished.

I take a deep breath. 'Sir, I work in the British Army section which is liaising with French Intelligence.'

'Yet, you tell me this presumably confidential information?'

'It will be common knowledge within a few days,' I respond softly.

He digests what I have said. His face is crushed into a mixture of confusion and despair.

'You are French?'

'Half French. Half Scottish.'

'Yet you are deserting us and leaving us to the mercy of the Germans?' he asks in anguish.

I nod. What can I say? He has a point.

He gets out at the next stop a broken man. His shoulders slump and he is unsteady on his feet - his proud bearing has vanished. 'Good luck, Corporal,' he whispers to me.

I alight shortly afterwards at my stop, *Le Peletier,* and am greeted by the sight of roads as crowded as the southbound *Métro.*

I hear a faint, distant rumble above the hubbub in the street. A few people stop and look up, puzzled by the unfamiliar sound. I am the only one to recognise the first Nazi bombs falling on the outskirts of Paris.

My visit to my former home is brief. I can see that the cleaner, to whom my bank pays a modest amount, is keeping the interior clean. I pick up my old school satchel hanging from a chair – it could be useful for my personal possessions - and check the post which she has placed tidily on a table in the hall. Only one letter catches my attention. It is a summons from the French Army to report for enlistment.

'Too late,' I say to myself. And, 'Thank God I chose London.'

I write a short note to the cleaner and tell her I hope to see her again soon.

I slip out the front door and head back towards the *Métro*. On the way I stop at a *parfumerie* which my mother used to visit regularly. It has closed for the evening. I have to ring the bell several times and then knock loudly before I hear a loud and impatient '*J'arrive, j'arrive!*' and the door is flung open.

I recognise the irritated owner and remind her that my mother was one of her customers.

'Of course. I remember Madame Bisset well,' she says, mollified.

'I was so sorry to hear she had died. And you, Monsieur Teddy, I remember you too. But what a surprise to see you in an English Army uniform!' she adds.

I ignore her curiosity. Does she have the item I'm looking for? Indeed she does!

'It was one of your mother's favourites. Only a woman of discernment would use this - it is one of France's best.' She puts a drop on the back of her hand and puts it to my nose. Ah yes, now I recognise it.

She hands me the blue-labelled bottle, carefully wrapped and I slide it into my bag. She grossly overcharges me. I don't mind; I have got what I want.

The bright, late summer evening is beginning to fade as I walk briskly back to the *Métro*. But I am blocked from going down the stairs into the station – there is a dense, angry scrum of people pushing and shouting. I set off on foot – it is nearly dark when I finally get back to the office.

The bottle of *Jicky* is nestling safely at the bottom of my satchel together with Win Marshall's calling card.

14.

Teddy

Whetmore orders me to start burning confidential papers. Just as we did in Lille. He disappears to brief our ambassador. We both know that this is largely a waste of time.

The French Army headquarters is in chaos, close to panic. Reliable intelligence from the field is difficult to obtain on the telephone. We know the Germans are using wireless to command their forces. The best source for the situation in Paris is the American *New York Herald Tribune*.

The feeling towards the British is now acidic. Our French colleagues are furious that France has been left alone after the evacuation from Dunkirk.

A French officer hisses at me, 'England has fought to the last Frenchman!'

Once night has fallen on the 10th June 1940, the French government flees the capital for a chateau east of Orléans, out of range of the Luftwaffe. We follow cautiously, meandering gingerly through the carts and cars of desperate, exhausted refugees. By the road are smouldering wrecks of cars and trucks hit by German planes. Now and then our headlights catch the bodies of civilians and soldiers in the sad, broken puppet shapes formed by people who die violently.

Three hours later tiredness forces our driver to turn into an *aire* – a layby - to snatch some sleep. I wander off into the trees to find somewhere comfortable enough to lie down and rest. In the darkness I have to step carefully to avoid treading on people lying on the ground with their possessions higgledy-piggledy in suitcases, wheelbarrows, prams and hand carts. I make a bed from leaves and branches and my jacket makes a comfortable pillow. I thankfully close my eyes.

I dream of the Christmas party in Lexham Gardens. Like the Cheshire Cat from Alice in Wonderland, Win Marshall's smiling face drifts in and out of my dream. I return her smile and imagine I am giving her the bottle of *Jicky*.

A bayonet pricking at my throat rudely wakes me up.

'Who are you?' a rough accent in French snarls through the grey dawn.

'I am an English soldier.'

The bayonet pricks harder into my skin. I feel a drop of blood.

'Impossible – no Englishman speaks French that good,' he shouts. 'You're a bloody fifth columnist, a traitor, a spy.'

'Kill the *Boche* bastard,' I hear voices in the bushes, egging the soldier on.

Still half-asleep I can't fully comprehend that this is how I am about to die; stabbed through the throat by a Frenchman who thinks I'm a traitor.

'Stop,' a voice in English-accented French orders.

My would-be executioner turns his head and stares into the barrel of a revolver six inches from his face held by a British Army officer.

Whetmore says politely, 'He is telling the truth – he is half French, half English. So don't kill him please.'

I stand and quickly don my jacket with its corporal stripes. The bayonet is grudgingly put away.

'Let's go Bisset, the car's waiting. I suggest we leave your compatriots before you come to harm,' he says calmly in English, slowly enough to dispel any remaining doubts that I am German.

'You were lucky. It took me about ten minutes to find you,' he says disapprovingly as we drive off, weaving our way slowly through hundreds of waking refugees.

I shake my head in disbelief as our car drives off through the paraphernalia of refugees dumped by the roadside: I was nearly killed by the English near Lille. This time it was the French. Thank God Whetmore found me in time.

Staring out of a window later that day in our new offices in the *Chateau du Muguet*, we are surprised to glimpse the rotund figure of Churchill, puffing on a cigar, going into a meeting with the French government cabinet.

Whetmore says *sotto voce,* 'He's buggered up twice now. Once at Gallipoli in the last show and this time in Norway. We can't afford another balls-up.'

Early the next morning our unshaven, pink kimono-clad leader wanders into the office we share with the French and demands, '*Où est mon bain?*'

I stand up and salute. 'Please follow me sir.'

The next time I see him is in the toilet, the bizarre location of the chateau's only telephone.

'You again, Corporal?' he grunts puffing on his cigar.

There is not much to do in the office. Contact with the French front-line forces is fractured and unreliable.

I write a friendly letter to Win Marshall, thanking her for the party. I don't mention she's been on my mind, quite a lot, actually, together with her *Jicky* perfume. I slip the letter into the post bag which is being taken back in Churchill's plane.

Later that day, shortly before Churchill is driven back to Orléans airport, I hear him describe the French junior war minister, Charles de Gaulle as *'l'homme du destin.'*

Whetmore tells the prime minister that the tall, lugubrious Frenchman has a big ego and recommends the prime minister should kiss him on both cheeks. 'I'll kiss him on all four if I have to,' growls Churchill.'

I glean that Churchill has refused further military aid. The attitude in the chateau towards Whetmore and me worsens – we are now detested.

We are on the move again. This time it is Tours and there is another meeting with the British leader.

'What's the point?' I ask myself. France has fallen. The best thing we can do is head for England and lick our wounds.

As if to prove my point the French government flees again, this time to Bordeaux.

Whetmore agrees with me. Continued liaison with a non-functioning French Intelligence is pointless and so does the new British general, Alan Brooke. We are ordered to St Nazaire to await the evacuation of British forces to England.

'You know St Nazaire. Bisset?' Whetmore asks.

'Yes Sir. We used to spend our summer holidays in La Baule, a bit further along the coast. It will probably be easier to find a billet there if St Nazaire is chock-a-block.'

15.

Teddy

My mother would start to hum a popular tune on the road from Paris to La Baule once we reached Angers and crossed the River Maine. We would stop for lunch and she would allow herself more than her usual small glass of her favourite *Muscadet*, as she, my father and I lunched on fresh seafood.

'Ah, Teddy, can you not smell the Atlantic in this glass?' she would ask me, every year, allowing me to sniff her wine. Once I reached sixteen, I was allowed half a glass.

My mother would then doze off in the car until past St Nazaire when she would gradually wake up and sing, 'Oh La Baule, La Baule,' as our car finally entered the smart resort for our summer holiday. She would open the windows of the small villa we hired ever year and let the cool Atlantic breeze wash over us, removing the sweat of hot Paris.

My parents would promenade arm in arm along the *l'esplanade Benoit*, enjoying the evening cool, looking down at the still gleaming white sand of the *'plus belle plage d'Europe'*. Shops and restaurants as good as Paris, my mother would claim excitedly. The same prices too, my father would grumble. She would gaze in admiration at the *Belle Epoch* villas and wonder what it must be like to be rich enough to own such magnificent homes.

Occasionally she and my father would take me to dine in one of the luxurious hotels. The Hermitage was a favourite.

I learnt from my mother the importance of good food to civilisation.

'Only the French truly understand this,' she would whisper in an exaggerated fear of not upsetting my father who would pretend not to hear.

She would shout and wave at me playing on the beach with my Lacroix cousins, building sandcastles and running in relay races in and out of the clear blue sea. I experienced my first kiss with a girl. To my surprise I found out that the opposite sex thought me attractive. And my fluent English was a bonus: I helped with their homework which brought me rewards. How I loved my holidays here.

'A penny for your thoughts, Bisset,' Whetmore says as we stand overlooking the beach a few steps away from our hotel, near La Baule's small harbour.

'Sorry sir. I was daydreaming about my holidays here as a boy.'

It is a sunny, mid-June morning. Whetmore and I are looking out over the beach, thinking about our evacuation from St Nazaire before the Germans arrive. Along the road wounded soldiers from the inland battlefields are being carried into the Hermitage, requisitioned for use as a military hospital.

There are ships dotted everywhere about five miles out to sea. Passenger vessels pressed into service to carry troops and Royal Navy warships, all looking like toy boats floating in a sparkling blue bath.

A plane flies low overhead and we crouch when we see the distinctive black *Luftwaffe* cross on its wings. It disappears quickly out to sea and turns sharply away towards St Nazaire as the navy ships open fire.

'Reconnaissance.'

'Yes, you're right,' Whetmore agrees. We both know it will only be a day, two at the most, before German bombing starts.

He points at one passenger ship, the largest vessel in view, with a big, single funnel.

'That's the *Lancastria,* Cunard line. A luxurious cruise ship, I hear. Perhaps we'll be lucky enough to get on board?'

We drive into St Nazaire the following day. Near the port the roads are full of troops waiting to be marched onto the quay. We have no luck in quickly arranging a passage.

'I don't care if you are in the Intelligence Corps, Captain. My orders are to get as many troops as possible evacuated in an orderly fashion, as directed by their commanding officers. You'll have to wait your turn.' The Royal Navy officer responds to Whetmore's annoyed grimace. 'Look, give it a day or two.'

The telephone rings and we hear a terse commanding voice. 'Yes Sir,' the officer replies dutifully.

He replaces the receiver and remarks half to himself, 'It's funny how telephone lines are the last thing to go. I was only speaking to Brest yesterday.' He gestures out of a window of the St Nazaire Harbour Master's office. 'You can see there are thousands waiting to get on a ship.'

Below there are long lines of soldiers, queuing in a disciplined, calm fashion being directed by sailors into tenders and launches. And snaking behind them on the road from Nantes is a three-mile-long queue of trucks and cars trying to get to the port. Now and then, on the quay below, tempers fray as Army officers try to pull rank and argue with Royal Navy seamen about whose turn it is to get into a boat. Many of the soldiers are in clean uniforms - they haven't seen any action. Their faces are tired and anxious, but nothing like those of their exhausted, defeated comrades that I had seen near Lille.

The naval officer wipes his brow. 'I'm told to expect up to 50,000 soldiers. At the moment I'm concentrating on the *Lancastria.* I reckon I could get up to 8,000 on her.'

Suddenly the men on the quay scatter and throw themselves down onto the quay stones as a German plane swoops down and drops a bomb – it misses and falls into the water sending up an enormous fountain. The soldiers jeer and enjoy the cool splash of water cascading down onto them. More German planes fly over but ignore the St Nazaire docks and continue out to sea.

Whetmore and I head back to La Baule in our staff car in the opposite direction to the traffic jam of army trucks inching itself forward. I am driving with Whetmore sitting next to me, something he'd started doing after we'd left the more formal atmosphere of Tours.

Whetmore taps his watch as we re-enter La Baule. 'Three-thirty old boy. Time for a spot of tea, don't you think?' I was well used by now to the English fanatical observance of after-noon tea.

Like a scene from an impressionist painting, we two men sit on comfortable cushioned chairs staring out to sea, in the shade of a matching pastel-yellow parasol, sipping tea and eating a fresh *tarte au citron*. A year previously the hotel would have been packed. Now we share the terracotta-tiled hotel terrace only with an elderly couple and their pet poodle. We gaze out to sea in silence at a plume of smoke from one of the passenger ships which has been hit by a bomb before we arrived. Through our binoculars we can see that its bridge has been demolished but the crew seem to have the fire under control. For now the skies are clear but we know another attack will be coming. We don't have to wait long.

I wince at the sound of a banshee scream, easily heard by us, as a twin-engine plane dives down almost vertically from the sky but pulls up at the last moment, dropping its bombs. Then another dives, and another.

'Ju-88 bombers,' Whetmore says matter-of-factly, a dispassionate intelligence officer, observing through his binoculars.

'They dive at over four hundred miles per hour. I haven't seen them before.'

The warm sunshine on our faces and the scenic view of blue, sparkling water would normally be idyllic, but contrasts starkly with the brutal drama unfolding before us. Much to our helpless guilt, we two British soldiers sit watching German planes bombing and machine gunning the ships of our country only a few miles away. Our fellow soldiers and sailors are being killed while we sip tea and nibble lemon tart, shamefully aware we look as uncaring as Nero watching Christians being thrown to the lions.

Occasionally fighter planes of the Royal Air Force and the *Armée de l'Air* do their best to defend the ships but, by and large, the vessels are left to protect themselves.

'The passenger liners have no guns. They're sitting ducks,' I say.

Most bombs miss their targets but then suddenly we hear a different noise. The muffled sound of a hit. Three times. Then a fourth. A large explosion.

'That's the *Lancastria*,' I say.

'Yes, but she's a big ship. She should be OK,' responds Whetmore.

He's wrong.

We watch anxiously as black smoke shoots out of the big ship's funnel.

Five minutes later the liner begins to list. Through our binoculars, we watch small figures jumping into the sea, a few at first then increasing numbers.

'Bloody hell, they're abandoning ship,' I exclaim.

'Oh God, how many men did that navy officer say were on board?' Eight thousand?' Whetmore asks and answers his own question.

The *Lancastria* is now tilted at a steep sideways angle and is beginning to sink, bow first. We can see a dark, ever-increasing smudge in the sea next to the ship.

'Fuel oil,' Whetmore says. 'The cold sea will make it as thick as treacle.'

Although we can't see them, we know there must be hundreds, perhaps thousands of people being blinded and choked by the oily sludge, fighting for breath and terrified of drowning.

In ghastly confirmation, the German bombers return at low level, machine-gunning the sea and dropping flares.

'The fucking bastards are trying to burn them alive,' I shout, shaking with a young man's fury.

'Quite so,' says Whetmore as calmly as possible, even though I detect a tremor of horror in the voice of a veteran of the bloody horrors of the First World War.

'Quick, come on, let's grab a boat,' he says, pointing to the small harbour at the end of the beach.

Others are running in the same direction. About half a dozen boats already have their engines started and are casting off - we manage to jump in one just in time.

A launch, half a mile in front of us, is strafed opportunistically by a German plane as it heads home. The launch survives. As we get closer, we see the *Lancastria* tip forward with its stern lifting upwards. We hear the screaming of men, clinging to its propeller, as the big ship starts its final plunge.

All the planes have gone. We join a ring of boats around the big pool of thick oil. The risk of fire or engine failure too great to enter, we try to pick up survivors who have managed to swim, paddle on pieces of wood, random flotsam, or row the lifeboats to clear water. Most are in a state of undress, some completely naked. All are coated in black oil and exhausted.

Their hands leave desperate smeared handprints on the side of our boat as they try to scramble up.

With two hands I grab a man under his arms, but he slides from my grasp.

'Let's try again,' I urge.

He smiles weakly and mouths, 'Bye' as he slips away and downwards, his eyes wide-open but unseeing.

We use ropes, boathooks, oars, whatever we can find to manhandle as many survivors as we can into our boat.

This is ghastly, filthy work. I see, not for the first time, how war can crush the human body. But I also experience how resilient and generous the human soul can be. Among those we rescue, there come croaked words of cracking gratitude. And from us, the rescuers, comes in return a surprising emotion of intense elation that we can play a part in saving their lives. Only the weak, white eyes staring through tar-black faces of those unable to speak, signalling despair before they cruelly fade into an eternal abyss, damage our spirits.

Our small launch is soon full so we head back to La Baule. People on the shore take the survivors to the Hermitage. We return two more times before we are satisfied there is no one left alive. We are now as filthy as the survivors and nearly as exhausted.

Our hotel-manger reluctantly agrees to let us shower and wash ourselves. I shower fully dressed. It seems the best way to wash my clothes.

Whetmore finds the lines are still open and uses the hotel phone to call St Nazaire. He arranges for a boat to pick us and the survivors up tomorrow morning.

'Probably the last ship back home,' he says, relieved.

We sit once more on the perfect terrace watching the setting sun, this time scowling through streaks of dirty black smoke.

'I feel like a drink,' Whetmore says. He still has lots of francs left so I order an expensive bottle.

We gulp the first glass, swishing it around our mouths to get rid of the foul taste of tar.

'This is nice,' Whetmore says as he drinks his second glass more slowly.

'Yes, it was my mother's favourite,' I reply. 'The best *Muscadet* comes from between the Sèvres and Maine rivers,' I add abstractly, repeating something from another life.

'You know your wine?' Whetmore asks dispiritedly, seeking to distract his thoughts away from the day's events.

'Certainly those from the Loire. My parents took me for a holiday along the river when I was old enough. My mother proudly showed me round all the big *Chateaux* while my father introduced me quietly to all the white wine *en route*.'

I take a sip, recalling my small family's expedition. 'We tasted as far as *Sancerre*. Some of the reds too, like *Chinon*. My mother was not particularly pleased with my father when she found out how much I'd drunk.'

Whetmore smiles. 'I had a similar experience. When I was eighteen my father took me to lunch at his club, the Travellers. He insisted the best way to learn about France's geography was through wine.'

He sees the fleeting question on my face. 'The Travellers is one of London's gentlemen's clubs. As the name suggests its members tend to be well-travelled diplomats, soldiers, explorers and so on. Not all British. As a matter of fact, your Talleyrand was a member when he was the French ambassador.'

He leant back in his chair. 'We started off with *Champagne*, went along the Loire for a bit, through *Burgundy* and then into *Bordeaux*. My father said it would be better if we left the *Rhone* for another time.' He shook his head at the memory. 'Christ, my mother was furious with him. I was completely sozzled.

'Anyway, I became a claret man,' Whetmore observes. '*Pomerol* wines are my favourite. I particularly like *Chateau Gazin.*'

I note his choice of a very expensive wine that my father, a canny Scot, would never have bought. I merely comment, 'My father liked *Bordeaux* too. He ignored the famous names, though. He called his favourite wine, 'Old Faithful' – from *Chateau Beaumont*, not far north of *Margaux.*'

We grimace guiltily at our heartless conversation but then reflect quietly that civilised life must continue, however traumatic the circumstances. How else can one cope with the terrible scenes we've just witnessed?

I break the silence. 'Do you think we will lose?' I ask. 'The war I mean.'

'What do you think? You're half-French. Will the same thing happen to England?'

'The French leaders gave up. Their spirit was broken,' I say, ruefully. I twirl my glass on the table and sip the tangy wine.

'I can never forgive what the bastards are doing to France. Both my French and Scottish halves will never surrender.'

'You have your answer,' Whetmore says softly and orders another bottle. 'Speaking of your two halves. You know that Winston offered a union of our two countries?'

'No,' I frown. 'What's the point of a union?'

He pours us another two large glasses. By now my tongue is like leather. We could have been drinking the roughest *vin de table*.

'That way Britain would have to treat the German invasion of France as if it were an invasion of its territory; it would have no choice but to go on fighting. Surrender by either France or Britain by themselves would not be an option.'

'That's incredible,' I say, accepting another glass.

Whetmore nods. 'Isn't it just?' He sighs. 'Even though the proposal was cooked up by a Frenchman called Jean Monnet, the French Government turned it down.'

I shake my head in disappointment.

'Just imagine if France and Great Britain had become one bi-lingual country like Canada. Would we have had one national anthem?' he says moodily, swirling his wine around.

Already tipsy, we look at each other, grin spontaneously and start to hum and then sing *La Marseillaise.*

Our voices are soft at first, then louder. The hotel front door opens and a shaft of light illuminates us in the dusky shadows. Our waiter, silhouetted in the doorway, joins in with a loud baritone. Above us the elderly couple fling open their windows and sing along too, their voices quivering with emotion. Their poodle barks with excitement. More windows open in nearby buildings. The world's most glorious national anthem reverberates along the seafront.

Then the singing finishes – the last words bellowed with gusto. It is followed by a moment of intense silence, broken only by the sound of soft waves lapping onto the beach, soothing our worries. I wipe away moisture from my eyes.

Whetmore smiles. 'France's leaders may be broken but its people have not given up.'

The waiter strides over with our unfinished but still edible *tarte au citron* and hands us each a *digestif* of cognac.

'You have heard that France is surrendering? Before we answer he demands, 'You English will come back?'

'Yes, without a doubt,' Whetmore confirms.

The waiter looks at our faces. 'Good, I believe you.'

Exhaustion engulfs our inebriation. We gulp our cognac down and manage to croak, *'Dormez bien.'*

I collapse in my damp uniform onto my hotel bed and kick my boots off.

***

Morning sunlight breaks through my open curtains. I look down onto low tide on the beautiful beach of La Baule and see about fifty, tar-stained khaki bodies scattered along the high-water mark.

We know we must check the pockets of those who are officers for anything useful to the enemy. Several of the dead are wearing life jackets with strange, lolling heads. Whetmore tells me, 'Poor bastards. If you don't jump properly, cushioning your fall into the water, your life jacket will break your neck.'

I am now immune to the oil-stained features of dead men as I rip open their uniforms and check for any documents. Lieutenants, captains, majors and a couple of colonels are searched. Maps and orders are retrieved or ripped up. My hands become covered with a red rash and oil seeps into split nails. All the while we are keeping an eye out for the Royal Navy.

By noon a frigate finally arrives offshore and lowers a couple of small launches. Men file out of the Hermitage, some carried on stretchers, and all make their way through shallow water into the small boats.

Whetmore and I are the last to be picked up.

Wading out, I suddenly remember something and turn back. '*Merde*, I've left something in the car,' I shout.

'Come back, you bloody fool, the Germans will capture you,' Whetmore bellows.

I ignore him and dash up the beach, sand filling my boots. Frantically I search my satchel on the back seat. Ah, there it is. I place the wrapped box and card onto my head and strap my helmet tightly down on top. I sprint back.

The water's up to my chest as I'm pulled into the boat.

'What can be so important?' Whetmore asks baffled.

'Perfume sir. Perfume for *my girl*,' I shout grinning from ear to ear. The boat roars its approval - even the wounded force a cheer and give me a thumbs up. Whetmore shakes his head and laughs along with the others. I like Whetmore. He's the first army officer I've met who seems a decent chap.

My girl? I surprise myself.

Yes, she may not know it yet, but she's going to be my girl.

16.

Win

Somehow we have managed to turn the disastrous defeat in France into a celebration of a miraculous escape by our army from Dunkirk before it is annihilated by the Nazi's *Blitzkrieg*. The expected invasion has not taken place. Instead, the Luftwaffe is trying to rule the skies. Above London people stare up at the vapour trails of the dog fights between Spitfires and Messerschmitts. In Churchill's phrase, this is the Battle of Britain, but life continues peacefully for most of those on the ground.

My lessons continue with Sol – which is how I'm now permitted to call him. Am I improving? His face is impassive. But he listens more and only makes brief comments. I feel most of my fingers are stronger but not yet to his high standards. Oh, Sol, for God's sake give me some encouragement.

'Win, in the ascending scale the thumb is in search of the note. In the descending scale the note is in search of the scale,' Sol lectures me.

But it is a measure of my progress under his tough regime that after six months I now understand and accept his method and style completely.

He even allows me to move my arms a tiny bit, although he says sternly, 'As a musical aid we can find no logical reason for the employment of arm-movement.'

He warns me that a pianist, 'Must be just as level-headed and controlled as a diplomat.'

But at last, in my notebook, I record, 'I do declare, a glimmer of daylight.'

As a reward Sol promotes me to five more exercises. These concentrate on the poor little fourth and fifth fingers and give each its individual control, not forgetting, of course, Sol instructs me, that the passing of the thumb underneath must be in as quiet and graceful a manner as possible.

I'm now permitted by Sol to play pieces which he selects – Beethoven's *Bagatelles* are his staple.

'Listen carefully to him, Win. They are like an artist's sketches before he goes on to major works.'

My steady progress continues but on and on I slog in the evenings with the exercises on my rented piano in the back of the music shop on the Kensington High Street – the two owners are delighted to accommodate one of Solomon's students. Occasionally they stay on and listen after they close the shop. But they don't stay long - listening to scales, however well-played is not particularly appealing. Oddly enough I do find that the marked increase in my fingers' strength means I'm enjoying playing the piano more.

I graduate to the exercise for the right and left hand to obtain the correct spacing of fingers to achieve, 'a moment of stillness and penetration through the keyboard.'

Then comes the blessed, magical day. Sol says that I am on course for a debut recital at the Wigmore Hall in September, two months from now, almost a year to the day since he started teaching me.

Leaving Sol at the college, I walk towards the music shop. More like I bounce along with glee singing the words, 'Wigmore Hall, Wigmore Hall, Wigmore Hall!'

Finally, I am going to be a concert pianist. I am bursting to share the news with someone.

I wave across the road at the statue of Prince Albert, sitting resplendent in his ridiculous golden Roman toga. 'Hi Albi, I'm going to play at the Wigmore Hall. I hope you can come too,' I wave.

I sit down at my piano in the back of the closed shop. Sol's practice routine goes out the window and I indulge myself with pure enjoyment: I dive into Chopin's *Nocturne*, Clara Schumann's *Piano Concerto* and finish with Debussy's *Clair de Lune*. Oh my God, I play with pride, freedom and passion. I conclude with a guilty flourish of my hands. Sol would definitely not approve. I giggle like a schoolgirl.

'Brava, brava,' accompanied by enthusiastic clapping greet my ending.

Astonished, I swivel round and see the two shop owners, shaking their heads in admiration.

'Oh, I'm sorry, I thought I was alone.'

'We apologise for startling you. We'd forgotten something. But I have to say, Win, that was truly magnificent.'

Red-faced I bow my head. They are my first audience. I beam with pleasure. Oh, how I wish the Mater and Pop (and even Lloyd) had been here. I play gaily on until seven o'clock, still a mid-summer light evening. Time to return to the flat.

In between the music sheets and my books, I fumble in my big carry-bag for the shop key to lock up; it clinks against glass. Peering down in the dark depths, I see an empty bottle of *Jicky*. Ah, so that's where it ended up. I wonder what happened to that good-looking French boy at Marjorie's Christmas party who promised to get me some more? Was I imagining it? Had he smiled at me in a way that suggested he found me attractive? Can't think why; I'd done nothing really to encourage him. I'd noticed he'd caught the fancy of quite a few other girls at the party, though. True, he had dropped me a short letter in June saying he was still alive after some exciting times. He hoped to visit me again before I left England. I'd barely glanced at his letter and thought no more of him. I suppose he was killed in Dunkirk? I know so many of them were. His name was Teddy?

'Hello Win, you've got a visitor,' Marjorie grins, surreptitiously girl to girl, as she greets me at the front door, before I have time to put the key in the lock. She must have seen me coming from the window.

'Visitor? Who me?' I look blankly over her shoulder into the sitting room.

'Hello,' the French boy says casually, walking over.

And then he hands me a small, wrapped present in paper which is badly frayed and stained. 'Here, I brought you this. I'm sorry it's a bit, er, weather-beaten.'

'Oh, I thought you were…'

'No, I'm still very much alive,' he cuts me short, chuckling.

I open the present. A bottle of *Jicky*.

'Oh, how much do I owe you?' I blurt crassly, as if he's just popped around the corner to buy it for me.

'Nothing.'

'No, I insist.' I reach for my bag.

'No, that won't be necessary.' As he speaks, I notice for the first time his eyes. They are teasing me – in a nice way, a friendly way.

He hesitates and then adds, slightly shyly, 'I thought perhaps we could go for a drink.'

'What, now?' I answer, flustered. I glance at a mirror in the hallway. My hair's a mess, I need some lipstick.

Marjorie interrupts. 'Oh for God's sake Win, you look fine. Teddy's only inviting you to go for a drink. Just go, will you.'

His eyes appeal to Marjorie for a suggestion.

'Oh, of course, you don't know London well, do you Teddy? Well, why don't you go to the Devonshire Arms? It's only five minutes' walk around the corner.'

17.

Teddy

We sit in the pub's walled beer garden. It's busy but people move over and we share a table - there's a war on and anyone in uniform gets a friendly reception. I buy her a gin and tonic while I order some white wine. I'm pleasantly surprised; the Devonshire Arms has some *Chablis*. I look around. Ah yes, the clientele seem well-heeled and probably know their French wine.

Our first words could be awkward but Win helps me out. She points up at the bright, white streak of a solitary vapour trail highlighted by the evening sun. 'I suppose he's just checking that Jerry really has gone for the day?'

'Yes, he probably is,' I agree and, keen to fill a gap in our conversation, I add, 'I think we're winning. Well, the Air Force is, at any rate.'

Nervously, Win looks at me over her glass. 'I'm so sorry that I was rude to you in the flat. I'm really very grateful that you managed to get some *Jicky* for me.'

'Please don't worry. I enjoyed hunting it down for you.'

She smiles, trying to make amends. 'Did you buy it in Paris?'

'Yes, I did. But not in the *Champs-Elysées*. I got it from the *parfumerie* where my mother shopped. In fact, my mother used to wear it sometimes. I thought I recognised it at your party.' My turn to smile. 'The *parfumière* said it was worn by women who have good taste.'

'You can't flatter me,' says her face, but I can see from the whimsical twitch at the corners of her eyes she enjoys my flirtatious compliment.

'How did you manage to get it out from Dunkirk without breaking it?'

Merde, I'm going to have to lie. She can't have noticed the date on my letter which was about a week after Dunkirk. I can't tell her that I left France from St Nazaire. The conversation might inadvertently lead on to the *Lancastria* disaster – there have already been rumours. We have been strictly ordered never to talk about the loss. Churchill does not want anything which might tarnish the joyous Dunkirk story, which turned 'defeat into victory'.

'I had to wade out to a boat with it on my head, strapped down tightly under my cap.'

She bursts out laughing. A full-throated guffaw of a woman who does not care about being considered unladylike.

She looks at me closely. No longer contrite, I can see she's inspecting me.

'Tell me about Australia,' I pause and, for the first time, call her, 'Win'.

She accepts the mild intimacy of her first name and responds jocularly. 'Well, *Teddy*, what do you want to know?'

'I've heard about kangaroos and koalas but not much else.'

'Oh God,' she hesitates and then grins impishly. 'Obviously we are,' she pauses to emphasise her next words, '*a sunburnt country, a land of sweeping plains, of ragged mountain ranges, of droughts and flooding rains…*'

A couple of Australian officers seated in the shadows next to the garden wall overhear her and continue, '*I love her far horizons, I love her jewel-sea, her beauty and her terror… the wide brown land for me!*' they bellow, their voices banging off the ivy-clad walls. Everyone else turns and stares at the noise.

'Good on you,' they chuckle, raising their glasses to Win.

She looks at them and puts a finger to her lips. 'Shh'.

I'm confused.

Win giggles. 'I'm sorry Teddy. It's a poem by Dorothea Mackellar all Australians learn at school. I couldn't resist. I just didn't know where to start about Australia.'

'You like poetry?'

'It's in my blood,' she nods. 'My second name is Wordsworth, he was my great-great-grandmother's uncle.

She sees my blank face.

'He was a famous English poet. You must know, *I wandered lonely as a cloud that floats on high o'er vales and hills, when all at once I saw a crowd, a host, of golden daffodils; beside the lake, beneath the trees, fluttering and dancing in the breeze.*'

She recites musically, giving the words cadence and feeling. I regret having to say, 'I'm sorry, I've never heard of him.'

She shrugs her shoulders. 'How about, *Entre les pattes d'un Lion, Un Rat sortit de terre assez 'à l'étourdie: Le Roi des animaux, en cette occasion, Montra ce qu'il était, et lui donna la vie.*'

I break in, laughing, my right hand conducting myself,'*Ce bienfait ne fut pas perdu. Quelqu'un aurait-il jamais cru? Qu'un Lion d'un Rat eût affaire ?*'

'You were taught French at school?' I ask, my chin resting on my hand, looking at Win in admiration.

'Yes, but I wasn't much good. I had to learn La Fontaine's poem off by heart to pass an exam. It's one of my party tricks to recite it and bluff people that my French is good.' She laughs. 'Wasn't he clever that Mr Lion? Sparing Mr Rat's life paid off in the end.'

A pause while she takes a cigarette packet out of her handbag and asks for a light.

'I smoke too much,' she says, puffing smoke out of the corner of her mouth. 'One of my bad habits,' she adds.

'I smoke too. I can't criticise.'

'So, come on, give me a French poem.'

I think quickly how to respond in a similar vein.

As she sees me smirking, she orders, 'No, don't you dare recite *Sur le pont d'Avignon.*'

'Alright I won't. Listen to this. '*La courbe de tes yeux fait le tour de mon cœur, Un rond de danse et de douceur, Auréole du temps, berceau nocturne et sûr, Et si je ne sais plus tout ce que j'ai vécu. C'est que tes yeux ne m'ont pas toujours vu.* '

She breathes. 'Oh my God, that was marvellous.

'It's not fair, is it? French is so much more beautiful than English. A French accent in English is charming. I know an English accent in French is awful.'

I shrug my shoulders. 'Like you: Just something I learnt at school.' Of course, I daren't say that I used to recite it to impress girls.

'My father, we call him Pop, says that French is the language of love, Italian is the language of song and English the language of business.'

'And what is German?' I ask.

'That's easy,' she says. 'German is the language of war.'

She has a point.

'But what a tragedy that a country that can produce Beethoven can also produce a murdering sod like Hitler.'

'Yes, awful. Simply ghastly,' Win sighs, puffing on her cigarette.

She lightens our conversation by playing a pretend piano with her hands. 'I've got to know Ludwig very well. My tutor, Solomon, is his greatest fan.'

Then she smiles sadly. 'Ironic really, seeing Solomon is Jewish.'

Another puff and she lays down her cigarette onto an ashtray and excuses herself; she needs to visit the Ladies.

I slowly swirl my wine around and idly pose myself the question that eventually confronts most men: What is it about a certain woman that attracts a man and makes him think maybe she's *the one?* My English Aunt Laura, feeling duty-bound to advise a nephew without parents, instructed me about a month ago.

'Teddy, whatever you do, don't marry the woman you *can't* live without. Marry the one you *can* live with.'

Although she was trying to be diplomatic, I could see that she was worried about a very pretty, but vacuous girl I'd brought to her home for afternoon tea.

Physical attraction is important, of course. Personality? Education? Common interests? A sense of humour? Yes, all those. But with Win I suspect there may be something else. Aren't we both outsiders? Am I right to sense she would share my ambivalent feelings about England? I know I don't fit in completely here. Although I love France too, I have felt not exactly a foreigner but always slightly detached growing up there. Perhaps I should live in a boat anchored in the middle of the English Channel?

And Win? She's Australian. Even though she has English and Scottish ancestry, I bet she sometimes feels a bit like a fish out of water in the 'Mother Country'.

I hear Win's voice and turn around to see her chatting to the Australian officers. One of them, a good-looking young man unsteadily gets to his feet and gently tugs her elbow, inviting her to sit down. I am kicked in the guts by a primal, intense male emotion. Jealousy.

'Let her go, you bastard,' an inner furious voice hisses. 'She's mine.'

My fists shake and clench as I fantasise about punching the Australian's face. My God, I've never felt jealousy like this. Ever.

I start to relax as Win smiles, shakes her head and disappears through the pub's back door.

I take a swig from my glass and light a cigarette. My hands

are no longer trembling.

She's back. Another sip of her gin and tonic. 'Come on, tell me more about France.'

I'm flummoxed. Win was so witty and entertaining. How am I to respond without appearing dull. I want to impress her.

I'm rescued. A hand suddenly taps me on the back. 'Hello Bisset. Didn't think I'd bump into you in this neck of the woods.'

I recognise the voice. Captain Whetmore.

He puts a hand on my shoulder. 'No, don't get up.'

The captain smiles at Win. 'Ah, this must be *your girl*?'

Her face registers surprise. Mine goes bright red.

Whetmore's social antennae twitch as he retrieves the awkward situation immediately. He holds his hand out. 'Hello, I'm Edwin Whetmore. Bisset and I were in France together.'

She shakes his hand firmly. 'I'm Win Marshall.'

No shyness, I notice.

'Has he given you the perfume?'

Win nods.

'Good. But has he told you yet that he risked his life to get it?'

Win shakes her head and says slowly, raising her eyebrows, 'No.'

'Well, he almost missed the boat,' he chuckles. 'Look after him, he's a good man. Knows his wine - always a good sign.' He nods at Win. 'I must dash. Nice to meet you.' 'I expect I'll see you again, Bisset,' he adds.

With that he breezes off with his companion.

'So, I'm *your girl*, am I, Bisset?' she says dryly, taking off Whetmore's manner and upper-class English accent to the tee.

In mock-embarrassment I cover my face with my hands.

My God she's funny. She makes me laugh.

'In that case, I'd like another G&T, please,' she murmurs, her oh-so-bright eyes dancing.

18.

Win

Teddy turns to me on the pavement, a few steps from the pub. I know what is coming and am looking forward to it. I'm glad he doesn't try to play tonsil hockey, which is what some of the girls at school had called it. Instead he kisses me slowly on both cheeks and softly brushes my lips. Twice. I'd forgotten how thrilling it is to be kissed sexually by a man. Funny how the mind works. I'm transported back to kissing Grahame on his father's boat, *The Victory*, scudding up and over white-crested waves. That was what, five years ago? All this reminds me nervously that I'm a virgin.

Teddy squeezes my hands and I squeeze back. 'Ouch,' he says, quickly pulling his hands back. 'Gosh, you've got strong fingers,' he adds, flicking the pain away in surprise.

'Oh God, what a start,' I scream at myself. 'I'm sorry. I've just done six months' strengthening exercises.'

'I had no idea pianists had to be so strong.'

I try to make light of it. 'Well, it's not called the piano*forte* for nothing.'

He laughs.

Then suddenly. 'May I see you again, Win?'

I stand still and look at him straight in the face. We both sense that my reply might set us on course to a serious relationship.

I take him by both hands and squeeze them *gently*. 'Yes, of course.' I grin. 'After all, I am *your girl*.'

'I wish I could stay longer but I've got to get back. I'm late.'

'I know, I know, you've got a train to catch. You men always have.'

Arm in arm, we stroll for ten minutes on the warm West London stone pavement slabs towards the nearest Underground station. We don't exchange more than a couple of words. Our minds are too busy churning over the implications of our mutual consent to explore a possible relationship.

We stop under the circular Earls Court station sign and, just before Teddy disappears through the turnstile, he turns and blows me a hugely exaggerated kiss.

I laugh and respond in kind.

He's funny.

Good-looking too.

A slim figure – well, we're all thin now thanks to rationing. And his voice? Oh, that charming, seductive French accent!

Is he, could he be *the one?* I ponder this fundamental question, walking slowly back to the flat. Miles away in my thoughts, I step out into the road without looking. A taxi swerves and just misses me. The cabbie toots his horn and I catch a furious cockney yell, 'Wotch it, yer bleedin' idiot!'

I turn into Lexham Gardens and realise I must calm down and gather my thoughts. My shaky hands fish around in my handbag for the key to the communal gardens. Sitting on a bench in the dimming dusk, I clumsily strike a match to light a cigarette.

'Well dear, what a-to-do!' I say aloud, blowing smoke up into the sky. Even though it makes me furious with myself I can't help asking, 'What would the Mater say?'

Then my father's advice about life springs up. 'The worst sin in life is to be dull, Win. There are too many dull people in this world. Avoid them.'

'Teddy's certainly not dull, Pop.'

From one of the bushes further into the dark gardens, I hear a man's ecstatic groan followed by a young woman's giggle, 'Shh…'

I recognize the voice of a girl from No 37 but I'm not too shocked. The pressures of war with its short holidays for serving men and women and their frantic goodbyes force couples everywhere to seek hidden places in London's parks, gardens and even back alleys behind pubs to have sex. What would it be like if Teddy and I were one of them? I stub my cigarette out and leave the gardens to the horticultural lovers.

Back at the flat, I can't wait to tell Marjorie and Katie about Teddy.

But there is something wrong. Horribly wrong. In the entrance hall I hear Marjorie sobbing in the sitting room. I find Katie with an arm around our flat mate who is weeping on her shoulder. I shudder. It must be news about her Paul. Bad news. We'd heard from Paul's parents that he'd been wounded in France and captured by the Germans.

There's a letter in Marjorie's hand, her knuckles clenched white around it.

My return seems to provide Marjorie with the resolve to stop crying. She sits up straight and dabs her eyes. 'I'm sorry. So sorry to make such a fuss.'

So *English,* I think, in admiration.

Katie tells me softly that Paul's parents have written to Marjorie - they'd never met - to tell her that their son had died in a French hospital.

I say nothing, but return from the kitchen with a bottle and three glasses.

'Here, drink this,' I say, handing Marjorie two fingers of neat Scotch, my other hand gently squeezing her shoulder. I surprise myself at how steady my hands are.

The Mater would be pleased at how calm I'm proving in a crisis.

She manages to swallow it in one go and splutters, 'Thank you, Win.'

I pour her another and some for Katie and me.

I hand Marjorie a lit cigarette.

She manages a stiff smile. 'Never mind me.'

Marjorie pulls from her grasp the crumpled letter from Paul's parents and hands it to me. I read they had been contacted by their son's commanding officer, someone called Captain Buckmaster, who had told them that Paul was a brave young man who had been badly wounded serving his country. He had heard via the Red Cross that Paul had died about a month ago. They had no information about where he was buried, except it was somewhere between Lille and Dunkirk.

I sigh and kiss Marjorie on the cheek. 'How very sad. I'm so, so sorry. I only met Paul the once but I thought he was a lovely chap.'

Marjorie nods bravely, draws heavily on her cigarette and takes another gulp of whisky.

'So, Win, how did it go with Teddy?' she asks, her voice straining with the effort to be normal.

I protest that they don't want to hear about my visit to The Devonshire Arms. But she insists.

Katie nods. 'Come on Win, we'd both like to know,' her eyes begging me to continue - anything to distract Marjorie from her misery.

I sit down. My turn to take a drink and puff on a cigarette.

'Alright, we got on very well. Much better than I expected.' I hesitate. 'I think I like him.' Another puff and sip. 'Very much.'

Katie smiles softly for me to go on.

'We kissed when we left,' I add.

Silence.

'I agreed to see him again.'

More silence.

Then Marjorie stares intently at me, leans forward and squeezes my knee to emphasize her words. 'Listen to me, Win.'

Her hands are shaking. 'Dig deep into your heart. As deep as you can.' She half sobs and recovers herself. 'Don't make the same mistake as me, darling. All I have of Paul is the memory of a few hugs and kisses on this sofa. If your heart tells you that Teddy might be *the one*, don't waste time.'

Katie and I look surprised - Marjorie was always a bit prudish.

Or so we thought.

Her eyes are bright now, her hands steady. 'This bloody war means we've got to seize happiness when we can.'

She sits up ramrod-straight, hands folded in her lap like a teacher. 'For God's sake you two, we could all be dead soon.' More whisky, but this time a measured, determined sip. 'If the Germans invade, we will never surrender,' she adds Churchillian-like. It sounds corny but I know she means it.

Really means it.

Like we all do.

19.

Win

I take Marjorie's advice and lose my virginity one Saturday afternoon in a large, pleasant house in north London.

Why does one say lose virginity. It can't be found again, can it?

Teddy had telephoned. 'Win, I've got to come up to London this week. But I'm free this Saturday. Would you like to have lunch?'

'Yes, that would be lovely. Whereabouts?'

'There's a lovely pub called The Spaniards in Hampstead.'

I think to myself, *Why such a long way from here?*

'I'm staying with my Uncle George. His house is in Muswell Hill, not too far from the pub.'

The long-distance line is crackly, almost as if the telephone operator is listening in, so he has to repeat himself. 'The thing is, Uncle George's away on Saturday. I thought after lunch we could go to his house and relax, listen to music have a drink, maybe...' His voice tails off. 'Win, Win, I can't hear you.'

He sounds anxious, worried that he's overstepped the mark.

'Yes. That sounds lovely.'

I place the receiver down and look at myself in a mirror. My face is blushing with guilt. And nervousness.

So now it's Saturday and my cheeks are flushed once again but this time because of my twenty-minute brisk walk from Hampstead underground station.

Teddy waves at me out of the pub window as I walk towards the door. He politely helps me with my coat and welcomes me with a kiss on both cheeks. I think, how French. I smell tobacco mixed with Old Spice aftershave on his close-shaved cheek. He smells like... like a man.

'You walked? I thought you would have got a cab from the station?'

'No, I wanted to see the view of the City. Sol, my teacher, recommended I walk. He told me he went to King Alfred School which is, I think, near here?'

'Yes, it's quite close. A good school, Uncle George tells me.'

He reminds me of Pop. Handsome in his tweed jacket, dark grey worsted trousers and a cravat. 'I hardly recognise you out of uniform,' I say.

I've made an effort too, but I needed help from Marjorie and Mary. The small allowance from Pop and the Mater means my wardrobe is lacking. My flat mates kit me out in a twin set and pearls and Marjorie's Hermes scarf - thank God we are all about the same size. It can be quite breezy on Hampstead Heath they warn me and the forecast says there's a risk of a shower. At least I have my own light raincoat.

Teddy ushers me with a gentle hand in the small of my back into a wood-panelled dining room with tables covered with starched white linen and glinting wine glasses.

'Champagne?'

Oh dear. If this is a sign of what's to come, I'm not sure I can afford to pay half of the meal.

He reads the menu fastidiously and asks what I would like to eat. I sense that he would prefer it if he ordered for both of us. Teddy sees me watching him.

'I'm sorry Win but my French side comes out in me with food. Which is why I suggested this place. Even with this war on they seem to provide good, er, *grub*.'

His English is near-perfect but he hesitates sometimes, searching for a colloquialism.

'I don't know why Englishmen don't pay more attention to their food. I don't live for food, but seeing that I have to eat, when I have the chance, I try to eat well,' he adds.

'I don't mind your French side coming out,' I smile.

I can tell we are both thinking the same thing: would our warmth during our last meeting prove merely a brief spark?

'Is fish okay?'

'Yes, I love it.'

Thank God. I thought for a moment he might order snails. Or frog's legs!'

He grins as he reads my mind.

The first course throws me. I've never had cold soup before. But I persevere. It is delicious.

'It's called *Vichyssoise,* Win. It's refreshing in summer.'

'I was surprised at first but now I like it. What's it made from?'

A second surprise. 'Potatoes, leeks and cream mainly. They grow a lot of them around Vichy.'

He ensures there's no awkward break in our conversation. 'Vichy is a pleasant town. It's famous for its spas and mineral water. My parents went there a couple of times.' He smiles at a distant family memory. 'My mother enjoyed the plush hotels and restaurants.'

He sips his champagne, glancing at me over his raised glass. He's checking that he's not boring me.

'Maybe I'll visit Vichy one day and see for myself why my mother liked it so much.'

Dover sole follows with a wine new to me, *Muscadet.* He says it goes well with fish and was his mother's favourite. (She sounds a bit like the Mater, always getting what she wants). And then we finish with a small crème caramel.

Any vestigial awkwardness dissipates as our conversation regains the conviviality of our last meeting. We chit-chat and laugh while we eat and explore each other's personalities.

I learn more about him and his life in Paris. Holidays with his parents in Normandy and somewhere called La Baule. I tell him about my parents. The Mater and Pop. And my brother Lloyd. He laughs admiringly when I tell him Lloyd keeps a horse next to the beach and rides him along the sand and into the surf. Our family holidays down to the cooler south near a place called Albany and day trips to a small island, Rottnest.

I refuse a cognac with my coffee.

The meal is just right: not too heavy, not too light.

'Teddy,' I say, 'That was *very* good.'

He's relieved. 'I was a bit worried that you might think I was being bossy.'

Relaxing, smoking our cigarettes over coffee, I offer to pay my share of the meal.

He shakes his head. 'All the time I was in France I had nothing to spend my money on. I saved all my pay.' He grins. 'Apart from your *Jicky*.'

A pause while we ponder the next step.

I fill it with, 'You said Uncle George's house is not far from here?'

'Yes, he's got a big house in Muswell Hill.'

'Win, do you fancy a walk in the park next to Alexandra Palace? It's five minutes from Uncle George's. I thought we could wander around for a while and let our lunch settle.'

I josh him. 'What a post-prandial perambulation? My father, Pop, is keen on Latinisms and always used to call it that when we went for a walk along the seashore after our Sunday roast.'

His turn to grin. 'Oh yes, I know from my father's family how important a Sunday roast is. And you have the same tradition in Australia too?'

'Too right, mate.'

'That's funny. Isn't it too hot?'

'It can be but not as hot as poor old Father Christmas in December!'

Teddy smiles politely but I can tell his mind is straying when he asks awkwardly, 'Shall I order a cab?'

I'm relieved he sounds as nervous as me.

'Vallence Road, Muswell Hill please,' he tells the driver. 'The house is called *Northfields*.'

'Alright Guv,' the cabbie says, grinning and throwing Teddy a surreptitious wink as he guesses our intentions.

We hold hands during the journey but do not speak. Our silence continues up to Uncle George's front door.

Any thoughts of a walk have vanished.

***

So, this is true love. Not a question.

Fact.

Complete emotional union with another being. This is what I feel as I study Teddy, lying next to me, dozing peacefully. For the first time I realise a man can be beautiful. So close to me, I touch the skin on his naked body which, glossed by the afternoon sun, is golden, peach-like. He seems to float over the mattress, almost out of this world, a demi-god, as he breathes in and out while his chest gently rises and falls. Physically he has everything: handsome face, lovely eyes and a taut body with long legs.

I run a caressing finger down his glistening, perspiring chest but stop as panic and self-doubt suddenly grab my throat.

I gasp for breath. Am I good enough for him? Why has he chosen me? Won't he jump into bed with the first woman who makes eyes at him? I remember some of the come-hither glances he got at our Lexham Gardens' Christmas Party.

He opens his eyes. 'What are you thinking of, Win?'

'You, me, us.'

'That, Babe, sounds too serious.'

Babe? I didn't expect to be called that. The Mater would definitely *not* approve. But I let it pass.

He leans over and starts to tickle me.

I shriek and twist my body, shaking off his hands.

'Stop Teddy, please.'

He relents. 'I will, seeing I've cheered you up'.

'Yes, you have.'

I lean back onto my pillow and giggle. 'Thank you Uncle George for letting me use your beautiful house. And thank you too, Marjorie,' I add more seriously.

'What do you mean, Win?'

I tell him about the two lovers in Lexham Gardens. I most certainly did not want to have sex under a rhododendron.

'But perhaps next to a fragrant lavender?' Teddy whispers in my ear.

I kick his ankles under the bedcover.

'But why thank Marjorie?' he asks perplexed.

'She told me to grab happiness while I can because, who knows, we could all be dead soon.' I squeeze his hand, *gently.* 'Just like your friend, Paul.'

He twists around, shocked.

'You didn't know?'

'No. I heard he's been wounded but he was alive and recovering in hospital.'

I squeeze his hand again. 'I'm sorry. Silly of me. I just assumed…'

He dismisses my apology with a sad shake of his head.

'Paul and I became pals,' he says. 'But we didn't really know each other that well. I suppose that's what happens in war.' He sighs. 'People from all different walks of life are chucked together. Some live, some die.'

There's a silence. I can see on his distressed face that he's thinking of something awful he must have seen in France.

He looks sadly at me. 'Win, Marjorie's right; we could all be dead inside six months if the Germans invade.'

'But we'll beat them?'

He ducks answering the question.

It's early evening and Uncle George must be on his way back, says Teddy. He insists on ordering a cab for me.

We kiss and hug goodbye.

Je t'aime,' he whispers in my ear.

'When will I see you again?' I respond.

'I'll be in touch as soon as I can. I've got to report to my HQ somewhere in Oxford but I'm not sure where I'll be posted,' he replies. 'Please thank Marjorie from me too,' he laughs as he helps me into the cab.

Sitting in the cab on the way back to Lexham Gardens, my mind barely notices the suburbs go by as I dare to believe. 'Yes, Teddy's definitely *the one.'*

20.

Teddy

Oriel College, Oxford. After the trudge from the railway station I am sweating in my heavy uniform with my satchel and, hanging from it, a gas mask.. I wipe my forehead and smear my palm dry along the college's cool, grey walls. Above I see busts of college benefactors looking down at me disapprovingly.

I step from the sunlight through a small door set into a larger wooden gate, entering a shady entrance way, leading to a bright green quadrangle enclosed by historic buildings. Apart from the grass, it reminds me of a small Loire chateau.

Almost tripping over the thick flagstones, I am confronted at once by a military police sergeant who steps purposefully out of an office. There is a sign above his head saying, Porters' Lodge.

'Stop right there, Corporal. What's your business?' he barks in a broad Scottish accent.

I now see two red-capped privates following behind him, rifles held across their chests. They are desperate for me to say anything the slightest bit incriminating which could be used to detain me.

'I've been told to report to Field Security HQ, Sergeant.'

'Ah yes, Field Security,' he sneers.

'You lot are now part of the *Intelligence* Corps,' he says sarcastically, stressing the word 'intelligence', implying the opposite.

'The Military Police wasn't good enough for you, was it?' he adds, cocking his head. His eyebrows jump up and down aggressively waiting for me to reply.

I'm used to sergeants with an axe to grind and remain silent. He reminds me uncomfortably of the sergeant near Lille who wanted to shoot me out of hand.

'Don't ask me Sarge,' I eventually say in the world-weary tones of ordinary soldiers used to stupid orders from above.

'That's Sergeant to you laddie,' he smirks, pleased that I've given him an opening to be unpleasant. 'And do your top button up,' he barks.

'Yes Sergeant,'

'Alright. Name?' he scowls, looking at a list on his clipboard.

'Bisset,' I answer, inadvertently using the French pronunciation by dropping the tee.

He frowns. 'What's that accent?' The two privates smirk and grip their rifles more tightly.

'I'm half French, half—' I hastily stop myself from saying British, 'half Scots.'

His eyebrows jump up and down furiously.

'My father was from Edinburgh.'

'Oh aye. What did he do there?'

'He worked for the Royal Mail.'

'*Go on,*' his face indicates.

'He got a job in a bank in Paris. That's where he met my mother.'

His eyebrows subside and his face becomes more receptive. He chews reflectively on the end of a pencil.

'That'll do, Corporal,' he says, reluctantly satisfied I am not a German spy. Disappointed, the two privates relax. He ticks my name off on his list and orders me to follow him.

He marches me through the quadrangle and into another. Then I'm surprised. Like the Alice in Wonderland rabbit, he leads me down some stairs into an underground tiled tunnel and then up into a narrow alleyway the other side. More surprise. I glimpse shops through windows along the alley. Amazingly I catch a whiff of something which I haven't tasted for months, real coffee. I catch a glance through the rear window of a smart café.

He strides in front of me as if on parade and opens a door of an innocuous-looking old building which blends in with its surroundings. The sounds of a busy office wash over us. Typewriters, telephones and chatter.

I walk in alone, ignoring the sergeant, not sure who to ask for. Pretty young secretaries in army uniform glance up and smile at me between the rings of their typewriter carriages and the clash as they push them back. One, with sergeant stripes on her arms, fishes a paper from her IN tray and walks over.

'Yes?' she asks sternly.

I ponder momentarily… why are sergeants always so unfriendly?

'Bisset,' I respond just as curtly.

As her eyes scan her paperwork, an avuncular voice booms from a nearby ajar door , 'Come in dear boy. I've been expecting you.'

The sergeant's eyes quickly check my name. She nods and stands aside.

Captain Edwin Whetmore extends his hand before I've even entered his small office and guides me into a seat in front of his desk. He's genuinely pleased to see me, proving once again that men who've served close together in the military and witnessed bloody events have a special bond - something that transcends all ranks.

'I told you I expected we'd meet again soon.'

'You did, Sir.'

'Well, how is er, Winfred?' he asks.

'She's fine, thank you.'

'I hope I didn't cause you too much embarrassment.'

I laugh quietly and shake my head. 'No, Sir. In fact you helped break the ice.'

'Splendid, splendid. Do you know Oxford?' he asks.

'No. This is my first time.'

'Um… I know what. Do you fancy a stroll while we chat about your next assignment? I can show you around a bit.'

Whetmore leads me back into the small alleyway with a brief, 'Back in half-an-hour' to the officious sergeant who forces a frosty smile of acknowledgement. After a few minutes of leaving Oriel we pass the back of a large college building.

'That's Christchurch,' he sniffs. 'A big college. Filthy-rich but a bit too left wing for my tastes. Oriel is much more sensible. Very good at rowing too.'

I learn Christchurch has its own cathedral completed by Henry VIII. A college has a cathedral? Yes, he nods. He leads me across a large green meadow owned, yes you've guessed by whom, he says, until we reach a river bank.

'The Charwell,' he says. 'But spelt c-h-*E*-r, ' he adds.

We saunter along a towpath and sit down on a bench, watching whirls drift by in the lazy, brown stream.

I accept a cigarette and wave back at people slowly punting by. Gales of laughter from the small boat's passengers ring out as the skipper with the pole almost falls in. Fun turns to fear as the violently rocking punt almost capsizes.

Prompted by the tableau on the river, Whetmore turns to me and asks casually, 'Do you ever think about the *Lancastria*?'

I bite my lip and gaze down at my boots to conceal unmanly emotion. I blurt, 'Yes, I do. I can't forget the horror. Sometimes I have nightmares about it.'

Whetmore's face is as anguished as mine.

'It's hard to keep bottled up since we can't talk about it to anybody,' I add softly.

He agrees. 'It haunts me too - haven't even told my wife. And I can't discuss it with anyone in the office. They all think I escaped from Dunkirk.' Another heavy draw on his cigarette. 'I saw some terrible things in the last show on the Somme but nothing as bad as what we saw that day.'

It may have only been for a few minutes but I can tell he's grateful to have been able to talk about the *Lancastria* – I realise that's why he summoned me to Oxford, rather allowing me to receive my orders at the Field Security depot in Winchester.

He sighs. 'Christ, war is shit!'

He draws heavily on his cigarette and blows out a thin stream of smoke, while he gazes into the distance. 'You know, all of us are fighting for different visions. For me,' he gestures with his cigarette to encompass our surroundings, - 'Oxford epitomises freedom of expression, no matter how much I disagree with some of it.

'Look at the German universities. The poor bastards risk being shot if they say anything against the Nazis. Whereas here there are plenty of conscientious objectors. We might despise them, but we don't shoot them.'

He reflects for a moment. 'But take a Liverpool docker; he is probably fighting for his family, city and, ludicrous as it sounds, Liverpool Football Club.' He pauses, his face more at ease. 'But you, *monsieur*, I think you are fighting for loftier ideals. The republican values of *Liberté, égalité, fraternité.*'

'*Bien sûr.*'

'But, like the people here, there are millions of French who hate the Germans for all sorts of different reasons.'

We relax for a few more minutes until we stub our cigarettes out on the damp ground.

Whetmore smiles. 'I don't suppose you've ever been to Dorset? A lovely county, I hear.'

'No, Sir. But I guess I will be going there shortly?'

'Correct,' he grins. 'Wraxhall Manor, actually. I've seen a photo. It looks delightful. The HQ of the 151st Infantry Brigade.'

He notices my flash of recognition. 'Yes, that's right, they were around Lille. They did well. Pushed the Germans back for a while. Made Dunkirk easier, I'm told.

'Anyway, they're getting ready to fight the German invasion.'

He explains that efficient field security is needed to look out for people shooting their mouths off in pubs and follow up on sightings of suspected spies.

'Every farmer seems to report enemy agents parachuting down at night. They all need to be checked - one of them might just be real.' He adds casually as we say goodbye, 'Oh, and we'll have to bump you up to sergeant to make sure you have a little more authority.' Whetmore laughs. 'You'll have a motorbike. Lucky devil. You'll be able to go on pub crawls with the army paying for your beer.'

21.

The Mater

'For Christ's sake John, listen to me!'

I glare at my husband. Sometimes I just want to shake him out of his perpetual, calm reverie. I wave Win's letter in front of him, almost knocking his glasses off. 'Take your nose out of that bloody book and read this again, damn you,' I yell. 'I can tell what's going on.' I pause and take a deep breath. 'She's sleeping with him. I know she is.' My face is red. 'I'm her mother. I can read between the lines.'

John's face is shocked. I've never spoken - shouted - to him like this before, and never about sex. I have his full attention now.

'Don't you see, she's softening us up for the next bit of news.' I shake my head, my voice beginning to crack. 'This letter took six weeks to get here.' Another deep breath. 'She's probably pregnant by now.'

'Calm down, Gladys,' he says, taking his glasses off to look straight at me.

'No I won't bloody calm down,' I say, conscious my voice is straining in fury. 'He's not even an officer. Just a bloody corporal.' I take a breath and say, conscious I now sound ridiculous, 'And to top it all he's French.

'How dare she? How dare Win get involved with a man without letting me vet him first! 'Where's Lloyd?' I ask brusquely. 'He'll know what to do.'

'Riding his horse,' John replies, almost monosyllabic, hurt by my attack on his lack of fatherly duty.

I drive quickly down to the beach. A pale winter sun is rising, still low in the cloudless blue sky, casting long shadows across the road. Sparkling, salty plumes shooting upwards from the breaking rollers are being whipped backwards, out to sea, by a stiff, early morning land breeze. The beauty of the day makes me even more furious.

Where is he?

The wind is picking up soft, dry sand and blowing it across the beach, masking the view. I can't see him.

Half out of the car and still furious, I nearly trip as I fumble for my sunglasses in my handbag. I can now see Lloyd, about half a mile along the beach, galloping towards me. My boy is closer now, still galloping hard, the horse's legs invisible through the fog of sand. Dismounted he leads his sweating horse up the dunes to my car.

'What is it, Mater?' he asks anxiously.

'Win,' I reply.

Alarmed he says, 'Is she alright?'

'Yes, but she's involved with a man.'

Lloyd smiles. 'Oh, Mater, calm down.'

'That's what your bloody father said,' I snap, wiping pin-pricks of sand off my lips. Startled by my language, he steps back.

'Shall we go home and talk about it?' he says.

I nod and twist on my heels back to my car. Dammit I say silently, I'm not going to win this family battle, am I?

I seethe in frustration as I angrily crunch through the gears jerking to a halt in our drive.

'I've got to go and bring her back before she makes a fool of herself,' I demand, my arms folded as I pace up and down in front of my husband and son, seated around the kitchen table.

Lloyd looks at his father and turns to plead with me. 'Don't be silly Mater. The government is allowing very few planes, for officials only, and there's a risk you'll be torpedoed if you go by sea.'

'I'll write to her and tell her she should come home,' John adds.

'Fat lot of good that will do,' I scoff. 'You wrote to her before, after the war started, telling her to come back. And she said no. She wanted *to do her bit* for London. For God's sake why can't she *do her bit* here?'

'Nonetheless, Gladys, I will write to Win again. I shall try to persuade her to come home,' John says firmly.

'A bloody corporal,' I mutter.

'Gladys, he's in the Intelligence Corps. They are probably full of people from all sorts of different backgrounds. I bet you rank does not count for too much.'

'And he's French. *And* we know nothing about his family.'

Lloyd rolls his eyes upwards. 'Mater, don't you think you're over-reacting just a little?'

I glare at him and John as I storm from the kitchen, slamming the door behind me.

In the living room, I sit down on the piano stool, still fuming. Win's book is open at the Moonlight Sonata. I inspect the music moodily for a moment and let the piano cover drop down with a loud bang.

I cradle my bowed head in despair, fingers pressing my temples.

Oh, why, why did I do it? Why did I push Win so hard to learn the piano? If I had left her alone, she might have stayed here.

And might have married a suitable boy from the tennis club? Someone like that nice boy, Grahame Deans?

'Christ, I was a fool,' I spit, furious with myself.

22.

Sol

There's something different about Win this afternoon. Her interpretation of the music is lighter – gayer. No, not frivolous but delightful. Her expression is less serious than usual. She is playing with a smile even during the more difficult parts. We are in her final rehearsal for her concert debut at the Wigmore Hall next week.

She makes a slight error and stops, irritated with herself.

'Why don't we take a break?' I say before she starts again. 'You've been playing for thirty minutes.'

She nods and turns around.

'Cigarette?' I proffer.

We light up and wander outside.

'How was your lunch in The Spaniards?'

That smile again.

'It was lovely, Sol. Delicious food,' she adds, happily puffing smoke upwards.

'What was your friend's name again?'

'Teddy.'

'Oh, I thought you said he was French?'

'It's short for Edouard,' she replies, emphasising the French pronunciation, not minding my gentle questioning. Her face is glowing and her eyes even brighter than normal as she mentions Teddy. I realise my Australian student is in love. My first thought is selfish. Will Win's new relationship affect her studies? I dare not admit it to anyone but my concert performances have drastically reduced in number and I have become more dependent on my teaching income.

A rooftop air-raid siren pierces the summer peace. We take little notice. There have been a couple of minor attacks, one in

Harrow north of London, and the other in Croydon, to the south.

Casualties have been few. The RAF has retaliated with a small bombing raid on Berlin.

We saunter slowly, deliberately placing our heels firmly down, pushing up from our toes, smiling at the memory of her first lesson with me.

The street next to the Albert Hall is quiet. Suddenly the peace is interrupted by a murmuration of frightened starlings streaking skywards from the trees. Then, we hear what scared them – a deep, threatening rumble. A few minutes later we hear the drone of several planes flying westwards, high overhead, so many that their vapour trails coalesce into fluffy, white clouds. Gazing upwards we lose count. Fifty? No, many more. One hundred? Two hundred? More? They arc gracefully towards the south, towards France. The rumble is noisier now. And continuous. Anti-aircraft guns open fire from nearby Hyde Park.

'They must be bombing the East End,' I say.

'The bastards,' Win swears, her face showing no fear, only hatred.

We part company, not sure when we will meet again.

It is September 7th 1940. Months of continuous bombing start.

We call it the *Blitz*.

The bombs go on falling through that afternoon until the early hours of the next day.

Once the all-clear sounds I take the first Underground train to St Paul's and walk to my old family home, Fournier Street in Spitalfields. The house is still standing. Keen to witness what's happened I walk further east towards the docks.

It's not long before there are bomb sites in every street. Some homes have completely disappeared. Others appear to have been sliced cleanly in half, looking like huge, opened dolls' houses, offering views of astonishingly undisturbed domestic life. Beds teeter at the edge of sheer drops to streets below, kitchens with shiny pots and pans hanging on walls, and cushions tidily arranged on sitting room sofas. But the strewn piles of rubble and smouldering rafters scattered nearby tell a different story. Here and there blood-stained bricks. Sheets thrown hastily over bodies awaiting collection. Steam from boilers and a whiff of dangerous gas. Desperate men and women, shouting the names of loved ones are still moving bricks by hand, seeking survivors. Others join police, firemen and air raid wardens shovelling dirt and debris aside to open blocked streets.

Now I hear people shouting angry insults and see police hurriedly escorting a smartly dressed couple heading in my direction.

'Fuck off,' says a man shaking his fist.

'Piss off back to your palace,' a woman screams.

'Coming down here to gawp at us. We need help not pity.'

A white-faced king and queen scurry by.

'God bless you, your majesty,' I shout at her.

The queen turns her head to the sole supporting voice. I mimic playing a piano.

Puzzled half-recognition on her face. 'Solomon?'

I nod.

There is a glimpse of a smile of gratitude as a policeman shouts, 'Make way' and pushes me aside.

Hostile glances are thrown at me within the crowd.

'It's them and us mate,' someone snarls.

I walk briskly back towards Fournier Street, head bowed but determined to do my bit to fight for London.

My London.

23.

Teddy

Oh Boy! Can there be a better sensation for a young man? The sun pours down on my head and the wind sweeps my hair back and dries my lips as I roar along the narrow Dorset country lanes on my motorbike. Accelerate, brake, lean left quickly, then right through the tight bends as flickering sunbeams reflect on and off the chrome on my headlight. Squawking birds flap their wings and scatter in alarm, protesting against the whirlwinds of chalky dust. Scared sheep stop munching and scuttle away from hedgerows, seeking sanctuary in the middle of fields.

Speeding over a small humpback bridge, I take off laughing in excitement, but almost lose control as I land hard on the other side. Tyres screeching. I have to skid hard right to keep on the tarmac and avoid a heavy metal gate straight ahead, my knee brushing the road. God, I'm a bloody idiot - I could have killed myself.

Relieved, I kill the engine and roll to a stop in a lay-by. I climb over a stile and wander unsteadily down to the gentle River Frome. Kneeling down on its grassy bank, I splash my face with cool water and wipe the dust away, my hands still trembling.

Now calmer, I lean back on my elbows looking at the rolling green hills. Whetmore had called it Thomas Hardy country. He laughed when I didn't recognise the name. I keep forgetting you were brought up in France, he'd said.

I lie on my back, hands behind my head and stare up at the clean, billowing clouds with their rainbow-coloured fringes as they fly under the sun. I close my eyes and drowsily think of Win.

'I wish you were here, Babe,' I whisper.

I'd arrived two days ago. A staff car driven by a pretty ATS corporal was waiting for me at Maiden Newton station *Are all female staff car drivers chosen for their good looks?*

'I thought you might be important, Sarge,' she says in a friendly voice, appreciating me choosing to sit next to her in the front seat. 'I usually drive Brigadier Nichols. He's the CO of 151st Brigade.'

I nod politely not saying I'd already studied the command organisation.

'I guessed you might be in Intelligence,' she says, looking at my shoulder flashes. 'I'm Jane Walters, by the way,' accompanied by a flashing smile. She glances at my fingers.

No rings.

Her eyes swivel sharply back to the lane with barely a hint of a grin.

'And I'm *Teddy* Bisset.'

She drives fast but skilfully. 'Shouldn't take long, Teddy. It's only about 4 miles to Wraxhall Manor from the station - ten minutes unless we get stuck behind a tractor. I'm to take you straight to a briefing for new arrivals.'

In fact, we are delayed for fifteen minutes by cows in the road. An irate farmer shouts through Jane's window as we weave past, 'You bloody army idiots have left a gate open.'

'We get a lot of that,' Jane says. Troops being trained as quickly as possible have other things on their mind than cows. We all know what's coming soon... a German invasion.'

She knows better than to ask me where I'd come from and what I'd be doing. Conversation falters after the usual pleasantries of how my journey had been.

'Fine thank you, and isn't the countryside beautiful?

'Yes, it is.'

I ask about pubs and restaurants.

'There's nothing around here. Wraxhall's not even a village. Hardly a hamlet really. We tend to go to Dorchester or Weymouth when we get a pass.'

A pill box being built next to a river bridge flashed by.

'Here we are,' Jane says, pulling off the lane into a gravel drive.

She looks at her watch. 'Blast, we're a bit late.'

Whetmore was right; the 17th century Wraxhall Manor was picture-postcard perfect. Limestone and leaded windows with climbing roses and wisteria creepers. But I have no time to appreciate its beauty. Jane leads me through the bustling entrance hall of an army divisional HQ, the khaki of soldiers broken here and there by the dark and light blues of the Royal Navy and RAF.

Jane hurries me up to the top of a spectacular wooden staircase where we tip-toe into a meeting, nodding silent apologies to a red-tabbed colonel standing in front of a large map showing plans of defence fortifications. He is briefing young newcomers – mainly young lieutenants with a scattering of sergeants like me.

There are two lines of defence says the colonel, 'The first is along Chesil Beach.' He sweeps his hand across the map to illustrate its long length. 'The stretch near Weymouth is defended by a tidal lagoon so is unlikely to be the site of a first assault. But the remainder of the beach must be a prime target for an invasion. As would Weymouth's famous beach. It's perfect for getting troops and armour ashore.'

He lets his words sink in for a few seconds and then follows, 'And the second line of defence is twelve miles inland along the River Frome. Which is where we are now, of course.'

He outlines the rushed construction underway of pill boxes, tank islands, and concrete blocks to hamper tank movements. Plans for mine fields and inundating flood plains follow.

'Jerry will be hit hard by the Navy and RAF as they attempt to land but we must accept that German troops and tanks will probably break through the beach defences and then hit the second line along the Frome. We must stop them here to give time for reserves to arrive – to the last man, if necessary,' he says firmly.

The colonel knew his stuff alright. I can see from his medal ribbons he is no novice. Unlike most of the small audience whose questions betray their inexperience and, here and there, ill-concealed fear. Nonetheless the colonel answers patiently, careful not to make anyone feel embarrassed.

I recognise him immediately.

Towards the end, he raises his voice to encourage his young recruits. 'This division was not defeated in France. Yes, we had to retreat but every time *we* engaged the enemy, we either forced them to halt or retreat. We will be equally successful here.'

'Gentlemen,' he coughs slightly as he finishes, 'and ladies, I don't need to remind you that *Careless Talk Costs Lives.*'

What he means, of course, is the opposite; that we all *damn* well need to be reminded to be careful in what we say when away from our posts.

His face becomes stern to emphasise his next words. 'Jerry is almost certainly trying to infiltrate spies around here. Weymouth is full of thousands of evacuees from France and the Channel Islands. It's entirely possible that Jerry spies have slipped through the checks. Pubs, cafes and restaurants in Weymouth, Poole and Shaftsbury will be places they'll visit, hoping to overhear tipsy conversations. Beware of total strangers offering to stand you a round.'

He points to the back of the room where Jane and I are sitting among my new colleagues. 'Our Intelligence friends are keeping a watchful eye to spot anything suspicious. Sometimes they'll be dressed in civvies. If they are, ignore them or pretend you've never seen them before.'

Momentary recognition flicks across his face as he spots me.

He continues, 'They might even get into conversation with your men, to test how careful they actually are. It's part of their job, let's face it, to spy on us to check for security risks.' He wraps up. 'That's it, chaps. Return to your companies and get weaving. We've got lots to do to get ready. It could only be a matter of weeks before the invasion starts.'

Smiling he walks over to me through the departing audience to shake my hand. 'I'm glad you got out. Bisset, isn't it? Near Lille?'

'Yes, Sir.' I salute. I take in the bright crown and two pips on his shoulder. 'Congratulations on your promotion, Colonel.'

'Ah yes,' he pauses, 'My predecessor bought it not far from Dunkirk.' His resigned expression said *life goes on*, meaning really *death goes on and on.*

He turns to my unit commander, a lieutenant who looks about nineteen, fresh out of Sandhurst, and chuckles. 'My sergeant wanted to shoot Bisset as a fifth columnist. He was dressed in civvies.'

He looks back at me but his words were for the benefit of my new unit, 'That was pretty brave to go crawling through the bushes to get close enough to find out what Jerry was up to.' The colonel grins. 'Well, at least I don't think you'll be shot around here if you're rumbled wearing civvies. You might get a black eye, though, if people think you're being too nosey.'

I can tell from the lieutenant's expression that he is impressed by the colonel's praise. It turns out that I am the only one, including himself, in his small command who has actually seen action.

He says respectfully, 'Sergeant Bisset, Jane will give you the address of your billet in Wareham. You'll be sharing it with one of our corporals and two women, one of them Jane, by the way. She'll take you to the transport pool to help collect your motorbike and maps. After that, why don't you go for a ride around our area. The air defence battery in Weymouth gives you a good view of the town.'

Jane, it seems, has been seconded to our unit. It makes sense - a couple going out on the town is much less obvious than a man by himself.

And now, not long after leaving the manor, my lazy break in a peaceful, green meadow, is interrupted. I hear the chain-saw buzz of an aircraft, very low, very fast, getting closer, chased by rifle shots like a chain of firecrackers. Guiltily, I jump up and absurdly draw my pistol. I can see the plane flashing along, further down the gently sloping valley, following the river towards me. It's a German reconnaissance aircraft - must be taking photographs. I shoot as it swoops low enough for me to catch in the blink of an eye its black crosses and for the pilot to salute me sarcastically. In an instant it's gone upstream, the pursing, futile rifle fusillades getting fainter. I holster my revolver and retrace my steps to my motorbike.

I kick my starter pedal and head off towards Weymouth, my spirits dampened by the sight of the Luftwaffe flying so close. I skirt the town centre and follow the sign to Portland Bill. On the narrow isthmus leading to Portland Island, I catch my first sight of Royal Navy ships anchored in the huge harbour. I stop for a while next to Chesil Beach and wave at a picnicking family. I am captivated by the serene family scene and walk over.

Don't they know there's a war on?

A mother, father and two children. The father is in civvies.

'Hello. Beautiful day for a picnic. You've got a lovely spot.'

'Yes, isn't it just,' the mother replies cheerfully. The father is a bit wary of me and gives me a hesitant smile.

'Here, would you like a ham sandwich?'

'Are you sure? I mean…' I hesitate awkwardly, 'what about your ration?'

She laughs. 'Things aren't quite so bad down here. It's not like London, you know.'

I accept gladly, trying not to scoff too quickly the welcome treat of the thick slices of fresh meat.

'You're not from around here, are you? Silly question, I know. All of you soldiers are from somewhere else.'

'You're right, I'm new here. This is my first day, in fact. I'm driving around to get a feel for the area.'

The small boy chewing his sandwich reads my shoulder badge and slowly says aloud, 'Intel… Intell… Intelligence.' He beams proudly.

'What's that? I mean what do you do, Mister?'

I squat down on my heels to his level. 'We keep a look out for anything suspicious which might help the enemy. People behaving oddly. Looking out of place. Asking too many questions.'

His eyes are popping out of his head. 'You mean spies?'

'Yes, could be.'

I pretend to be very serious. 'And you can help. If you see somebody snooping around, please tell a policeman. He'll tell me and I'll investigate.'

'Like a detective, you mean?'

'Yes, just like that.'

His father notices me glancing at his clothes. He says sadly, 'I failed my medical.'

I shrug my shoulders, walk down towards the small waves breaking on shore and pick up a smooth, flat pebble. The boy and his father join me in skimming stones.

The father says defiantly in well-worn words. 'I do my bit as an Air Raid Warden.'

He looks along the beach. 'Perfect place to invade?'

'Yes, I'm afraid it is.'

With a well-practised arm, the father flings one pebble hard and is rewarded by six bounces as it heads out towards the Channel to where the blue sea seamlessly meets this never-ending summer's perfect sky. 'You know, nothing good for England ever comes from over there.'

'I mean, there were the Romans, William the Conqueror, Napoleon and the Kaiser. Now there's this bloke Hitler.'

I don't mention I'm half-French. We walk back to the picnic rug.

Sitting down again the father puts an arm around his boy. 'Don't worry son. We'll be OK. We'll stop Hitler.'

The mother places her hand on his knee in solidarity with her family unit. I can tell from their clothes they are not poor but it's not hard to imagine every penny counts. Even though, in terms of material goods, they have probably not much to lose. But in their quiet, modest way, they are determined to fight.

I'd noticed from my bike that, not far away, on the other side of the narrow isthmus, at the edge of the navy harbour were about twenty large fuel-oil tanks. I stand up, turn to the mother and say softly and casually, so as not to alarm the children. 'I saw a German reconnaissance plane not long ago this morning.' I pause. 'That big fuel depot must be a target for bombers.'

The mother conceals her concern, my message understood. 'Come on kids. We've finished lunch. Let's pack up.'

I leave, fearful for this small English family's future. If the Germans land here, most of Weymouth will be destroyed in the fighting. Will they survive?

I wave a friendly goodbye, speed past the sign saying Mere Oil Fuel Depot and accelerate up to the Heights, the highest point of the island.

The boom gate is down at the entrance to the heavy anti-aircraft battery that I'd seen on my map. A couple of Royal Artillery guards appear from a tent. Welcoming the chance to alleviate their boredom, they give away information freely without checking my identity card and asking simple questions to check my *bona fides*. I feel sorry for them because I'll have to report their carelessness. The guards tell me the battery has four three-inch mobile guns.

'And you know what Sarge? They're training women to fire them. Well, they're girls really, a couple aren't even twenty.'

I steer my way to the tented command post where the CO, a Royal Artillery captain, checks my identity card and quizzes me about the people he knows at Wraxhall Manor.

'I suppose you're here to check on security?' he asks.

I nod in agreement.

Satisfied with my replies, the captain shows me around. 'The sappers are building four permanent concrete emplacements for 3.7-inch guns and a proper command post. We need them urgently.'

He points down to the navy harbour. 'Until July 4th we had *HMS Foylebank*, an anti-aircraft artillery ship as the harbour's main defence. Unfortunately, three Stukas dive-bombed her.

About 170 people were killed when she exploded. One of the crew was awarded the Victoria Cross.'

I shake my head. No, I hadn't heard about the *Foylebank*. I wasn't too surprised. Gossiping about bad news was frowned upon.

He stoops down into a heavily-sandbagged small enclosure. 'Come on, I'll show you our box of tricks.'

Inside on a table there is, as he said, a box with dials and wires. Two young ATS privates are going through a training exercise, looking through two telescopes pointing skywards, turning wheels on the side of the box. The captain gives one a nod of permission. 'Morgan, give the Sergeant a brief summary please.'

The private, who can't be long out of her teens, looks at me. 'This is our computer, Sarge, a Vickers Predictor. We use it to measure the speed of the enemy aircraft, take into account the wind and the curved flight of the shell because of gravity. We've got a separate range finder for the height. So we fire where the aircraft is going to be, not where it was when we first spotted it.'

She takes a moment to check I've followed her and then continues, as if reciting from a memorised training manual, 'The Predictor is wired up to the four guns. The gunners adjust the elevation of the guns and set the fuses. And then fire.' A cheeky grin and a flutter of flirty eyelids from under her helmet. 'Simple really.'

'So you shoot them down every time?'

'No, of course not.' It's on the tip of her tongue to add 'silly' but she continues, smiling at me. 'The pilots weave and duck as they approach the target. But when they start their bombing run, they have to run straight to get their sights on the target, otherwise they'll miss. That's our opportunity.'

Her captain adds, 'Forcing them to miss is almost as good as shooting them down.'

The way she rolls her Rs is the same as the picnicking family did. It must be the local accent. She's seems different from Jane and the other ATS women I've met before. Less reserved and more frank. Left school early, I'd guess, and probably jumped at the chance to get involved in something more exciting than serving in a shop or milking cows on the family farm. She reminds me of the country girls from around my mother's village in Normandy.

She says reassuringly, 'Don't worry, Sarge, we've been well-trained. We're ready.'

Back in the command post the captain confirms the battery will be a mixed company. 'As well as Predictor operators, some of the gunners will be women. All of them are as good as my men. That did surprise me, I must confess.'

He had also seen a reconnaissance plane earlier on. 'It flew low and fast over the harbour before heading inland. It was already gone by the time the navy's ack-ack woke up. And it was too low for us anyway.'

I mention, 'I was in France on the Atlantic coast when we had a bombing raid. A reconnaissance plane had flown overhead just a few hours beforehand.'

He winces as he shows me his map of the Channel and points wearily to Cherbourg. 'They're only half an hour or less from here. Jerry can hop over and bomb our ships in the harbour whenever he feels like it. Cup of tea?'

Sweet, milky tea, as thick as treacle in tin mugs is offered by a soldier. I'm polite and accept a steaming mug.

Sipping the hot drink, I suggest diplomatically, as a sergeant advising an officer. 'Forget the navy ships, Sir. Now the *Foylebank* has gone, I think the fuel depot is a more attractive target.'

He agrees. 'Because of this hill, I'm certain they'd rather fly in from the east, unless they dive bomb, of course.'

We drink our tea outside the tent and gaze silently towards France. The captain, no doubt, sees it simply as the location of the enemy. But for me it is torture. I see beautiful Normandy, the home of my mother's family, now under brutal foreign occupation.

The wireless operator lifts his head, listening intently and scribbles a message on his pad. 'Enemy planes spotted heading due north, Sir.'

'How many?'

'About twenty, Sir. Believed to be heading towards Bristol.'

The captain seems unsurprised. He tells me since the *Blitz* started a few weeks ago the Luftwaffe has turned its attention more to bombing cities instead of solely military targets.

An air raid siren starts to wail down below in Weymouth. Soon after we spot the bombers ten miles or so east of us, like migrating birds, still over the Channel, arrowing through clouds and glinting sunlight. We relax expecting them to hold their course for Bristol. But then we spy two peeling away, heading west directly towards us and Portland Harbour. Even from a distance, I don't need binoculars to identify JU 88s – the same, fast fighter-bombers that had sunk the *Lancastria.*

The captain bellows, 'To your posts,' and under his breath, 'now we'll find out how good the girls really are.'

The two planes approach quickly. One begins its bombing run towards the fuel tanks. The other alters course, climbs and starts circling.

The battery opens fire and accurate flak starts to explode around the plane on its bombing run.

'That's good shooting. Look, the pilot is finding it difficult to hold his line,' the captain shouts above the din. The plane flies past overhead; its bombs fall past the fuel tanks and explode on Chesil beach. The battery cheers.

But now the second JU88 attacks. This one dives swiftly at about 45 degrees directly at the fuel tank depot.

'Fuck,' the captain screams, 'we won't be able to predict its position!'

The bomber is now low enough for us to see clearly the two pilots through the Perspex fuselage. The plane swoops like a hawk, releases its bombs and its engines scream as it climbs rapidly upwards. Over the noise of the screeching engines, we hear the sound of a direct hit - a fuel tank exploding and thick black smoke billowing up higher than our position on the hill.

The bomber veers away towards France. Almost instantly it is attacked by an RAF Hurricane.

'Go on. Get the bastard,' one of the young women screams excitedly.

The exchange of fire between the bomber and fighter lasts less than a minute. The JU88 seems to have more firepower than the Hurricane which comes off second best. We groan as the RAF fighter flips on its side, starts to burn and crashes into the sea.

A moment of utter miserable silence follows. Is there no stopping this powerful enemy?

'Don't believe everything you read in the papers, Sergeant. Around here, at any rate, we're losing more planes than Jerry is,' the captain whispers despondently.

I leave the battery and head off to my allocated digs. Jane has given me a letter addressed to my landlady, Mrs Clarke, Everley, St Martins Lane, Wareham. Along the isthmus I am forced to slow down through thick oily smoke lit by flames from the fuel depot. I can barely make out the shape of ghoulish men fighting the fire.

There's no sign of the family who were picnicking on Chesil Beach.

24.

Win

Sol and I are standing high and precariously on the sloping rooftop tiles of his 120 Kensington Church Street, home. Like watching in the 'gods' of a theatre, we have a clear view eastwards over Hyde Park. It's four days after the start of the *Blitz*. Today's raid had started at four o'clock in the afternoon and had continued through the evening and into the late-summer night.

I have been rehearsing on Sol's own piano in his flat for my Wigmore Hall debut in a couple of weeks' time. We could hear the crump, crump of bombs but we feel safe - they were falling miles away on the other side of London.

At about ten o'clock we finish and take a cognac with us onto the roof.

All London is blacked out - a barely visible, ghostly-grey domain. In the distance giant rods of bright light desperately hunt the sky until they illuminate their prey: bombers, like silver moths, frantically fluttering left and right, trying to escape. For an unlucky few, starbursts turn the moths to flaming red and they fall to the ground. I inwardly cheer each fallen enemy's demise.

We can just make out St Paul's Cathedral, a flickering, orange cupula in the distance, silhouetted against sparklers and fireworks shooting into the night sky.

'My God, they're getting a pasting,' Sol says. 'You know Win, that's where I was brought up,' he adds furiously.

I'm surprised. Sol's accent does not suggest an East End boyhood. I'd assumed a prosperous Jewish suburb like Golders Green.

So far, we feel safe here in the West End. The raids have been on London's docks. Yes, there have been a few bombs scattered here and there but we assume they were unintentional. But tonight, something changes. The bombs are creeping closer and not by accident. One falls only a street away and the force of the explosion shakes our building and cracks a window. Glass tinkles down onto the street. We scuttle down the stairs.

The war has come to the West End and I must do something to help my neighbourhood. I refuse to go back to the ambulance service but hear the Women's Voluntary Service is looking for people to run their mobile tea canteens for the fire crews and police. I volunteer and tell the South Kensington WVS manager, a redoubtable society matron called, Mrs Miller-Sterling, clad in fur with diamonds sparkling on her fingers, that I am prepared to drive into dangerous areas.

'But can you drive a lorry?' asks Mrs Miller-Sterling, doubtfully. 'You look very young. How old are you?'

'Twenty-two. But I've been trained to drive an ambulance,' I say without hesitation. I can tell she's not made up her mind.

'And what is your occupation, my dear?'

I explain I'm being taught how to play the piano by a private tutor. She is unimpressed - clearly students are not high on her list of reliable recruits.

'Oh yes. And what is your tutor's name?' she asks making polite conversation before she fobs me off.

'Solomon.'

She recognises the name. 'Oh really, Solomon, you say? I've been to one of his concerts.' I have impressed her.

Quite what the link is between driving a mobile tea canteen and being one of Sol's students is beyond me. But Mrs Miller-Sterling, it seems, believes there is one.

She looks closely at me and says graciously, like the King bestowing an honour, 'Alright you'll do, Miss Marshall.'

I'm paired up in my mobile canteen with a beautiful actress who tells me her name is Tessa Bouchier. I've never heard of her but she seems naggingly familiar. Is she really someone famous I ask myself? Her flashing smile brushes off my questions about her work.

We laugh the first time we hear the fake, upper-class-sounding English traitor, William Joyce, we call Lord Hawhaw, on German radio. We soon learn he's no joke.

'Alright Kensington, it's your turn tonight,' he snarls. Sure enough, as punctual as a German train, at 8.45 pm, right-on time, the bombs start to fall.

We three flatmates decide to remain in our home during the bombing. Bravado? Probably. Every night, once the all-clear sounds, I hurry to my South Kensington WVS station to get the tea and van ready. Our Kensington customers are grateful. Putting fires out and rescuing the wounded is thirsty work.

The phone rings at Lexham Gardens just after a raid. 'Miss Marshall? Good. I'm confirming you are reporting for duty tonight. We are going to be busy. Jerry's dropped more than usual on our patch,' barks Mrs Miller-Sterling.

I hear a loud noise at her end.

'Good God,' she gasps. The phone goes dead.

Worried about Mrs Miller-Sterling, I open the front door without thinking about the blackout and the hall light illuminates a group of teenagers and small boys outside on the road. I catch their faces and get a snap impression they are all brothers. They are pushing a handcart laden with bits of twisted metal. I know what they're doing - picking up fallen shrapnel from anti-aircraft shells. Someone has told me it's lucrative but dangerous work during a raid. The government is desperate for metal; it can be melted down and used again for ammunition.

'Come on Freddie,' I hear one of the older ones say. 'Keep this up and you'll be rich one day. Dad says let the others do the fighting and we'll be quid's in once the war's over.'

Noticing that I've overheard them, they give me an embarrassed thumbs-up. 'Orl' right darlin?'

But I'm already half-way down the street.

I trot along the pavement haphazardly lit by the flickering flames of burning buildings, my shoes crunching on bits of glass and masonry. Two policemen suddenly loom out of the gloom nearly knock me over as they manhandle a handcuffed prisoner along.

They see my startled torch-lit face. 'Looter, Miss,' they say. 'We caught him bang to rights,' they add proudly.

Not everyone in London is motivated by patriotism.

I never see Mrs Miller-Sterling again. Apparently she'd been caught in the blast of a bomb armed with a delayed fuse.

25.

Teddy

I have a Saturday evening date with Jane by the seaside in Weymouth. Strictly work – on the look-out for anyone suspicious or shouting about stuff they should keep to themselves.

Jane scrubs up well – it's marvellous what women can do with a little lipstick and makeup. Out of uniform she looks a different woman in her slacks, blouse and a silk head scarf knotted up tightly. She's a good-looking woman anyway – she now looks distinctly glamourous.

Jane drives us in an army car. Although both in civvies, we don't stand out in the crowded seaside centre. There are several civilians adding colour to the dominant army khaki: evacuees from the Blitz in London, refugees from the Channel Islands, land girls and factory workers, all out for a good time. Here and there I overhear depressed French sailors discussing the situation in their homeland.

We blend in with the jolly crowd promenading around the harbour, licking ice cream, drinking lemonade and gossiping. The town has a relaxed, pre-war holiday feel. Some people are popping into pubs for something stronger.

Jane links an arm with me. 'Come on Teddy, we're meant to look like a couple. Let's have a drink.'

She leads me towards a pub whose white walls are glistening with reflected sunlight.

'Come on, let me show you the Black Dog. Great pub. Apparently it used to be The Dove until a landlord brought one of the very first Labradors into the country.'

'Really?' I ask, mildly intrigued by the local folklore. Smiling I ask, 'Was that recently?'

She laughs. 'No. Back in the 1700's. It came from Canada. Tough on the Dove, I suppose. But I love Labs. I was brought up with them. Mind you, perhaps it's apposite - the symbol of peace being replaced by a gun-dog.'

The pub is heaving - standing room only - so we have to push and jostle our way to the bar. I order a pint of bitter for myself and a cider for Jane. We join half the pub's customers standing on the warm cobbled street near the beach and I return to our conversation. I must admit I enjoy Jane's company. Her looks are complemented by a bright personality.

I return to the topic of dogs. 'My mother's family in Normandy had a couple of Labradors. I learnt to shoot with them.'

Her face registers the answer to the question I guess she's wanted to ask for some time about my accent.

'We hunted *les sangliers* – wild boar.'

'Gosh, that sounds more exciting than my father and my brothers – they only shoot pheasant. Oh, it seems ages, but that was only about a year ago. We have a farm in the Cotswolds. I started to go shooting with them during my boarding school holidays.' She chuckles quietly. 'They objected at first but when I became just as good as them, they became rather proud of me.'

I look at Jane again. She looks and sounds different from the ATS girls at the anti-aircraft, ack-ack battery. Judging by her clothes and manner she comes from a comfortable background. Despite her casual clothes, she still manages to look *chic*. She reminds me of the stylish women I used to see in the fashionable Paris 16th *arrondisment*.

I can't help comparing Jane to Win. My Australian girlfriend definitely shares Jane's self-confidence. But Win was not *chic*. Yes, she is attractive and could certainly dress well – however, her clothes were not too expensive. I know Win's family is not wealthy but she comes, I guess, from a more intellectual and cultured family, possibly.

'A penny for your thoughts,' Jane says.

'Sorry, I wandered off.' I decide a white lie would be opportune. 'I was thinking about shotguns. Hunting was good training for me as well. I became a good shot too,' I said purposefully.

She understood the implication. When the invasion came, we would both be able to play our part.

We finish our drinks and wander from pub to pub. But they are all as full and noisy as the Black Dog with their patrons spilling out onto the streets. We give up trying to overhear conversations or spot suspects. At our second port of call, or is it our third, Jane introduces me to the local cider – scrumpy. Strong stuff – I drink slowly.

'We call it *Cidre fermier*.'

'Well, for once I think the English name sounds better,' she says finishing her scrumpy quickly, licking her lips for another.

Soldiers from rival regiments and too much drink seldom go well. Things are becoming rowdy in some places. Redcap Military Police intervene to break up fights. We avoid them and move on to other pubs.

A sixth sense tells me someone is following us. I use my training to try and spot who but the milling crowds provide perfect cover.

'Hello Sarge,' a young woman, arm linked with a friend, both dressed for going out on the razzle, says suddenly out of the melee. I don't recognise her.

'Private Morgan from the ack-ack battery. You visited us the other day when the fuel depot was bombed.'

Now I see who it is - the girl on the Predictor with the cheeky grin. 'Hello! Of course!'

She flashes a bright smile. 'Look, we saw you and your lady friend,' a quick glance at Jane, 'earlier in the Black Dog.' She surreptitiously glances back from where she has come and holds a palm up to forestall me. 'The thing is, we weren't the only ones who spotted you. Those two guards you reported are after you. And they've got their mates with them.' She raises eyebrows. 'They've had a skinful. If I was you, Sarge, I'd scarper. Otherwise, you and your friend will get hurt.'

We heed her warning and quickly head off to our car, checking we have thrown off any pursuers.

Jane says, 'That was awfully nice of that girl to warn you.' A few hurried steps later. 'Girls are usually nice to you Teddy, aren't they?'

She's right. I've always been popular but not just with girls. Boys too. My mother said I'd inherited my father's easy-going nature. My father, on the other hand, said I'd got my mother's good looks. *Parfait?*

We quickly get out of Weymouth. I drive. Even though I realise I have had a bit too much to drink, I'm in a better state than Jane who's had far too much scrumpy. She laughs as she leans against my shoulder while I struggle to concentrate on the road lit feebly by the dimmed-out headlights, obeying black-out rules.

Jane uses the excuse of me steering unsteadily around a corner to let a hand flutter below my waist. I can hear her giggle in my ear as she feels my reaction.

'Let's stop Teddy,' she whispers in my ear.

I veer off the road through an open gate along a track and stop near a river. We stumble, arms around each other, over the dew-laden grass to a felled tree on the bank.

Jane kisses me desperately, fiercely. We stop as her scarf gets in our way. She rips it off her head and chucks it onto a branch. She grabs me again.

144

I shout at myself, *What are you doing? You love Win don't you?*
I gently push Jane back.

'Oh Christ, there's someone else!' she sighs, stepping back.

'Oh, Paul,' she whispers to herself and slumps down onto the tree trunk. 'Oh dear, I'm sorry Teddy. I had a boyfriend called Paul. You might have known him? He was in Field Security in France, near Lille, like you.' Slowly she starts to weep. 'He got killed. I heard months afterwards.'

Oh God, Paul. It has to be my friend, Paul. 'No, I never knew him.'

It's too dark for her to see that I'm lying. But, in a sense, I am partly telling the truth. I never knew Paul was carrying on with two women, Marjorie and now, I discover, Jane.

'Oh fuck,' she screams suddenly, repeatedly smashing her palms into the tree trunk, 'it's this bloody war.' Furious with herself, she hisses, 'Here I am behaving like a bloody tart with a man I've only just met.'

I say nothing. There's no need and we both know it. The harsh reality is that there are thousands, tens of thousands of young women like Jane, whose hearts have been broken and who are desperate for some affection. And the supply of young menfolk is diminishing all the time.

We sit on the tree silently side by side in the dark.

Calmer now, Jane breathes in deeply. 'Give me a cigarette, soldier,' she orders in a mock sergeant major's voice.

The tears on her cheek glisten from the flame of my Zippo lighter. Oh God, I feel awful I've caused her so much anguish.

She rests her head on my shoulder and I silently put an arm around her. I am comforting myself as much as her.

Our tender silence is shattered by the wailing of distant sirens in Poole and Weymouth. We hear the drone of German bombers heading swiftly inland, chased frantically by search-lights and anti-aircraft fire. Although we can't be the targets for the planes, both of us wince in fear at their sound.

'Bristol again?' Jane says relieved, as the planes quickly pass. Searchlights are switched off and guns fall silent. An inky-black stillness hides us from the rest of the world. And from looking at each other.

Her flicked, glowing cigarette arcs through the darkness and lands, hissing into the river where, for a split second, we see it floating away with the current.

'Teddy, don't you find this damn war makes one feel – oh, I don't know – as helpless as a Pooh stick being carried along by a river to only God-only-knows-where?'

'Sometimes I just wish bloody Hitler would invade and get it over with.'

Jane's right. Not knowing our immediate fate can induce a gut-wrenching feeling of terror in all of us. We struggle to keep it hidden but every now and then it pounces and catches us unawares.

26.

Win

The September breeze, gently rippling off the English Channel, feels cool, prickly-salty on my cheeks. '*Fin de la saison,*' Teddy says, tenderly wrapping his army greatcoat around me.

'*Fin de la saison,*' I repeat.

Teddy smiles, kind amusement crinkling around his eyes, at my pronunciation. Sitting on an old bench next to the sandy beach, he gestures towards the narrow gap between the two headlands protecting the entrance to Poole Harbour.

'I wanted to bring you here because Brownsea Island is the closest I could get to my mother's family in Normandy.' He gently squeezes me closer. 'I'm going to teach you more French. I want them to be impressed when I introduce you.'

The significance of his words do not register at first. I turn to stare at his face. He is blushing, pride tinged with a sliver of fear. I see a polished ring gleaming in the palm of his free hand.

'*Winfred Wordsworth Marshall, veux-tu me faire l'honneur de devenir ma femme?*'

Before I can respond he removes any doubt lost in translation. 'Winfred Wordsworth Marshall. Will you do me the honour of becoming my wife?'

I don't hesitate. 'Yes'.

And yet my head is swimming in conflict. The thought of marrying Teddy makes me extremely happy, delirious even. But, oh my God, what will the Mater say? Even Pop?

He pulls me closer and slips the ring onto my finger. The silver is well-worn and slides on easily.

'It's beautiful, Teddy,' I say, holding my hand out and twisting it to and fro so that the ring twinkles in the sunlight.

'It was my mother's. She would be delighted that I have given it to you.'

His mother's ring! I am doubtful at first. Is wearing a dead person's ring acceptable?

He senses my nervousness.

'You are sure, Win? Aren't you?'

I smile. 'Yes, yes, of course! I knew from after our lunch at the Spaniards.'

'Me too,' he grins.

We stand, kiss and hug each other closely, staring silently into each other's eyes, reluctant to break the spell.

'Come on Babe, let's go for a stroll.'

Teddy had telephoned a couple of days ago. 'Sorry for the short notice, Win, but do you fancy coming down to Wareham this weekend? It's fine with our landlady. One of the girls billeted here had to move away suddenly so there's a spare bedroom for a few days.'

When I arrived at Poole railway station from Waterloo on the Saturday, he'd greeted me with a laugh. 'We're going on a sea cruise, Win. I'm taking you to an exotic island.'

***

As we stroll along the small island's shoreline, a yacht sailing slowly close by into Poole Harbour catches our eyes. A couple in the stern wave at us and we reciprocate. Two young boys are manning the sails. The skipper shouts an order and the mainsail is carefully lowered, the yacht moving on powered only by its engine.

'It's a peaceful scene, isn't it, Teddy? I never imagined people were enjoying themselves like this outside London, as if there's no war.'

'Yes, but look carefully, Win. The couple in the stern look as though they're in their 70s, at least. And those kids must be their grandchildren.'

He didn't need to add that the boys' parents were probably somewhere else, serving in uniform.

'Have you ever been sailing in a yacht, Win?' he asks, as we walk on, holding hands.

'No, but I had a boyfriend whose father owned a lovely, big launch. We had great fun cruising up and down the river.'

That is until the Mater reminded me that I should concentrate on the piano rather than Grahame, I recall silently.

'It's not the same, Win.'

He thinks for a moment, choosing his words purposefully. 'A motorboat often has to fight against nature. It forces its way into a head wind and smashes through the waves.' His voice takes on a softer, dream-like quality. 'When I'm steering a yacht, even a small dinghy, I feel as if I'm being gifted with the power of nature. I tack into the wind and ride diagonally over the waves, smoothly and elegantly. At the top of the wave, I love the brief sensation of being still before the bow dips down the other side. I feel,' he pauses again, 'almost serene, God-like. As if my emotions are being ordained by the heavens.' He turns and laughs in embarrassment. 'You must think I'm a bit odd.'

I squeeze his hand. 'No, funnily enough, I don't, Teddy.' My turn to express myself. 'I can experience something similar when I'm playing the piano. Sometimes I feel in complete union with the sound. And there is also a pause, sometimes a split second, between notes. And when I'm playing well, I feel, as you say, ordained by the God of Music.'

'Apollo, wasn't it?'

'Yes, he was some God, wasn't he? Good at everything. A bit like my brother, Lloyd. To whom I will take great delight in introducing you. You'll like him.'

Not like the Mater. She'll interrogate you like Gestapo-man in Heidelberg.

'Well, one day I'll teach you to sail. I'm no expert but I've sailed many times on summer holidays.'

We saunter into a large open area.

'You've heard of Boy Scouts, Win?'

'Yes, of course.'

'I hadn't, but this is apparently the site of their first camp. An English general called Baden Powell was in charge. I've heard he's famous.'

'Yes, we've even heard of him in Australia,' I say dryly.

A sudden, very loud screech of a bird makes me jump. 'What the hell was that?'

Teddy squeezes me. 'Don't worry. That was a peacock. The eccentric owner of the island has several, wandering around.'

Sure enough, a large peacock struts out of the bushes towards us, trailing its magnificent plumage.

'I had no idea they were so loud. Louder than a kookaburra,' I say, still a bit shaken.

'He's looking for a mate, Babe.' He mock-glares at the bird. 'You're too late. Win's mine. We're engaged!

'I've read somewhere they're meant to bring bad luck. We've just proved that wrong.'

We turn and kiss, tightly again. No longer the nervous virgin, I look forward to making love with Teddy later on at his digs. The peacock, seemingly in a huff at being ignored, disdainfully furls its display and pecks his way through some scrub towards a treeline on the other side of a small lake.

'This part of the island reminds me of Rottnest - you know, the holiday island I told you about - it's a bit dull away from the sea. But the beaches. Oh my!'

'Tell me about the beaches, Win,' Teddy says.

'Well, for a start, they are so much more beautiful than the beaches on the mainland which can be a bit boring to look at. They just go on and on in a straight line for miles and miles before they disappear into the heat haze.' I smile, remembering happy times. 'There's every type imaginable from big to small if you like surfing, spear fishing, sailing or paddling with kids.'

He twists around, grabs both my hands and spins me about in a big circle, as if we are dancing.

He laughs and says, 'I like the sound of paddling with kids.' Then more seriously, pulling me towards him in the middle of our circle. 'Our kids. By the way, what's a kookaburra?'

'Like a big brown and white kingfisher. They sound as if they are laughing. Very loudly.'

He says wistfully. 'I have so much to learn about Australia. I must write it all down so I don't forget.'

In the distance I see soldiers laying large tubes and wood on the ground. Teddy answers my unspoken question. 'They're laying the fires and lights to fool Jerry's bombers into thinking this is Poole. It's been quite effective so far. They've dropped tons of bombs here instead of on the town,' Teddy explains. 'We need to get to the jetty, Win. We don't want to miss the last boat.'

'My landlady, Mrs Clarke, is laying on a tasty supper. She makes a great stew.' That gorgeous Teddy smile. 'She's looking forward to meeting my fiancée.' He holds his hands up to forestall me. 'I told her you are my fiancée. I had to, otherwise she would have said you couldn't stay.'

I punch him playfully. 'And if I had said no?'

'I guessed you wouldn't.'

151

I punch him harder. 'Oh you great, big conceited man.'

'Ouch that hurts,' he shouts and picks me up off my feet and spins me around in his arms, laughing.

'Stop Teddy, you're making me dizzy,' I plead.

He places me down carefully. Our eyes lock and our arms bind us together.

Oh, what a great kisser he is!

Two young lovers, cocooned in our *own* world, we saunter along until we see the jetty.

'Oh, damn it, come on, Babe. The launch has almost sailed.'

We shout and wave and finally get a reply. 'Hurry up you two. We can't wait forever.'

Some soldiers lend us a hand onto the launch. As we head off back towards Poole, I hear the faint sound of a peacock crowing.

***

'Pleased to meet you, dear,' says Mrs Clarke. 'Teddy's told me a lot about you.' Her eyes check my hands. 'That's a lovely *old* ring, isn't it?'

'Yes, Mrs Clarke. It was my mother's,' Teddy interjects.

'Arrr, that's lovely me darlin,' Mrs Clarke says approvingly, the local accent rolling like warm syrup around her tongue.

Mrs Clarke ladles out stew from a large earthenware pot. The walk on Brownsea Island and the fresh sea breeze have made me hungry. Teddy's right. The stew smells and tastes delicious. Mrs Clarke notices me chewing my meat, trying to identify the animal - not lamb nor pork. Chicken perhaps?

'Rabbit, dear,' she smiles, all mother-like. 'What with all the meat shortages we're getting, I think we'll all be eating it a lot more.'

I conceal my distaste at the thought of eating a rabbit and stop myself from saying that rabbits are regarded as vermin where I come from. There's even a two-thousand-mile-long rabbit-proof fence to keep them out of Western Australia. I metaphorically shrug my shoulders and pretend it's chicken.

There are five of us sitting around the large table in Mrs Clarke's kitchen. We've been joined by two of Teddy's army colleagues, one of them a young woman, about my age. Her name is Felicity. I catch her eye now and then and smile. I get a guarded, neutral response. The stew finished, we sit back, relax and light up. Teddy lights a pipe and grins at my surprise.

Mrs Clarke does not let the conversation flag and quizzes us each in turn. I sense Teddy's landlady wants plenty of ammunition for a good gossip with her friends.

My turn. 'Well dear, Teddy tells me you are studying the *pianoforte*,' showing off she knows the full name of my instrument.

Felicity sniffs, making clear her disapproval that I'm not 'doing my bit'.

'Yes, Mrs Clarke, but I also drive a canteen lorry.' I pause and look at Felicity. 'Apart from topping up the firemen and ambulance nurses with hot tea, we often join in and help get survivors out of bombed buildings.' I look down at my plate, recent experience colouring my tone. 'Some of them are so badly wounded, a bloody mess really, men, women, kids, that they die right there and then.' I fiddle with my fork and cough awkwardly. 'Right in front of us.'

Silence while the table absorbs my words.

Felicity looks at me - her eyes now say respect - and she smiles. 'Where are you studying music, Win?'

I explain about my lessons with Solomon and that how disappointed I am that the war has interrupted my chance to play my first concert.

Felicity says, 'He's famous, isn't he?'

'Who?' asks Mrs Clarke, puzzled.

'Solomon, Win's teacher,' replies Felicity. 'He was a child prodigy. He even played for the King and Queen in Buckingham Palace,' she adds.

The table quietly mulls over the fact someone in its midst is a student of somebody *famous*.

'I know, dear,' Mrs Clarke says brightly, 'We could do with a bit of cheering up. There's a pub, the Lord Nelson, around the corner. It's got a piano.'

She looks around the room. 'Let's go and have a sing-song. You can play *Roll out the barrel* – you must know that, dear.'

I nod, hiding my panic. I've never played popular songs. Solomon would be shocked.

Mrs Clarke must have noticed my reluctance so says craftily when we've finished eating. 'There's no need to clear any dishes away. I'll do it later.' She smiles at me. 'There's nothing like a good old knees-up.'

Teddy takes my hand and shines his torch for me along the blacked-out street. Mrs Clarke leads the way – she could find it blindfold, I realise.

The Lord Nelson is full with a happy Saturday-night crowd. Farm workers, soldiers on leave, and local shop keepers.

I'm saved - the small, hideously out-of-tune upright has plenty of music sheets. I quickly pick up the tunes and my education begins. I belt out the songs: *Run Rabbit Run* or rather, the pub sings, *Run Adolph, Run Adolph, Run, Run, Run...* and *Bye bye Blackbird*, and *Bless 'Em All*, which becomes *Fuck 'em all!*

The long and the short and the tall;
Fuck all the Sergeants and W.O.l.'s
Fuck all the corporals and their bastard sons;
For we're saying goodbye to them all,
As up the C.O.'s arse they crawl;
You'll get no promotion this side of the ocean,

So cheer up my lads, fuck 'em all!

I giggle uncontrollably and blow Teddy a kiss as I thump out for the second time. 'Fuck all the Sergeants…'

Oh, how Solomon would be shocked. And my, oh my, the Mater would be scandalised, I giggle deliciously.

After forty-five minutes or so of continual banging of the keys, I'm exhausted. The voices in the Lord Nelson are hoarse from raucous bellowing. Men are quickly downing pints of beer, slaking their thirst and soothing their throats.

Mrs Clarke sees the dripping sweat on my forehead and hands me a small cotton handkerchief.

She raises her hand and calls for silence. Her call is amplified by masculine whistles and shouts of 'pipe down' to the rest of the pub. 'Ladies and gentlemen our piano player has had enough. All good things must come to an end. But I am going to ask her a favour.' She smiles proudly at me, speaking loudly so everyone can hear. 'Many of you don't know she's training to be a concert pianist. She'll be famous one day.'

'Oooh,' the pub shouts in mock awe.

She holds her hand up and the hubbub stops. 'So, Win, will you play something for us please?'

How can I refuse?

Teddy, standing next to the piano as my page-turner, hands me a glass of water which I gratefully down in one.

Hands relaxing on my lap I choose from the extensive off-by-heart catalogue in my head a piece which is simple, beautiful and sad. Appropriate for the times, I think.

I play very well despite my battered piano.

Sometimes in a musician's life, he or she completely captivates the audience and holds them transfixed by the hypnotic power of the music. It might be Solomon in the gilded pomp of the Albert Hall or me, now, in front of a tipsy, happy crowd in a tobacco-stained, smelly old pub on England's south coast. I feel intense emotion behind me and realise this is such a moment. The pub is hushed now. Not a sound. Rapt attention binds my audience as I carry them along with my music, like a babe in arms being soothed gently by a mother's lullaby.

I finish softly and place my hands on my lap.

My head bowed, I await applause.

Nothing, only silence.

Has my performance fallen flat?

Mystified, I turn my head.

I see embarrassed men, avoiding my eyes. Soldiers, farmers and yes, a policeman, staring down into pints, trying to hide the hint of glistening eyes. One young soldier has his back to me, sitting on a bar stool, slumped forward, head down in his arms while his shoulders shake in silent sadness. The women are less inhibited - hankies are dabbing tears. Slowly the crowd recovers and starts to smile gratefully at me.

Mrs Clarke says hoarsely, 'That was lovely, Win…'

The spell is broken.

All of the Lord Nelson breaks out in loud, thumping applause and shouts of, 'Well done, me darlin'. Bloody well played!'

Teddy bends down and kisses me tenderly on my cheek and hands me a rough cider. 'Here drink this scrumpy, Babe. You look as though you need it.'

The drink goes to my head but helps me recover.

Teddy lights me a cigarette and, on a whim, tells me to keep his new lighter to remember my 'Wareham concert'.

'See how generous I am Babe. First a ring, now a cigarette lighter.'

There's a queue of people who come up one by one to thank and entreat me. 'Please come back again.'

'Of course, I will.'

Walking back through the darkness to her house, I ask Mrs Clarke who owns all the music sheets in the pub.

'The son of a friend of mine.'

'Well, please thank him. He saved my bacon.'

'I'm afraid I can't dear.'

She looks down and says sadly, 'He was killed at Dunkirk. He loved playing the piano.'

Death is now commonplace, unremarkable even. Condolences for someone you don't know can sound insincere. I say nothing.

Back at his digs, Teddy says, 'I told you Win was a great pianist, Mrs Clarke. She'll be famous one day'.

'You're right Teddy. I think she will be.'

She clucks off, 'I'd better get the things ready for breakfast tomorrow. Good night you two,' she says from the kitchen, stressing the words *you two* as if we are a proper, respectable couple while we climb the stairs towards our bedrooms.

Teddy takes my hand and slowly closes the door of his room behind us.

'Win, I'll never forget what you played tonight. It was utterly beautiful. I think I've heard it before but can't remember its name. What was it?'

'Debussy's *Clair de Lune*.'

'Well, let's have some moonlight,' he whispers, stepping towards the blacked-out window.

He switches the light out and throws open the curtains.

The bed in my own room remains unslept-in.

27.

Win

33 Lexham Gardens,
London W8
Mon. September 16th 1940

My dear Teddy,

I'm sitting as usual waiting for the 'All-Clear' to go before I report for duty. I've received no letter from you yet, but I suppose it's like the rest of the bombs – delayed.

I enclose the snaps, and the negatives, if you feel any of them are worth taking off. Myself I don't.

Well, the invasion hasn't come yet, but I expect it will. As a matter of fact, I shouldn't be in the least surprised if you haven't shifted from Wareham already.

Marjorie and Katie have been writing anxious letters, but believe me, I shall be alright. I simply can't work up any sort of fear, and I sleep regularly from 12p.m, to 7a.m. Music is not suffering in the least and I go to and from the studies – raid or no raid.

The cigarette lighter is working magnificently, and I smoke far more than I need to – just in order to use it.

Rang old Sol this morning and found him full of beans and very anxious to know if I was suntanned.

I believe the All Clear might go at any moment so must don uniform and prepare for work.

Keep smiling Ducky.

All the best to Mrs Clarke.

For the moment I send all my love and best thoughts from <u>Win</u>.

***

What was once a small, terraced house, is now a mound of rubble under a fine mist of brick-red dust and lazy smoke from smouldering wood. There are other wrecked homes along the street, their guts spilling out onto the tarmac. There is a whiff of gas which makes us rescuers uneasy. But the air wardens, ambulance drivers and nurses shout at us to join in and help ferry the wounded. And stretcher the dead onto the road where their faces are covered in coats and whatever else comes to hand.

'Be quiet,' a doctor suddenly yells, his hand raised in urgent appeal. He is kneeling and bending down, his head disappearing down a gap in the broken bricks, a torch in one hand. A fireman is on all fours next to him.

We strain our ears and pick up what they hear; a pathetic mewing sound, like a terrified kitten. But, oh dear God, it's a person.

The doctor's head disappears and bobs up ridiculously red, covered in dust. He shakes his head.

We strain forward and catch the fireman's words, 'There's about four down there. I reckon they are all dead apart from the one whose head you can see sticking out. He's trapped. There's no chance we can get him out for at least an hour, doctor. Poor bugger's in terrible agony.'

And then, as we strain forward listening to the pitiful sound of the man in agony, the fireman adds, staring at the doctor, 'We can't leave him like that. He's dying.'

The doctor, a middle-aged man, nods. He glances quickly at one of the young nurses, mentally measuring her slim waist against the gap. His hands tremble as he beckons her over to him. He speaks softly into her ear and turns to the fireman who nods his head in agreement. The doctor fishes around in his black leather bag and pulls out a large brown bottle. He splashes a liberal amount of liquid onto a pad. We all watch guiltily, sideways out of our eyes, as the nurse strips down to her bra and knickers, flicks her suspenders open and removes her stockings. The doctor hands her the pad.

'Chloroform,' someone mutters.

I catch the nurse's eyes briefly. They show grim determination. Only her teeth biting her lips betray nerves. The doctor and the fireman brace themselves and hold the nurse tightly by her ankles and slowly lower her down into the hole. All we can see are her legs. The two men hold the nurse for a couple of minutes. To me it seems like hours. The mewing sound slowly fades away.

We, the watching group, bow our heads in sorrow, our faces betraying guilty shame that we are the lucky ones, still alive.

The nurse is hoisted out of the hole. Her face is white, contrasting with her filthy hair. She falls onto her knees, her head bowed and chest heaving while she sobs silently. The doctor covers her shoulders with her dress and places an arm around her.

'Jesus,' I mutter.

A policeman who is watching says, 'Alright everybody, let's get on with our own work and give that brave, young lady some privacy.'

***

I write to a friend in Perth telling her what life is like in London's Blitz, little knowing she would pass it on for *The West Australian* to print it.

In an American clipper airmail letter just received, Miss Win Marshall, the West Australian writer and pianist says:

'Here is a true story of the way the British are 'cowering and shivering in frightened numbers in their air-raid shelters'. Last night I was at a promenade concert in the Queen's Hall, London. The hall was crowded

out, and the Brahm's Symphony had just commenced at 9.15 o'clock when a man came forward and announced that the sirens were sounding outside, and anyone who wished to go to the public shelter must leave immediately as the concert was certainly going on. Exactly five people walked out. The rest, with a simultaneous movement, looked at their watches and remarked that 'he' was a quarter too soon. For the last two nights we have received the warning at exactly 9.30 o'clock.

'Sir Henry Wood then picked up his baton, and the symphony proceeded as if nothing had happened. When the last item was finished, the manager came forward, picked out some tunes with one finger and gave us a guessing competition, all the while carrying on a running fire of dry humour – which was supplemented by the audience! The crowd by now was in an extremely good mood and thoroughly at home. They hung their feet over the edge of the circle and galleries, while those in the promenade stretched themselves on the floor with cups of tea, and frankly went to sleep.

I don't add that many of the audience, including me, gradually drift away and seek shelter in an Underground railway station. At 4 am the All-Clear siren sounds - Christ what a persistent, irritating, piercing noise it makes.

Where they can, the Underground trains, buses and taxis slowly start operating again. I make my way as quickly as possible to the WVS station and start to brew the tea and fill up biscuit tins.

Another dark, early morning of helping exhausted and parched firemen, police, air raid wardens, doctors, nurses and ambulance drivers – men and women awaits me.

28.

Win

Looking down expectantly from our flat window, I watch two big black, shiny saloons drawing up outside our block of flats, right on time. As if in military convoy they reverse smartly to park, one after the other, their hot exhaust fumes turning the cold November air into miniature steam clouds.

A few minutes later a uniformed chauffeur, all shiny buttons and polished leather gaiters, rings the front doorbell at our 33 Lexham Gardens flat.

'Miss Marshall?' he salutes, a hand raised to his peaked hat.

'Yes,' I reply, barely suppressing a giggle. I know Marjorie and Katie are smirking behind me.

In his spotless gloves, the chauffeur gingerly lifts up my battered suitcase and I follow him down and out onto the pavement. He has a limp but he shrugs off my offer of help.

'Nice car,' I say, as way of thanking him as he puts my suitcase away in one of the cars.

'Yes,' he smiles. 'A Buick Century - the best and fastest car in the world, Miss,' he adds as he opens a rear door and assists me into the passenger compartment. A thick carpet and the warm, leathery smell of clean upholstery wafts over me.

A middle-aged woman resplendent in a silky fur jacket - she purrs later that it's Russian sable - and wearing an Astrakhan lambswool hat greets me. I smell Chanel - not a scent I often encounter these days.

'Hello Win. It's very nice to meet you at last.' She pats me affectionately on my arm. 'Your mother has told me so much about you.'

'Hello Mrs de Bernales.'

'Call me Helen, please dear.'

The chauffeur closes his door with a barely audible click.

'Alton Lodge, please Simon,' Helen commands. She whispers to me, 'In case you're wondering, Simon was injured in the last war.'

She's right to tell me. There's so much bile directed at people suspected of not 'doing their bit'.

'I thought we'd spend tonight in our Roehampton town house before we wend our way down to Selsey tomorrow. We've got a beach house on the south coast. She fiddles with her large string of pearls. 'Claude is already down there. We can have a good chat this evening. I'm looking forward to hearing you play the piano.' She flashes a friendly smile. 'If that's alright with you, Win?'

How can I demur?

Even though signs of bomb damage decrease the further west we go from central London, after our Buick has crossed Putney Bridge, there are still wrecked buildings here and there. Our chauffeur has to slow down occasionally to drive around craters in the road.

'Claude tells me that even if Luftwaffe pilots have missed their targets, they'll still want to get rid of their bombs after they turn left and fly over us on the way back to France. It's much worse where you are in Kensington, isn't it Win?'

She takes my silence as gloomy affirmation.

'I promised your mother I'd get you away from the Blitz,' she says patting my arm. And you can practise on our piano until it's safe to go back.'

I smile gratefully but feel guilty that I'm abandoning my WVS canteen.

'War is ghastly. It seems like yesterday when my brother was killed in the last one. And here we are fighting the Germans.' She sighs in exasperation. 'Again.'

Simon turns our car through Alton Lodge's large wrought iron gates. I catch glimpses of roses, rhododendrons, a vegetable garden, greenhouses and immaculately-edged lawns as the Buick gently crunches up the gravel drive. A grand Georgian mansion appears between the tall trees and we come to a smooth stop in front of a Grecian-columned porch.

Out of the corner of my eye I see the other Buick entering a garage bigger than most people's houses.

I never find out why there were two cars in our little convoy. Had Helen been shopping?

The front door, as shiny black as Simon's Buick, opens quickly and a maid dressed in a black dress with white apron and cap bobs as Helen sweeps me into a vast chequered-floor entrance hall.

Is this a house or a museum I ask myself as I stop and stare at an impossibly beautiful, white marble statue of a nude woman in the middle of the hall.

'She's called *The Greek Slave*,' Helen says gently.

I tell from her voice she's surprised I haven't heard of it.

'Claude bought her off a Russian prince. He also managed to get some paintings and furniture from him which had belonged to the Tsar. Come on, I'll show you to your room upstairs.'

Room? It's a suite. Bedroom, bathroom and a sitting room. Like a swanky hotel, the house has about three suites.

'You'll join me for drinks at 6.30 pm? There's no need to dress for dinner. Claude's not here.'

I luxuriate in a hot foam bath. I giggle as my toes play with the gold taps and laugh out loud. 'If only Marjorie and Katie could see me now. Oh, how the other half live.'

Despite Helen's request not to bother to dress for dinner, I can't help feeling out of place in my plain skirt and blouse compared to the simple elegance of her black, silk cocktail dress. She sees me admiring it and tells me later, 'Chanel, darling.'

A butler serves me champagne off a silver salver in a drawing room. Red and orange highlights from the enormous fireplace reflect off the cut glass flute as I slowly twirl it around in my fingers.

'I met your mother at the Cottesloe tennis club,' Helen says between puffs on her black ivory cigarette holder. The club was close to our home, Overton Lodge.' She smiles to herself. 'An odd name for a Spanish *hacienda*, people used to say.

'Claude named it after the Brixton house he was born in.'

What's a hacienda? I don't add Pop always wondered how the enormous, sprawling house got planning permission.

'I know, I used to look up at your house when I played tennis there too.'

'Ah, happy days,' Helen says. She continues dreamily, 'I used to love playing on those manicured grass courts under the blue sky. Mind you, it was a bit windy once the Fremantle doctor started after lunch.' Her eyes quiz me. 'You're probably wondering how Claude and I met?'

I was but was too polite to ask.

'Claude's first wife died. Her brother was my husband who got killed in the last war. So we already knew each other very well.' She taps her holder on an ashtray. 'Perth's a small place really. All the people who matter usually know each other. Claude met your father during his Kalgoorlie gold mining days.

'He's very proud that he won international recognition for our state for its mining. We're no longer just known for wheat, cattle and sheep.'

She coughs awkwardly behind her hand and watches my reaction to what she says. 'You know your father doesn't approve of Claude.'

I lie. 'Oh, I didn't know that. Pop hardly ever talks about his work.' That part's true, at least.

Helen adds, 'But I've always got on well with your mother.' She smooths her dress. 'She always calls a spade a spade, doesn't she?'

I nod.

Our meal shows no sign of wartime restrictions: crab, venison and raspberry *soufflé*. And red French wine I've never tasted before.

'Claret, from *St Emilion*,' Helen says.

And then sweet dessert wine with the pudding. Helen advises me to have a spoon of the *soufflé* first to adjust my palate.

'*Chateau d'Yquem*,' she smiles sweetly, knowing I haven't a clue about the wine. It tastes really yummy though.

'All the vegetables come from our garden. And Cook makes our own bread,' she adds proudly.

After the meal I choose a grand piano in one of the drawing rooms and play for Helen and her servants – there were about half a dozen of them.

'That's all from memory?' Helen asks. 'Incredible,' she shakes her head.

'Yes, my first teacher in Perth, Miss Ida Roberts, insisted I learnt everything off by heart. And Solomon is just the same.'

I don't play terribly well but I realise my audience doesn't notice.

Shown to my bed afterwards by a maid, I feel uneasy as I try to fall asleep. I know Pop would ask, 'Who's paying for all the opulence and grandeur of Helen's life?'

For me there's also the unsettling realisation that the wartime rationing and the shortages of everyday life don't apply to the very rich like Helen, despite the fact *we're all in it together*.

***

Something's not quite right in The White House. Helen's beach house turns out to be – I'm now not surprised – more like a seaside mansion with Chippendale furniture, Dresden china and a private beach.

Helen's Claude, a tall, good-looking man, always impeccably dressed, is suspicious of me. I catch snatches of conversation, hastily broken off when I'm in earshot. Helen seems embarrassed by what I might have overheard.

I try to practise during the day but the tense atmosphere in the house means I can't concentrate.

After breakfast on the third day Helen takes me for a long walk along the seafront, past the lifeboat station, with its railway leading down into the sea, and crabbing boats tied down on the shingle beach. We cheerily smile good mornings to other walkers, dogs straining at the leash desperate to chase teasing seagulls.

We loiter on a bench for a while and watch the brown breakers slam down on the shore. The stiff November breeze whips up spray as the waves hit the beach protection timber boards and pilings. White foam rushes up and down the slope, sucking and rolling pebbles.

Black and grey clouds zoom swiftly overhead, switching the sun on and off.

'Come on Win, let's go on. I want to show you one of my favourite spots down here.'

We walk on for another mile or so along the sea front, shingle gives way to sand and tufts of wiry, stringy grass. We branch inland, bordering a muddy marsh until we arrive at a small, ancient chapel and cemetery. St Wilfred's, Helen tells me.

A shower threatens so we seek shelter inside. Helen takes a small card from a box on a table near the entrance.

'Here read this Win,' she suggests. 'It's by Rudyard Kipling. I think it's quite wonderful.'

I read it aloud:-

Eddi, priest of St. Wilfrid
In his chapel at Manhood End,
Ordered a midnight service
For such as cared to attend.

But the Saxons were keeping Christmas,
And the night was stormy as well.
Nobody came to service,
Though Eddi rang the bell.

"Wicked weather for walking,"
Said Eddi of Manhood End.
"But I must go on with the service
For such as care to attend."

The altar-lamps were lighted, --
An old marsh-donkey came,
Bold as a guest invited,
And started at the guttering flame.

The storm beat on at the windows,
The water splashed on the floor,
And a wet, yoke-weary bullock
Pushed in through the open door.

"How do I know what is greatest,
How do I know what is least?
That is My Father's business,"
Said Eddi, Wilfrid's priest.

"But -- three are gathered together --
Listen to me and attend.
I bring good news, my brethren!"
Said Eddi of Manhood End.

And he told the Ox of a Manger
And a Stall in Bethlehem,
And he spoke to the Ass of a Rider,
That rode to Jerusalem.

They steamed and dripped in the chancel,
They listened and never stirred,
While, just as though they were Bishops,
Eddi preached them The Word,

Till the gale blew off on the marshes
And the windows showed the day,
And the Ox and the Ass together
Wheeled and clattered away.

And when the Saxons mocked him,
Said Eddi of Manhood End,
"I dare not shut His chapel
On such as care to attend."

I've never considered myself as particularly religious, so I'm surprised that my voice trembles slightly with emotion as I read the final few words.

Helen says she too has, 'Difficulty with the last verse.'

I reflect on Kipling's words. 'I agree Helen, it's a lovely poem.' I place the card down onto my lap and look around the chapel. 'And this is a special place.'

'Yes, isn't it just. It's a pity that the Victorians took down most of the church and rebuilt it in the centre of Selsey where there were more people.' She smiles ruefully. 'I think they realised it is often *wicked weather for walking* around here.'

'Who was Eddi?' I ask after a moment.

'I've read Wilfrid was a bishop around here in the seventh century. He was Eddi's boss.'

'And Manhood End? It seems a funny name.'

'I've no idea. Perhaps the shape of the land?' Helen says mischievously.

More seriously she looks towards the chapel's altar. 'I come in here often and think about what Eddi meant.'

I'm not sure how to respond.

She smiles awkwardly at me. 'I think he meant that God doesn't care who you are, the King of England, a small child or, yes, even a donkey. Rich man, poor man.

'And Eddi keeps his chapel open to tell us God is always there for everybody.' She glances at me to see how I will react to her next words. 'Win, I come here and pray for Claude.' She takes a breath. 'He's having a very difficult time with his business. I know he's doing his best but his critics won't let up.'

She continues fiercely, 'And now that awful man, Lord Beaverbrook – you know, he owns the Daily Express – is starting to ask questions. Claude now thinks all reporters have it in for him.'

I can see she's twisting her hands nervously.

She recovers her composure and says slowly and deliberately, looking at me, 'And that includes journalists in Australia.'

I am a bit slow but eventually the penny drops. She means Pop. That explains the painful silences and odd looks in their house when Claude is around. Of course: he's worried that I might overhear something and repeat it to my father. I sit up and smile sympathetically at her difficult position.

'I understand Helen. Don't worry, I'll go back to London.'

She squeezes my hand, grateful for my understanding. 'I'm so sorry, my dear.'

As we leave St Wilfred's, a gust of wind slams shut the centuries-old front door behind us.

I still have Kipling's poem in my hand.

29.

Sol

The concert manager holds his hand up and Pachelbel's Canon in D stops.

The Albert Hall is hushed as he bellows through cupped hands to the audience, kept to no more than five thousand, 'Ladies and gentlemen, Lord Haw Haw has announced that it's Kensington's turn again tonight.'

He looks theatrically at his watch. 'It's about 8.15pm and the German bombers should, as usual, be punctual and overhead in half-an-hour.'

His message is quickly relayed around the hall to those who could not hear him.

He looks around the audience. 'If anybody wishes to leave, we quite understand but we would be grateful if you could do so now.'

Even though the Queen's Hall has been destroyed by a fire bomb – fortunately empty at the time - nobody stands up.

We all share a feeling of proud courage that we will not let the Luftwaffe bully us. Our bravery is bolstered by widespread rumours that the Albert Hall's huge dome is being spared as a useful landmark by the bombers.

From our front seats I catch the eye of the pianist who is accompanying the violinists and smile fondly.

I tap Win's arm and point. 'Look, that's my great friend and tennis partner, Gerald Moore. I've told you about him.'

Gerald returns Win's wave with a discreetly raised hand.

I say, 'I hope one day we might be able to arrange some mixed doubles.'

'Yes Sol, that would be marvellous.' She grins. 'I've only ever played on grass.'

I chuckle. 'Well, I could always try and book a Wimbledon court. Do you play, Sergeant Bisset?' I lean forward and ask Win's companion.

'Alas no, Mr Cutner,' he smiles.

I instinctively think I will like this young man, Win's fiancé. He is polite with a friendly, handsome face. But Pachelbel resumes and interrupts our first attempt at conversation.

Win has invited me to the concert to meet Teddy. We can go for a drink and a chat afterwards, she said.

I'm the first to stand when the music stops. The conductor recognises me and bows gratefully as I clap enthusiastically.

Of course I am applauding dear Gerald, not him.

The concert over, we join those who are wandering uncertainly out into the darkness of the blackout, their throng incongruous in comparison with the deserted streets. Many remain inside, waiting for the All-Clear.

Flak bursts high above are reflected randomly across our faces. Searchlight beams still criss-cross the sky like fencers' rapiers but the drone of bombers and the whistle and thump of bombs are receding into the distance.

My work as an Air Raid Warden and Win's as a mobile canteen driver means we are less nervous than most about venturing outside during raids. In fact, I believe one is safer in the streets than in buildings. Teddy Bisset is similarly unperturbed.

I hold Win's hand. 'Thank you so much for inviting me. I loved it. Seeing my dear friend, Gerald was a bonus.'

I'm guessing that the young couple are not exactly flush with money. 'I know, instead of a pub, let's pop into my room at the college. I've still got some Champagne. And a cigar too for the Sergeant. We should celebrate your engagement properly.'

'Are you sure, Sol?' Win asks.

'Of course, of course. I was given a dozen bottles not too long before the war. I keep them for special occasions. Come on Sergeant, Win knows the way; it's just around the corner.'

We walk away from the dispersing crowd along the deserted side street to the Royal College of Music. As luck would have it, we bump into one of my Air Raid Warden colleagues who kindly helps us on our way with his torch to the front of the college's grandiose red-brick Victorian front facade.

I lead us briskly up the front stairs into the big entrance hall and draw the thick black-out curtain back across the front door.

Grabbing a bottle from the communal office fridge I usher my guests into the privacy of my own separate room.

'My inner *sanctum*, Sergeant. Win knows it well.'

Teddy's eyes roam around my cluttered room with its books, dog-eared music papers, photos, and overflowing ashtrays. His eyes settle on my black, polished Steinway.

'So, this is the famous piano?'

'Yes, this is where Sol took a nervous young Australian girl and turned her into a proper pianist.'

'Yes, and you did very well,' I nod proudly.

'You were a hard taskmaster. You put me through the ringer, alright.'

But she smiles.

And there's no bitterness in her voice.

'You came through all the better for it?' I ask.

'Yes I did. But this damn war is continually interrupting my lessons.'

I nod. 'But let's hope it's temporary for all of us and we can continue sometime in the not-too-distant future.'

She gently squeezes her hands in her lap, betraying, unusually for her, a touch of nervousness.

'What is it?' I ask softly.

Teddy puts a supporting hand on her shoulder.

She hesitates. 'I've been called up. I've been in England for two years now.' And then she gabbles. 'I'm starting my training to be a nurse at St Mary Abbott's Hospital.'

'Oh, that's convenient. It's just about around the corner.'

'Yes, I know, but the thing is once I'm trained, I'm going to be sent to somewhere called Arlesey. There's an emergency hospital there.'

'Oh! Where's Arlesey?' I ask, expecting her to reply it's an outer London suburb as I stand up to fetch some glasses. I gently twist the bottle and carefully pop open the Champagne.

I don't want her French fiancé to think I don't know how to open Champagne properly.

I pour her a glass of *Pol Roger* and then turn to Teddy and ask in French, 'Would you like a glass too, Sergeant? And a cigar?'

Startled by my good pronunciation, he replies in kind that he would indeed like both. And please, call me Teddy, he adds.

'And I'm Solomon or Sol. But never Solly. That's reserved for my mother.' I continue in French and raise my glass, 'Here's to your engagement, Win and Teddy. I wish you all the best of luck in these difficult times.'

Teddy replies, 'Thank you very much, Sol.'

He drains his glass in one. Shamefacedly he says, 'I'm sorry. It's some time since I've drunk decent Champagne.'

'No matter,' I say and top him up. 'I can understand why this is Churchill's favourite,' I add.

Win is staring at me. Her eyes, appealing for understanding, bring the conversation back into English. 'Sol, Arlesey's about 50 miles north of London.'

It takes a couple of seconds before I realise the implication of what she's just said… I won't be teaching her again for a long time, if ever.

Silence.

'I see.'

Then my fist bangs the small side table next to me. An ashtray rattles up and down.

'Bloody, bloody hell.' I calm down and add despondently. 'So, this could be the last time we'll see each other, at least for a while.'

To break the sad silence which has fallen across my room, I force a smile and say, 'Come on Win, play something to say goodbye.'

'You mean, *Au revoir*?'

I nod.

'Of course, Sol,' she says.

No longer my deferential student, she hands me her glass. 'First, give me a top up please.'

Win takes a gulp of Champagne, shakes her long, strong fingers free of stiffness and sits down onto the piano stool, her back to me, face towards Teddy who takes her glass.

Once I've settled into my chair, Win starts.

My signature piece, Beethoven's Moonlight Sonata, of course. I realise quickly that, despite my invitation, she is playing for Teddy not for me.

And how she plays! She's never played quite as well as this for her tutor.

Elbows tucked in and hands and wrists relaxed - no silly melodramatics insult the composer or instrument. And her fingers articulate every note with my mantra of a 'remarkable stillness.' But there's more. She's not slavishly following my instructions. Her interpretation colours everything she plays.

I am simultaneously proud and sad. Proud that my student has shown that she is capable of a standard well above a competent concert performer.

Sad that the extra tuition she needs from me to rise even further and become a *virtuosa* on the international stage will not now transpire.

She finishes, looks up at Teddy, turns around and challenges me for my opinion.

I clear my throat with a sip of my Champagne. I tease her by drawing out the suspense further by taking a puff of my cigar.

'That's not how I would play it,' I say, pretending to be stern.

'Why Sol, what was wrong?'

I stand up and laugh. 'Nothing Win. Absolutely nothing.'

I gather my thoughts and say slowly, 'I'm going to repeat what Lazare Levy,' I see from Teddy's face that he recognises the famous French pianist's name, 'said to me in Paris, many years ago.'

Another sip. 'Now listen Win, that was your interpretation. It's just as valuable as any I could produce. Any music lover or newspaper critic would recognise it as such.'

I deliberately place my glass and cigar on a side table and walk over towards the piano. Bending down, I take her hand and gently kiss her cheek. 'Well played Win. That was magnificent.'

She bows her head at first and then tilts her chin up.

Her eyes are welling with tears. But they are tears of pride in her performance, tinged with sadness that she will probably never play so well again.

The three of us are quiet, appreciating the bitter, sweet moment.

Teddy takes Win's hand and lifts it to his lips and kisses it tenderly.

So French!

Our silence is punctured rudely by the All-Clear sirens.

177

'We must go, Sol,' Win says unsteadily after glancing at Teddy. I see she is managing to keep her composure, even though her eyes are still glistening.

I hug her and shake Teddy's hand.

Will I ever see them again?

Pulling the heavy curtain covering the college's front door to one side, I see them out.

At the foot of the steps, holding hands tightly they turn around to wave goodbye, their faces spotlighted by the bright hall lamps.

I have never seen such intense love between a couple before.

30.

Win

'Over to you, Marshall,' Matron commands, handing me the bedpan in a tone that's as stiff and starchy as her apron.

'You've had enough training,' she adds sternly.

Yes, but that was watching others do it.

I neither blush nor flinch one *iota*. The sight of a naked Teddy means I'm familiar with a man's nether regions. Pulling the bedclothes back over the young man's knees, I tug his pyjamas down, place my arm under the back of his knees, lift them and hoist his bottom up in one movement.

With my free hand I try to push the bedpan underneath his backside. It's impossible to be gentle with the hard, cold porcelain receptacle. Even though Alf is a big, tough fellow – a London fireman badly injured by falling roof rafters - he winces in pain as I twist and shove it into place.

'I'm sorry.'

'Don't worry, nurse,' he says.

To give him some privacy we look away while he defecates. He takes at least five minutes.

'My goodness, you must have been desperate,' I say cheerfully, withdrawing the pan and inspecting the large mound of faeces for blood. All clear, my eyes signal to Matron. She nods in agreement. I carry the bedpan into the toilet, flush its contents away and return quickly to the patient where I wipe his bottom with a small, damp towel. This is placed in a bag hanging from my trolley for collection by one of the hospital porters. Once Alf is tucked up, I offer him a cup of tea.

He chuckles mischievously. 'You seen parts of me only my missus has seen, nurse.'

I nod impassively - Matron does not approve of familiarity with patients.

The three trainee nurses, who are observing, look white-faced and nervous at the realisation of what their duties will entail. Whereas I, with the benefit of six weeks training just completed, am an 'old hand'.

I smile encouragingly at them and whisper, 'Don't worry. You get used to it quickly.'

'Thank you, Marshall. That will do,' says Matron, irritated that I have addressed her trainees directly without her permission.

So, I'm not just a pianist and journalist. Now I'm also a nurse. Well, not a proper nurse, *just an auxiliary nurse*, as Matron warns me when she thinks I'm getting too big for my boots.

I must confess that I feel a bit of a fraud. I only had 50 hours training at St Mary Abbott's in Kensington. Yes, I saw two dead bodies on my first day and on the second I helped lay out a third in the morgue. The hospital porters were surprised at how I took death in my stride until I explained how I had often helped move corpses from bombed-wrecked homes, while driving my WVS canteen van. I still drove my mobile canteen every other night - bloody Jerry was not going to stop me 'doing my bit'.

Arlesey is an emergency hospital. We take the overflow from London. There is a steady stream of Blitz injuries: civilians, firemen and ambulance drivers. Occasionally we have shot down RAF pilots and civilian traffic accidents. I have a lot to learn about nursing. Our ward sister sees I'm keen and is happy to teach me.

The morning after a heavy night's bombing in London, casualties start to arrive. Experienced nurses and doctors triage arriving patients into: hopeless; need immediate care; and those who can wait.

The news that I'm used to dead or dying people spreads and I'm given the task of giving pain killer pills and morphine injections to the hopeless cases. I get used to holding hands with people slipping away from life. I talk to relatives who come to collect bodies and reassure them that their son's or brother's - there are no women in my ward - last remaining moments were as pain-free as possible. I have to lie sometimes about the cases when screams of agony were only partly reduced to exhausted whimpers.

Blood from weeping wounds colour my hands and stain my apron. Forgetfully I wipe sweat from my brow, leaving crimson streaks across my face.

After my shift, I vigorously mop the floors clean - it helps banish guilty thoughts that my inexperienced hands may be overdosing some of my patients with morphine, hastening their death.

Gradually I'm given more responsibility and, once I've learnt the surgical instruments' names, am even asked to attend emergency procedures in the operating theatres, where a steady hand and a calm manner under pressure are the main requirements.

During the less frenetic periods, I resume my normal duties tending our patients. Feeding, dressing wounds, changing bandages, taking temperatures and accompanying the doctors on their daily rounds.

I like our patients. And they like me too. I enjoy larking around with them. God knows, some of them badly need cheering up, stuck in hospital counting the days till they can get out again. I entertain them by whistling and singing. Thermometers are surreptitiously placed in cups of tea behind my back and we all have a good laugh at the ridiculously high temperatures.

But Matron does not like my familiarity with the patients. What a surprise!

I'm hauled into her office. 'Look here Marshall,' she barks. 'You may be able to behave like that in Australia. But this is England. Over here you must behave like we do.'

But my ward sister approves of me. She thinks the Matron fails to see how I cheer everyone up.

The ward sister watches me approvingly as I go about my work and tells me that I should consider a career as a nurse. And I'm on course for promotion to a senior nurse.

Being a nurse. Is it worth considering?

For the first time in ages, I'm saving money. A small amount is deducted from my salary for food which means I manage to buy a second-hand upright piano in good condition from a music shop in Bedford. There is a hospital meeting hall where Matron allows me to store my instrument and practise during my off-duty hours.

Word soon gets around that Nurse Marshall is a whizz on the piano.

She's been taught by Solomon. Who? You know, the famous concert pianist.

Even the non-musical have vaguely heard of Sol.

Anything up to a dozen patients, walking or in wheelchairs, porters, doctors and nurses regularly drop in to hear me play. Even Matron pops in occasionally to listen.

I don't just play serious stuff but also popular songs which I first played in the pub when I visited Teddy down in Wareham.

'Well, Marshall, I can see you are gifted when it comes to playing the piano,' Matron says. I can tell she's being sincere. 'Let's see how we can put your talent to good use,' she barks, reverting to type.

Not for the first time, I think to myself she would have made a good sergeant major. Even the Mater would have met her match.

I am summoned to her office. For once, she asks me to sit down.

'Here, look at this,' she says handing over a large poster.

Give all you can to
Mrs Churchill's
RED CROSS
AID FUND

'A worthy cause?' she asks.

I nod.

Unnervingly, she smiles. 'Mrs Churchill's fund has its flag day,' she checks a letter on her desk, embossed heavily with the Red Cross symbol, 'on the 16th December. I have in mind a concert to raise money for it. Would you be agreeable?'

'Of course, Matron,' I stammer.

She informs me, under her management, naturally, an organising committee will be set up to publicise the concert, decorate the hall with bunting and sell little Red Cross flags.

'On the night, I will introduce you and all you have to do is play,' she says as if my contribution will be incidental.

'May I choose what to play?'

'Of course. But I'd suggest something similar to what I heard the other day. Something classical, not too heavy, followed by popular songs towards the end, so we can all join in. Finishing, of course when we all stand for the National Anthem.

'And, Marshall, I want you to play in your uniform. It will help with fund-raising. Please see to it is clean and well-pressed.'

'Of course, Matron.' She does not need to add that she's ticked me off a few times for being 'scruffy'.

I am dismissed. 'Good. That's settled then.'

The night of the concert, after an encore of *Roll Out the Barrell,* Matron stands and signals everyone to rise for *God Save The King.*

Then she leads the applause for my performance.

Afterwards, Matron kindly thanks the organising committee, after which, she graciously accepts a bouquet of flowers for all her hard work!

The next day I am summoned to Matron's office where I am shocked to be greeted by a beaming smile.

'Well done Marshall. I've had nothing but praise for our concert.'

She now astounds me by standing up and shaking my hand. 'We have raised a total of 3 pounds, 5 shillings and sixpence. I am sure Mrs Churchill can use it for some good.'

Matron pauses and with her normal authoritarian face, looks me in the eye, 'We will have to do it again.'

I realise this will be a command performance rather than a request.

31.

Teddy

'The Inter-Services Research Bureau. How does that sound, dear boy?' Whetmore greets me back at Oxford in a jovial, avuncular mood. But, I notice somewhat disconcertingly, his eyes are studying me much more closely than when we last met at Oriel College.

'Well, sir, anything would be better than kicking my heels up at Trentham Park.'

'I can imagine. What precisely *were* you doing in that Victorian pile?'

Of course, he knows what my duties were. But I enjoy his friendly joshing. 'Liaising and translating for a few hundred Free French sailors.'

'And?'

'Rescuing them from run-ins with the police when they got drunk or too friendly with the local girls. Well, it was Christmas,' I say shrugging my shoulders.

'And what else?'

'Trying to spot Nazi and Vichy sympathisers. There weren't any. The Free French weeded them out some time ago.'

Whetmore lights a pipe and grins. 'I hear you enjoyed swimming in the pool?' Leaning back, he blows his match out. 'Wasn't it a bit cold?'

'Not much more than the baths in the main house.'

'The changing rooms are a fine example of Art Deco, I understand.'

So, he's been keeping more than a casual eye on me, I realise. Well apart from a few beers too many while joining in pub sing-songs and the odd game of British vs French basketball,

185

there's nothing to report. I was bored out of my mind for most of the time.

God, how I missed Win.

Playing the sergeant major he stands and barks suddenly, 'Come on Bisset. I'll buy you a pint and a sandwich.' Grabbing his bulky briefcase, he nods towards the busy typing pool and its officious supervisor. 'The walls have ears here.'

Outside, the contrast with the summer of 1940 is stark. Where sunshine had glinted off bright stone, the low February sun struggles though Oxford's misty murk.

Gazing out of Whetmore's car everything and everyone appears a greasy-grey. We pass some khaki-clad soldiers, kit bags over their shoulders, trudging along the High Street. Their weary faces down, they show no interest in our army saloon – just another bloody officer, I imagine them thinking.

A gaggle of female undergraduates, laden with books and gas masks requires us to stop at a pedestrian crossing. One of them raises a tired hand in a faint gesture of thanks.

In their black gowns, to me they look like forlorn crows searching for scraps of food.

'Always depressing this time of year,' Whetmore remarks. 'Christmas is over and spring has not yet sprung.' He sucks his pipe. 'Of course, the war news doesn't help.'

'No sir.'

Onwards through north Oxford. I smile at an incongruous sign which says, Summertown. Twenty minutes later we are sitting on a pub riverside terrace, sipping watery beer and chewing stale, white bread sandwiches.

'Sorry Bisset. The food was good at The Trout before the war started.' He reflects moodily, 'Well, one can say that about nearly everywhere at the moment, I suppose.'

'Do you mind if I smoke, Sir?'

Whetmore smiles at my well-mannered recognition of our difference in rank - he could hardly say no as he puffs away on his pipe. 'Of course not.'

I don't need to ask why he had chosen to sit outside on a murky February morning.

We are alone.

'The Thames,' Whetmore says, pointing with his pipe at the swirling stream flowing swiftly past. 'A small river here, not far from the source.'

He takes a mouthful of beer and grimaces.

'Sod this bloody, watered-down, war beer.' He walks over to the river and tosses the drink into the water. A silver flask appears from the folds of his coat. He rinses his beer glass out with a small amount of spirit and then pours himself a generous tot. 'Cognac, he says pursing his lips.

He knows I'm half Scots.

'Would you like a wee dram, laddie?' He hands me the flask and its silver top.

'Here, help yourself.'

He clears his throat while I pour. 'What I am about to tell you is *Most Secret*. You must not, I say again, must not repeat anything I tell you now. Not even to Win,' he says, pleased to recall her name. 'By the way how are you two getting on?'

'Very well. We're engaged.'

'Congratulations, my boy.'

He sips from his flask and says sympathetically, 'It must have been hard for you both to be apart over Christmas?'

'Yes, it was tough. But I say in a letter to try to cheer her up, *Oublie tous les ennuis de la vie à l'occasion de Noël.*'

Whetmore hands me his flask and pushes his pipe to the side of his mouth. 'The Inter Services Research Bureau – God, what a mouthful, is the cover name for a new secret organisation, let's just call it the Firm, shall we, which has been established to work with the Resistance movements across occupied Europe.'

I take a swig of brandy as he continues.

'The Firm's primary aim is to supply and train the Resistance in each country to carry out sabotage.'

He hunches forward across the table, glancing around to check we have not been joined on the terrace. 'In fact we've already started training agents for France down near Guildford in Surrey.'

He nods at me. 'Yes, another country mansion. Wanborough Manor this one's called.' And then he chuckles and oddly says in mock Cockney, 'The stately 'omes of England. You've been posted to Wanborough. Field Security duties, maybe more,' he hints. 'You'll be able to see more of Win too. It's on the mainline to Waterloo.'

Lunch over, Whetmore drives me to Oxford's railway station.

At the station, after I've hoisted my kitbag over my shoulder, he shakes my hand and smiles, 'Good luck, Teddy. I think this posting will be the making of you.'

Teddy? Not even at La Baule had he called me by my Christian name.

The weather changes as the train leaves Oxford. The murk becomes a fine drizzle, weaving odd, distorting patterns on the train windows as we climb up towards the Chilterns escarpment. I peer out but don't recognise anything.

32.

Win

Oh God! Teddy tells me in his latest letter that he has written to Pop in Australia asking for my hand in marriage. Of course, we had already agreed he should. But now the deed is done, I feel that there is no holding back. We will push on together as a united couple, come what may. Exhilaration and trepidation make me dizzy.

I pick up Teddy's letter. Although his spoken, colloquial English is now almost perfect, I know the Mater will pick up on his lack of written fluency in this letter. I find his mildly stilted sentences quaint, almost old-fashioned, but she will surely disapprove. I read every word…

Guildford 6th June, 1941
Win Darling,

   You must make a note of this date. I sent today to Mr Marshall a letter by Air-mail, all the way, asking the hand of his daughter in marriage. I did not make any mistakes which could tell him that I knew something about the cable he sent lately. Neither did I mention the letter from your mother. I thought it was better not to say anything about these two factors which are more or less against my request. Luck is on our side and I am quite confident about the answer.

   I told your Dad that I had been promoted to the rank of Lieutenant and that it was through your moral support that I did so which is perfectly true.

   J'ai une jolie Australienne qui m'aime – et ça fait toute la différence!

In my excitement I skip through the rest of Teddy's letter to me until its loving finale:

'Good bye, your Toots is thinking much of you, he would love to hold you in his arms and kiss you good night, waiting for that moment he only says à demain and t'envoie ses plus tendres baisers et amours.

Teddy'

Ironically, because of the irregular nature of wartime postal deliveries, I receive Teddy's latest letter to me just before I dash off to catch a train to meet him at somewhere called Normandy near Guildford in Surrey, twenty miles south of London.

Oh, how we laugh at the name. See, Teddy says, I told you I'd take you to Normandy.

In fact, the station name is Wanborough after a nearby manor house.

Teddy tells me that even though he is working at Wanborough Manor, we have to use his Intelligence Corps, Guildford office address for our mail. 'Army red-tape,' he says. I know his job is different now but he is even more elusive about what he actually does.

I sit and read again Teddy's letter in my lap, glancing out of the train window, gripping the paper so tightly that it almost rips apart. I barely register the names of the suburban stations as the slow, stopping train chuffs its way through the sooty, Victorian-terraced housing of outer London, pockmarked with bomb sites.

Oh, how I wish I shared Teddy's confidence that Lady Luck is on our side and Pop and the Mater will relent and finally give their permission to our marriage.

The train speeds up and we are now in the undulating bright green fields and the flashing bosky, black shadows of the English high-summer countryside. The time between stations increases and I carefully check their names at every stop.

Eventually I hear a station master shout out along a platform through the train's steamy smoke, 'Wanborough, Wanborough.'

I nearly slip down the carriage step and fall onto the platform in my haste to alight, caught off balance with my small suitcase in one hand and mac in the other - one can never trust the English weather.

The station master grabs my arm. 'Steady on, luv,' I hear him say as he slams the door shut behind me. In one well-practised movement he blows his whistle and waves a flag. The driver hoots goodbye twice.

Recovering my poise, I shout, 'Hello Toots, over here,' as I recognise Teddy appearing through the steam that swirls behind the departing, hissing locomotive.

'Babe,' he mummers in my ear while we hug tightly.

I relax my hands and step back. 'Oh my, look at you. Don't you look dashing in your officer's uniform,' I tease.

He salutes stiffly in mock retaliation. 'At your service, Miss Marshall.'

He grabs my suitcase handle and leads me by my arm. 'Come on, I've managed to get us a room at the New Inn, an old pub in Send.'

I'm baffled. 'Send?'

'Yes, funny name isn't it?'

At the pub I watch Teddy change into slacks and a short-sleeved shirt. Not for the first time I notice how neat he is. His uniform is carefully folded, shirt hung in the wardrobe and shoes stowed tidily away. I've read somewhere that children without siblings are often like this - parents can concentrate on the behaviour of one child without the distraction of others.

He feels my gaze, smiles and reaches out for my hand. 'Fancy a walk?'

I beam happily, sitting for over an hour in a grimy train means I'm keen for fresh air.

We stroll along a canal next to the pub. A narrow boat passes slowly by, small whirlpools lazily spinning off its rudder in the calm, brown water. A terrier on top of the cabin barks, warning off potential boarders.

'Never mind him,' the owner says cheerfully, both hands on the tiller as a bridge looms ahead.

The backs of modest bungalows with large gardens full of tomatoes, beans and fruit trees run down to the canal path. All are obeying the government's exhortation to 'Dig for Victory.' Families spill out into the sunshine to enjoy the weekend break. The hum and laughter of conversation, glasses clinking, cutlery rattling against plates and children shrieking in excitement smother any thoughts of the War. Hand in hand, Teddy and I pause to enjoy the peaceful, idyllic scene.

Pointing with my chin I ask. 'Do you think we will ever have something as perfect as this, Teddy? I mean a home, garden and children?'

'Of course we will, Babe.'

'But how will we be able to afford it?'

'Don't worry about money, Win. Once this damn war is over, I'm sure Uncle George will help me become a stockbroker like him in London.'

He pauses and twists around in front of me to emphasise his next words. 'Or we might go and live in Normandy. I can join my mother's family business. I know they like me. Don't forget I own a house there and one in Paris.'

'Yes, I know, Toots. But will they accept me? I'm Australian, from the other side of the world.'

He reassures me. 'They are not snobbish Parisians, Babe. They are down-to-earth country people. Not much different from your Perth, I think. After all I accepted you. And you accepted me.'

Mollified, I kiss him softly on the cheek.

'Hmm, I can smell *Jicky*,' he says, his seductive eyes suggesting it's time to return to our room.

Making urgent, passionate love, clothes chucked higgledy-piggledy over the floor, and then relaxing, cuddling up in each other's arms in an unfamiliar bed feels, oh, I don't know, so delightfully decadent. I am so, so happy. I love my Frenchman, my Toots. And he loves his *Australienne*, his Babe.

Later we change for dinner and find a seat in the saloon bar. I've learnt from experience that in English country pubs, the public bar might as well have a sign above its door: Men Only.

We are sipping gin and tonics when Teddy's eyes narrow as he sees two men entering the pub. One of them checks his progress as he spots Teddy.

After a quick aside to his companion, he approaches us in a cheeky, effeminate manner. The smell of alcohol wafts over us as he slurs in a mock-flirtatious voice, 'Good evening, Teddy.'

My God, I swear the man almost blows Teddy a kiss.

'Good evening,' Teddy says curtly, his face reddening in embarrassment.

'Why don't you introduce me to your friend, Teddy?' the man giggles archly.

'Of course. Win, this is, er…'

'Denis Rake,' the stranger interjects.

'Hello Denis, I'm Win Marshall.'

'It's a pleasure to meet you, Win,' he says, offering a limp hand.

Teddy suddenly interrupts, speaking rapidly in French. The man responds in the same language and a short, heated conversation follows. I catch the words *putain* and *merde* but not much else in the rapid crossfire between the two.

Then just as suddenly as he started, Denis Rake stops, shrugs his shoulders and grins at me. 'Teddy's reminded me of another engagement I have this evening. I'm sorry Win. I would have enjoyed chatting to you.' And then, incredibly, he pokes his tongue out. 'Sorry Teddy. I thought today we were off-duty.'

And with a laconic, mischievous grin he saunters off. I see him affectionately squeeze his friend's arm to signal they should leave.

'Teddy, who the hell is Denis Rake?'

'One of our trainees.'

'What on earth are you training him for?'

Teddy grimaces. 'You know I can't tell you much. Part of my new job means I'm helping observe a group of trainees. The training will take place around the country and I will be going with them.

'Getting trained myself too,' he adds half to himself. 'And in case you think the British Army has gone mad, that particular gentleman has a skill that is in short supply. Otherwise, he would have been chucked out long ago.'

'His French sounded good,' I mutter *sotto voce*.

'Quite,' says Teddy enigmatically.

33.

Win

They are very young, Tony and Hope. He's still only nineteen, not yet twenty, and she a few years younger. I can tell from Hope's strained face that she is a nervous teenager who is determined to put on a grown-up face in front of Tony's new, older friends.

Old? We're still in our twenties, for God's sake!

We are sitting hugger-mugger in the packed York Minster pub in London's Soho. The hubbub is very loud and very French, like nearly all of its customers - it's widely known as De Gaulle's Free French pub. Which is why Teddy enjoys popping in now and then to soak up a bit of Gallic ambiance. I can see that Tony is also revelling being immersed in a French crowd. His eyes are darting around taking in the French uniforms as he cocks his ears, trying to overhear the buzzy conversations around us.

Despite Teddy's best attempts, inevitably after catching snatched conversations at boozy parties in pubs and flats, I gradually put two and two together and realise Teddy works for an organisation which is training people to fight with the French Resistance. Its official name is the Inter Services Research Bureau, but called simply, *The Firm,* by everyone who works for it. Which is why I know that Tony Brooks will soon be sent on a mission to France. But it seems Hope is unaware of this. At least so far.

In the meantime, Teddy is taking an impatient Tony around London, getting him fitted with 'French' tailored clothes and personal possessions while relaxing with him in the evenings, trying to mollify his irritation at being kept waiting.

Tony smiles at me. 'Teddy took me under his wing when I joined the Firm. Nearly everyone else was in their thirties. I was very grateful.'

But Teddy has told me that, in reality, Tony didn't need any support. 'He gives the impression of someone at least ten years older and very confident. Some find him a bit cocky. I think he's grown up quickly because of his experiences in France and the tough training he's had from us.'

The two of them had clicked immediately. Teddy had explained that just like him, Tony was bilingual and sometimes felt English in France but French in England.

Hope looks around at the unfamiliar uniforms, wide-eyed. She whispers, 'I think we're the only English people here. Everyone's speaking French.' 'Oh, I'm sorry,' she gushes. 'Although you don't sound it, I'd forgotten you were Australian, Win.'

Hope's right, my Australian accent has almost disappeared. I've not tried deliberately to lose it, but it seems to have gradually faded.

Hope goes on, 'And you're really French, Teddy, or so Tony tells me.'

Teddy smiles. 'Yes, I was brought up in Paris.'

'Where do you come from, Hope?' I ask.

'Leverington,' she replies. 'It's a village in north Cambridgeshire.'

Hope sounds and looks like what she is: a pretty, fresh-faced, young country girl not used to the big city.

She blushes slightly. 'The father of one of Tony's school friends was our village vicar. We met during the school holidays. Tony got a job fruit picking for my father.'

'So your father's a fruit farmer, Hope?' I ask, easily imagining her swinging her brown legs in the autumn sunshine, sitting on the back of a farm trailer, surrounded by baskets of freshly-picked apples.

'Hope's father is a bit more than that, Win,' Tony says diplomatically. 'He buys lots of fruit from farmers and supplies markets.'

He drops into the conversation that Hope's family live in the rather grand-sounding Leverington Hall.

Ah, so not humble farmers, more like well-off English country squires.

The noise in the pub suddenly tails off into a stiff silence. I glance towards the door and see a tall French officer leading a group of colleagues through the throng. Judging by the two stars on his *képi,* I assume he must be a general.

'De Gaulle,' Teddy hisses, glancing at Tony.

All the uniformed men in the pub spring to attention as the famous Frenchman strides briskly by. Glimpsing Teddy and Tony's British uniforms, he twists around and barks suspiciously. '*Vous êtes Français?*'

Both reply in French. Teddy answers yes, while Tony says no.

De Gaulle recognises Teddy's Intelligence Corps insignia and asks where he is serving.

'The Inter Services Research Bureau, General.'

De Gaulle snorts derisively. 'You mean Buckmaster's little band of saboteurs?'

Teddy remains silent.

De Gaulle glares at him and moves on without another word.

The bar breathes out a collective sigh and the men all retake their seats.

'Gosh, if looks could kill, Teddy,' I say, puzzled by the French leader's reaction, watching the lugubrious figure stride upstairs into the *Chez Victor* restaurant. 'I thought we were on the same side.'

Teddy buys some time by tapping his pipe over an ashtray. 'I'm told De Gaulle wants anything to do with France to be under his command. He is furious that Churchill won't agree.'

'And,' I add, 'he was a little less than discreet with regards to what he called you all.'

'Quite,' Teddy agrees, glaring at the restaurant stairs.

'At least it confirms a few more things for me,' I say quietly and squeeze Teddy's hand. He returns my tight smile and in our shared glance we know to speak no more of it, but Hope looks puzzled.

Her apprehensive voice interrupts the silence, 'Does that mean you are going to France, Tony?'

Tony flashes an embarrassed glance at Teddy, not knowing how to reply.

Before the conversation blunders further into sensitive military matters, I suggest we drink up and catch a cab. I had thought earlier that we might make our way to the Oddenino Hotel and enjoy its atmosphere of gay wartime abandon and saucy cabaret. But I fear now it might prove too *risqué* for our young, country girl, Miss Hope Munday.

I announce, ignoring Teddy and Tony's smirking at my accent, '*Nous avons mangé une tranche de la vie française. Maintenant nous allons en Australie. Tout de suite!*'

***

'To the Boomerang Club,' I tell the cab driver.

'Orlright luv, Australia House it is.'

The name suggests a scruffy, Australian watering-hole. But the Boomerang Club's main room has the decor of a luxury hotel with walls and lofty ceilings of grey marble, as befits part of Australia's plush High Commission in London. The chairs and sofas are upholstered in pink leather and our shoes sink into a deep wall-to-wall matching carpet.

Although filling up, we manage to grab a table and four comfortable armchairs. I queue with Teddy to order pies, sandwiches and tea from a snack bar. Cooking smells emanate from a small kitchen behind the counter, staffed by Australian women who've lived in London for ages.

In the background a piano tinkles. I know the pianist but have resisted her entreaties to play - I'm wary of being pestered every time I visit.

Australian officers, sergeants, pilots, seamen, army privates, Red Cross nurses, men and women from Down Under mingle and gossip. Anyone over thirty-five looks out of place. There is a well-thumbed message book on the counter which is grabbed by newcomers desperate for news about friends who they think may have visited. Not unreasonable - every Australian in London will pass through the Boomerang Club at some stage or the other.

Later on in the evening, when people flock from closing pubs and night clubs, the atmosphere will become more raucous and sing-songs will start around the piano.

'My, these pies are good,' Tony says, wiping his lips. 'And this is the best tea I've had for ages.'

He nibbles his sandwich, frowns and raises his eyebrows. 'What's this?'

'Vegemite,' I chuckle. 'Like Marmite but not so salty.'

Tony looks uncertain how to respond without sounding rude.

I feel an affectionate hand on my shoulder. 'Hello Win. Did I overhear you introducing Vegemite to our British friends?'

I start to stand up but the hand gently restrains me. 'Good evening, Mr Troy,' I say.

'Come on Win, I think you can call me Frank, now,' he says.

I look around our table. 'Tony, Hope, Teddy, this is, er, Frank Troy. He is Western Australia's Agent General in London. Our state's ambassador, if you like.'

Teddy and Tony stand up and shake hands.

'So you must be Win's fiancé?'

Teddy smiles in acknowledgement.

This is a bit awkward. I never told Teddy that the telegram from Pop refusing permission to our marriage came via Frank Troy's office.

'You're a lucky young man. Win comes from a great family. I've known her parents for years. Her father is one of our state's best journalists. No, I shall rephrase that. He is our best journalist.' He squeezes my shoulder. 'And her mother is famous for being the first woman to fly from Perth to Sydney. She's quite a woman - just like her daughter.'

Yes, he's familiar with the Mater's reputation alright.

'Win, I've heard from your father. Lloyd has started training with the Air Force. He's doing very well, apparently.'

Troy turns to the absurdly young-looking Tony. 'And you work with Teddy?'

Tony nods slightly.

'You must be a very brave young man,' he says quietly, recognising conversation about Tony's occupation would be fruitless.

In that moment I realise Frank must have made enquiries for Pop about Teddy. And that if he knows what De Gaulle alluded to, then my father would now know Teddy works for an important secret organisation fighting the Germans. Self-centredly, I hope that my parents might now think more highly of Teddy. Frank promises to tell Pop he bumped into me and my fiancé. I even hope now he's met Teddy, however briefly, he might report that he looks a decent chap?

Frank Troy responds to a wave from across the room and moves on.

'Your family sounds very interesting, Win,' Tony says, watching our Agent General disappear into the crowd.

'I suppose Lloyd's your brother?' he asks.

'Yes, he's my younger brother.' I smile, trying to hide sibling rivalry. 'He's always top of the class. At everything.'

'Except playing the piano,' Teddy says, supporting me with a quick hug.

Gratefully I reward him with a peck on the cheek.

'When are you two going to get married? Hope asks.

'Ah,' I say. 'The thing is...'I clear my throat. 'My parents haven't given their permission yet.'

I pause, looking at Teddy and squeeze his knee. 'It shouldn't be long now.'

Tony, coughs on his cigarette, looking embarrassed. 'Forgive me, Teddy,' he says. 'This is probably not the right moment. But I may not see you for a while.'

Gosh, he really does sound much older than nineteen.

'But Hope and I have decided to get married.' He presses on, 'And I'd really like you to be my best man.'

'Of course,' Teddy smiles proudly. 'It would be an honour.'

I lean across the table to give Hope a congratulatory kiss. I glance at her young eyes. They belong to those of little more than a schoolgirl. Will she regret marrying someone from the Firm?

34.

Teddy

My hands are red and sweat drips from my brow. If I'm not careful, I'll get blisters from all this strenuous rowing in the summer sun.

'In out, in out,' my naval colleague bellows cheerfully as our oars in our clinker-built, naval whaler pull us away from *HM Yacht Sunbeam II*. Although *The Sunbeam* is kitted out for war as a floating depot, anchored in Cornwall's Helford River, her beautiful schooner lines are barely discernible under the ugly camouflage grey.

'If her former owner could see her now, he'd weep,' says Royal Navy Lieutenant, Richard Townsend.

I sweep a hand over the panorama of a blue, secluded river mouth, nestling between gently-rolling, green farmlands. 'But he'd love this beautiful anchorage though, wouldn't he?'

Richard concedes my point. 'Yes, he would.'

'God we're lucky, aren't we? Let's enjoy it while we can.'

I tell Win in a letter that I'm living the life of a rich man somewhere in the West Country. Rowing in the morning, sailing and swimming in the afternoon in a sunny river. There's delicious fresh seafood to eat – no rationing here. The fishermen are doing well – having a good war, some people say jealously - selling most of their high-priced catches onto the plates of London's expensive restaurants and hotels.

Fresh air and exercise make for grumbling stomachs. I join Richard for an early supper in the Ferry Boat Inn, close to the beach and a short walk from the Firm's quarters in a requisitioned large house called Ridfarne.

We order large helpings of crab and pints of local beer. I've got used to Cornish beer; it's not too different really from some Norman *bière artisanale*.

We're well into our second pint when Richard recognises someone through the crowd of fishermen and service people, ordering a drink at the bar. I can tell from his serious face that the person might be important.

Waving his hand in polite welcome, Richard says, 'We are honoured Teddy. Commander Fleming has just arrived.'

He whispers, 'He's the deputy head of Naval Intelligence.'

'Only a Commander?' I say, quizzically.

I don't really need to ask; it's not uncommon among intelligence personnel that nominal rank is not necessarily an indicator of importance. It probably suits Fleming to have a middling officer's rank.

'You know he started my outfit, the Inshore Patrol Flotilla,' Richard adds.

I smile at another name that means little. Far from Inshore, the job of Richard's five or six boat flotilla is to deliver and fetch messages and people from the Firm and our sister secret service, MI6, to and from France by passing themselves off as part of the French fishing fleet, right under the eyes of the German patrol boats. Gossip has it Richard's already been ashore in occupied France himself a couple of times.

He responds to my expression. 'Well, our name's not as stupid as your Inter Services Research Bureau moniker.

He grins and shakes his head in mock exasperation, 'We all know it's a cover.'

He has a point - a silly name which is fooling fewer and fewer people. Increasingly I notice military personnel, like Richard, are becoming aware of the Firm's real name, the Special Operations Executive, SOE for short.

The joke of the stately 'omes of England has worn thin.

'Fleming comes down now and then to check up on us and make sure we are properly briefed for any special ops… Like ours,' he adds.

Richard nods at a jerk of Feming's head towards the door. We follow the Commander outside towards a spare table lit by the evening sun. Fleming brushes left-over food from the tabletop with a monogrammed silk handkerchief. I can tell by the curved rings on his jacket sleeves that he is not a regular officer but a member of the Navy Reserve – nicknamed the Wavy Navy.

I also guess from his expensive, well-tailored uniform - *definitely* not standard issue - that Fleming is *not short of a bob or two*, a delightful English expression I've learnt recently from Richard.

The Commander sips from a glass of neat whisky and grimaces slightly - clearly not to his taste.

Ostentatiously, and slightly effeminately, Fleming takes a cigarette with a thin gold band near its filter from a blue packet, embossed with the name *Moreland of St James* and twists it into a holder.

This man seems to like the good things of life.

He turns to me and asks in passable French, 'Would you like a cigarette?'

'Thank you, Sir.'

Surprising me with his friendliness, he now holds his hand out, 'Fleming.' He pauses to smile. 'Ian Fleming.'

I soon notice he chain smokes.

God, his cigarettes are strong. Is that why he uses a cigarette holder, to stop his fingers from becoming stained?

I can see him summing me up. 'Teddy?' A quick glance at Richard for confirmation of my name. 'Teddy Bisset, isn't it? You come highly recommended. Buckmaster speaks well of you.'

Rubbing his chin, he reflects, mainly to himself, 'Good chap Buckmaster. I just missed him at school.' Looking around, he checks nobody is within hearing distance. 'So, are you two prepared for Operation Guillotine?' he asks softly, his eyes hooded, concealing his expression.

'Yes, Sir,' Richard confirms confidently. 'The *Ar-Miscoul* is ready. She's a bit of an old tub but that just makes it easier to blend in with the French boats. We've taken her out for a sea trial and didn't encounter any problems.

'We'll load her with the cargo of guns and ammunition from the *Sunbeam* tomorrow afternoon and leave early the next day for the Scilly Isles, where we'll refuel. Unless the weather turns bad, we'll leave the following day, first thing for our rendezvous with *l'Audacieux* near the Ile d'Yeu, south of Saint Nazaire.'

'Excellent,' Fleming says. 'You both know that this is a trial to see how easy it will be to get a sizeable load of arms and ammunition by boat to the Resistance halfway down the French Atlantic coast?'

He looks intently at both of us through his cigarette smoke, 'It could be a bit dicey,' he adds, carefully watching our reactions.

Yes, our faces acknowledge we both know the dangers of sailing deep into enemy waters, close to the major German naval base at Saint Nazaire.

Satisfied, he draws heavily on his cigarette and coughs behind his hand. 'You've got family in Normandy, haven't you Teddy?'

I nod.

'So, you'd easily spot if someone's not speaking with a local accent?'

I smile confidently. 'That should be easy, Sir.'

I eye Fleming closely as we talk. He has a hard, sardonic face. It's difficult to read what he's thinking. Handsome but not a pretty boy. Like me, a man whom women find attractive, I think conceitedly.

The conversation becomes more relaxed as we drink another round and chat about the various parts of France we like - Paris, Nice, Bordeaux.

Midway through our conversation, through his cigarette smoke, Fleming asks casually whether I know Dieppe. I tell him that I've visited the seaside resort a couple of times for short holidays.

Watching his cigarette smoke rising slowly, he asks, 'Did you like Dieppe?'

'Yes, I did. I remember walking around the harbour and eating in some of the fish restaurants. I got to know the place quite well.'

Fleming rubs his chin thoughtfully at my reply, seemingly thinking of a visit he made himself to Dieppe.

Then he grins. 'Did you ever have a flutter in the casino?'

'No, Sir,' I chuckle. 'My parents definitely did not approve of gambling.'

'Whereas I, Teddy, was fool enough to lose money at the casino, damn it.' Jokingly he adds, half to himself. 'At least the barman there was happy to make my favourite Martini.'

'And what was that, Sir?' asks Richard, humouring our senior officer.

Fleming stubs his cigarette out and says good-humouredly, 'Well, since you ask, three parts gin, one of vodka, half of vermouth and a slice of lemon peel. He lights another cigarette and adds, grinning, 'Shaken, not stirred. It preserves the flavour of the drink better.'

***

'Etes-vous Espagnol?'

'Non, mais moi, je suis Français.'

Merde! The password reply should have been, *'Non, nous sommes basques.'*

'Christ, Teddy, do you think he's German?' whispers Richard.

He holds an outstretched palm, restraining our two-man crew, crouching in the cabin stairway, holding Sten guns, their strained eyes intently waiting for Richard's orders.

'Where are you headed?' I shout over the heavy swell.

We've been circling around searching for this boat for about four hours. He wasn't at the first *rendez-vous* and he's twenty miles off the second. A German patrol boat had passed close by earlier but are satisfied by my French and our typical Breton fishermen's colourful smocks.

After a tense few minutes' conversation I reassure Richard that the captain's Norman accent is genuine and *l'Audacieux* comes alongside.

Over coffee in the *Ar-Miscoul's* galley the French skipper shrugs his shoulders at our worries about how far we were from the agreed *rendez-vous*. He also refuses to take the full consignment of explosives, Colt pistols and ammunition. Too risky he says. Spot checks by the Germans will detect an unusually large cargo. He wasn't sure what boat or its name to expect so was cautious about using the password. Nobody had told him the details.

'You are from Paris?' he asks me disdainfully, in half-decent French, as if that was the reason for our initial communication problems.

I nod.

'Well, tell your English friends that next time you must have proper fishing gear. Your boat must have sails as well. Fuel is in short supply. You are lucky the Germans haven't noticed these obvious mistakes.'

Feeling disgruntled and let down by our side, we part company; *l'Audacieux* towards its French fishing port, and the *Ar-Miscoul* back towards the Scilly Isles.

I'm not sad to return to England. I look across the sea towards St Nazaire, just over the horizon, and painful memories of thousands of drowning soldiers and washed-up dead bodies from the sinking *Lancastria* come back to haunt me.

That night we spot a damaged U-Boat being escorted back to St-Nazaire. A sitting duck for bombers - we try to radio our base. There is no response.

'Fuck this, Teddy,' Richard says furiously, throwing the microphone down onto the chart table.

'We've risked our lives for a bunch of idiots.'

35.

Teddy

They're a good bunch, these French-Canadian anti-aircraft gunners. I'm training them in street and house-to-house fighting, using the British Sten gun and hand grenades, for a special raid to grab some new German anti-aircraft gunsights.

I know I've got their confidence and my sessions are going well. In effect, I'm passing on the excellent training I've received from the SOE, strengthened with my own field experience.

Out of the corner of my eye, I see five figures approaching my group as we practise shooting on the target range. As they get closer, I recognise some of them immediately: the head of SOE, Major General Gubbins, my commanding officer, the head of SOE's French section, Colonel Maurice Buckmaster, and my friends, the towering figure of Jacques de Guélis, and Peter Harratt who is going to lead our SOE team on the special mission I'm training the Canadians for. As my commander I've seen Buckmaster at least a dozen times since our meeting in Lille, before I went off with Captain Whetmore, tagging behind the disintegrating French government as it fled west towards Bordeaux. Gubbins, I've only met once before, when he was inspecting a parachute training course at Ringway near Manchester. Once seen, his steely-eyed stare and twirled up moustache were not easily forgotten.

Now they get closer, I recognise the fifth; Commander Ian Fleming.

The group observe the training session, watching as I advise and encourage each soldier in French. I see a grimace flash cross Jacque's face as he hears the replies in their French-Canadian accents – a coarse version of Norman French, too unrefined for my French aristocratic friend's taste.

After the shooting stops, I am invited to follow my visitors to the range's office, a nondescript Nissan hut, for a briefing. I thought I already knew the ostensible purpose of the mission for which I am training *my* Canadians. It soon turns out, I was wrong.

Walking along I overhear the casual small talk between Buckmaster and Fleming. I remember that Fleming told me they'd gone to the same school but had missed each other by a year or so. They were chuckling over common acquaintances and the idiosyncrasies of their teachers at Eton. I mentally shrug my shoulders. I've grown accustomed to how the British military places great importance on its officers' backgrounds to make sure the '*right sort*' is appointed to positions of responsibility. Even so, it's common knowledge that the SOE is regarded by many outsiders as ludicrously snobbish about the British who are permitted to join its senior ranks.

We wait at the hut door and follow Fleming. Inside there are several army red tabs on lapels and plenty of silver and gold rings reflecting off the sleeves of RAF and navy uniforms.

There is tension in the hut as we stand around a large map-table. The atmosphere relaxes as a large tea urn arrives.

Fleming turns to me. 'Would you like a cigarette, Teddy? I recall you like mine.'

'Thank you, Sir.'

Eyebrows raise at hearing Fleming calling me by my Christian name.

By now everyone else has lit cigarettes, except de Guélis who puffs on a cigar.

Where on earth does he get them from?

The tea is poured by a private who disappears quickly, unnerved by the sight of too many red tabs and gold braid. I eye Fleming closely as he starts the briefing with an air of authority. I'm not surprised now to notice he chain smokes.

'Tell me Teddy, have your Canadians asked why you are training anti-aircraft gunners in commando-style street and house to house fighting?'

'Yes, Sir,' I nod.

'I've told them the truth. That we may have to fight to capture the new type of gunsights Jerry's using on its anti-aircraft guns. We've all guessed that it will be a raid somewhere in France.'

Fleming's eyelids briefly retract as he glances around the table. He nods approvingly. 'Excellent, Teddy. Please keep it that way. The truth is always the best lie,' he adds *sotto voce* to everyone.

The Royal Navy's deputy head of intelligence now unrolls a large map of the French coast. Cups, saucers and ashtrays move to secure the corners and edges.

'Teddy, you know all intelligence briefings are secret.' He smiles to himself. 'But this one is Ultra secret. You understand?

I nod uncertainly, not sure of what is to follow.

'In fact, you're the last person in the room to hear what I'm about to say. But one of the most important at this particular juncture,' he says softly.

He stares hard at my face to check that I have indeed grasped the sensitivity of what he is about to tell me. Another puff of smoke and then he says slowly, emphasising each word. 'You won't have heard of Enigma.'

It is not a question but a statement.

He places a photograph of a wooden box on the map and then carefully, deliberately, another photograph next to the first. The second one shows the same box with its lid off displaying what, at first sight, looks like a typewriter.

There is intense focus around the table on the photographs: I realise that I'm not alone in seeing them for the first time.

'You will have to be fully indoctrinated into the classification Teddy, but for now, just so you know, that word I used, Ultra, is what it is called. It is above Most Secret.'

He pauses to let that fact sink in. Then he points to the photographs.

'This is Enigma. It is the machine which the Germans use to code and decode their messages. For example, to and from their U-Boats. There would be an Enigma used by the German navy in Dieppe and one on each submarine.'

He sighs. 'The Germans have recently modified the Enigma machine I'm showing you. This one has three rotors,' he says, pointing to three cylinders. 'The new one has four,' he adds.

'It's absolutely vital to the war effort that we get our hands on this latest version,' he says fiercely, his eyes are furious slits and his fist clenches on the table.

Like everyone, I've heard the rumours of the high number of ships being sunk in the ship convoys crossing the Atlantic. A year ago, we thought we were beating the U-Boats. But our food rations have recently been reduced. I notice wryly there's not a single fat person in the room. In fact, I can't remember when I last saw anyone overweight, except Churchill. But now it seems the Germans are winning in the Atlantic. Is it because of this four rotor Enigma?

Fleming leans over the map and pencils a large circle around a northern French port. He looks at me. 'You are training for Operation Jubilee which is a major raid on Dieppe.' His eyes crinkle as he reminds me sardonically, 'Yes, we spoke about Dieppe before, didn't we?'

For the benefit of the others in the room he raises his voice. 'Lieutenant Bisset knows the town well. 'Unlike me though, he didn't get stung in its casino,' he adds, raising a laugh which lowers the tension.

'Teddy, thousands are involved in Operation Jubilee. The Navy and RAF will have a heavy supporting presence. Planning and operational control falls under Lord Mountbatten's Combined Operations.'

Standing up straight, he chews on his cigarette holder. 'The landing force will get in and out on a single tide, before the Germans can mount a major counter-attack.

'There are various reasons for the raid, most of which don't concern this meeting. But the most important, as far as I, and therefore you, are concerned is the capture of the latest Enigma machine, in whole or in part, and related documents, code books and so forth, so that our boffins can examine them.'

He looks round the table. 'Gentlemen, there could be more than one Enigma in Dieppe. For example, the German army or the Luftwaffe may have their own in convenient locations in Dieppe town centre, not too obvious to prying eyes.

'After the initial waves of our attacking troops clear the way, there will be more than one small search party entering identified buildings as swiftly as possible and capturing whatever booty they can find.'

He wipes some cigarette ash from the map with a red polka dot hanky, pulled theatrically from a shirt sleeve cuff.

Fleming stabs a finger at the Dieppe street-plan. 'This is the location of the Hôtel Moderne. We believe that this is the location of the German Navy HQ and the most likely position of an Enigma machine. It is the target of my specialist commando team.' A pause for emphasis. 'And nobody else.'

He stabs at another building. 'Teddy, you and your Canadians will concentrate on the Town Hall here.'

He twists around and stares intently at me again. 'Now listen carefully. Just as important as actually obtaining an Enigma is making sure the Germans don't realise we have pinched one and therefore believe they need to develop another version.

'Which is why the office or the building where the Enigma was kept must be completely wrecked. It must appear to the Germans that it was destroyed beyond trace incidentally as part of the attack and wasn't singled out for special attention by us. That way we hope they will not realise what we were actually searching for.'

Now he locks my eyes. 'Your personal task will be to seize the Enigma you find and spirit it away without too many eyes, even among your Canadians, seeing what you're doing.'

He gestures towards Peter Harratt. 'You'll carry it yourself and pass it on to Peter. His task is to get it as swiftly as possible onto a Royal Navy ship.

'After that you will, using grenades or whatever may come to hand, blow up, burn and smash the location where you found the Enigma.' He pauses and blows smoke upwards towards the ceiling, lost for a moment in his thoughts.

'Mounting a large raid means that the Germans shouldn't suspect that pinching an Enigma is the major objective,' he mutters softly, half to himself.

Christ, has he let slip that this whole raid on Dieppe is an elaborate smokescreen to, as he says, pinch an Enigma without the Germans realising?

'Your Canadians, if captured, won't know the real purpose of the raid. The fact they also speak poor English will impede the Germans.'

Another laugh echoes around the table.

Fleming blows cigarette smoke up towards the corrugated iron roof. 'In any case, they can truthfully say they are simply anti-aircraft gunners searching for the latest German gunsights. You too will be French-Canadian, wearing a Canadian Army uniform, which should allay any suspicions if you are caught. As consolation, you'll be promoted to a Captain in charge of an anti-aircraft battery. 'More details will follow but that's enough for now.'

The briefing is finished.

Fleming lights another cigarette and disappears with Buckmaster.

***

On 19 August 1942 our small armada sets out for Dieppe.

The raid is an utter disaster.

I spend hours in a boat offshore, German shells whistling overhead, waiting for the signal to land. But no signal arrives. Hundreds of Canadians are slaughtered on the Dieppe beaches and get no further. Thousands more are wounded and captured. The Royal Navy lose a destroyer, the RAF lose over 80 aircraft. We do not recover a single Enigma machine or even a code book. Fleming's own specialist commando team are wiped out before getting close to their target. Only one makes it home physically unscathed.

Furiously I shout at Peter Harratt, 'What a fucking cock up!'

I wonder who's to blame? Mountbatten? Fleming?

Some poor Canadian general will carry the can, you can be sure of it. That, or they'll shove the blame at a lack of intelligence and planning.

With our tails between our legs, we retreat back to England.

Defeated once more by the damn Germans. Will we ever win?

36.

The Mater

It's a blustery, soggy sort of day. Pop and I are walking arm in arm along the seafront, the collars of our raincoats turned up and our eyes half closed against the stinging salt and beach sand. I have a silk scarf wrapped tightly around my head. The brim of Pop's hat is flapping in the breeze.

The seagulls are circling around above us, enjoying the opportunity to use the wind to hover and glide effortlessly, while keeping their beady eyes upon us for any food we might drop.

The late winter afternoon sun, shining obliquely through the scudding grey clouds, casts fleeting shadows across the footpath.

'It's funny how life turns out,' I say, thinking aloud.

'Yes,' Pop responds. 'Who would have thought that only twenty years after the last war, here we are fighting the Germans again.'

'And that damn Churchill, of all people, is leading us,' I remark.

Unspoken is the ill-feeling held by many Australians towards the British prime minister - whom they hold personally responsible for the disastrous Gallipoli bloodbath in World War One.

'Yes, but I have to admit his speeches are powerful. I don't think I've ever heard a politician be so inspirational. A real orator!'

'Cometh the hour, cometh the man?'

Pop nods at the *cliché*.

We've left the golf links behind us and walked past the de Bernales' *hacienda* mansion, scowling down at us from its sandy heights.

I remind him that Helen de Bernales had invited Win down to her Selsey home on England's south coast for respite from the German bombing of London.

Predictably Pop grunts disapproval at Helen's surname.

'Come on, Pop. Win said Helen had been very friendly. She was very grateful. And so should we be.'

Pop grimaces. 'Yes, and she also said they live a life of luxury. Sorry, that sticks in my throat. So many people lost their entire savings investing in his company.'

'I suppose he won't be the last to persuade people to invest in the dream of finding lots more gold in Western Australia?'

Pop grunts his affirmative. 'Some people will never learn.'

We move on in silence, approaching the imaginatively named Ocean Beach Hotel, its outline blurred by the windswept air.

Pop wipes specks of beach sand from his eyes. 'Let's go and have a drink, Gladys.'

'It's a bit early?'

'We'll, it's Saturday. I think we can make an exception. And the weather seems to be getting worse.' He twists his face towards me. 'And we have a major decision to make, don't we?'

Pop's right. We've dodged the question over lunch. Which is why we've agreed to take one of his 'post-prandial perambulations' and delay the uncomfortable matter even further.

We take a table at a window overlooking the sea, its wave tops turning foamy white as they break near the beach.

'Cheers, my dear,' Pop says, lifting his schooner of beer.

I sip my gin and tonic.

He reaches into his jacket and pulls out an envelope with a British stamp. Pop hands it to me, even though I've already read the letter over lunch.

Frank Troy's words leap out at me again.

By chance I bumped into Win and her fiancé, Teddy, at the

Boomerang Club – don't laugh, that's its silly name for obvious reasons. He looked and sounded a decent chap. He's a lieutenant in the British Intelligence Corps.

I've already told you that our military attaché says he works for a hush-hush organisation set up on Churchill's orders. It is quite prestigious. The gossip is that it is staffed by very well-connected British.

As you know, he's French which should give you a clue as to what his work involves. He must be a very brave young man.

Pop smiles gently and takes my hand. 'He's an officer now, Gladys. Frank says there's nothing objectionable about him. In fact, he sounds a courageous young man. Yes, we both know that young people can be swept up in an intense, wartime romance and rush to the altar.' He swallows a mouthful of beer. 'But, you know, they've been engaged for some time now and he's already done the honourable thing and written to me, asking for my permission to marry our daughter.' He cups his chin and says in a measured tone, 'It doesn't sound like a quick fling, does it?'

He searches my eyes and pushes on, 'I don't think we can reasonably refuse any longer for them to marry, do you?'

I sigh. He's right.

'It won't be long either before Lloyd's in England too, flying with the RAF.'

That means both our children will be in England soon. Please God watch over them.

The bar is beginning to fill up with men. Some are scruffily dressed and already tipsy.

Respectable women are absent.

I check my watch, half past four. The boozy 'six o'clock swill' drinking session is starting and will soon be in full swing before the barmen shout, 'Last orders,' at six o'clock.

Pop says, 'Come on Gladys, we've made our decision. Time to walk home.'

37.

Win

'You want a *Methodist* minister to marry you *here*, you say?'

Shock, perhaps, would be too strong a word. More like strong surprise was writ large on the Church of England vicar, the Revd Eric Loveday's face.

'And you are Australian? Your fiancé is French?'

He takes a deep breath and asks me to sit down next to him on a pew near the front of the church, not far from the altar.

My face betrays my anxiety. This is my first step towards arranging our wedding since we got the - *hallelujah* - news that the Mater and Pop have finally given us their blessing.

'Win, may I ask why you particularly want to get married in St Martin-in-the-Fields?'

I bite my tongue. I can't possibly say because it's conveniently situated in the heart of London, making it easy for our travelling guests.

And I can also boast that I got married in a famous church, I self-confess shamefacedly.

I fib. 'I often pop in here when I'm walking to Australia House.'

Well, I have on occasions.

So far, so good.

'It's such a beautiful place. I say a little prayer for my fiancée, Teddy, and my brother, Lloyd. He's in the RAF.'

Well, that's all true, at least.

'Hmm…,' he mutters doubtfully.

He absent-mindedly picks up a hymn book in front of him and flicks through the pages while he ponders what to say.

'Win, in order to marry in St Martin-in-the-Fields I have to formally ask, Do you or your family have close pastoral connections with this church, or regularly attend services here?'

I shake my head despondently. 'I live in Kensington and Teddy's job takes him all around the country.'

He says wryly, 'I think then we can safely say the answer is no.'

There's a painful silence broken after a minute or so by the Revd. Loveday who asks gently, 'Tell me a bit about yourself and your fiancé.'

I start to summarise our story. First me: Australia; piano scholarship; Solomon; mobile canteen for firemen; and nursing.

Then Teddy: France and then the Intelligence Corps doing something *hush-hush* with a branch of the army called the Inter Services Research Bureau.

'Ah, yes, I've heard of them,' he says quietly, astonishing me.

'You'd be surprised by what we hear in this church, Win.'

Another silence.

'And why do you want a *Methodist* minister to marry you?'

'He was our church minister back home in Australia. He knows all my family. In fact, he became a friend of ours.

'He returned to England and now has a church in south London, in Lewisham. His name is Nicholas Richardson.'

'Would you say he is a good vicar?'

'Oh yes. I'll never forget Nicholas teaching me in Sunday school that Jesus had a sense of humour.'

'Did he, by Jove,' says the Revd Eric admiringly. I can see he's never considered before whether or not Jesus could laugh. *I imagine him storing the thought away for a future sermon.*

He pauses again and reminds me of Sol turning over in his mind whether to take me on as a student.

'Alright Win, I'm happy to let your *Nicholas* marry you and Teddy in my church.'

'Oh God, thank you so much,' I blurt out and then apologise immediately for my words.

'Don't worry. I'm not prissy about people saying God. By the way, you're from Perth, you say? Have you ever visited Melbourne? I have friends there.'

He's surprised when I say that I'd never been out of Western Australia before coming to England. 'It's a big, very big country,' I say, used to reminding people in London how enormous Australia is.

He returns to our marriage and warns me, 'There are still a couple of hurdles. Because neither of you have got a connection to this parish you need to get what's called an Archbishop's Licence. I'll tell you where to go to get the ball rolling.

'And also, I'll need to get my boss, the Bishop of London, to agree to a Methodist minister performing a marriage ceremony in this church. His name is Geoffrey Fisher. He'll be startled, like I was. But he's a good man, he's working incredibly hard to hold our church together during these terrible times.

'You see, this is one of London's most prestigious Anglican churches and has been for hundreds of years.' He chuckles. 'But we must have had Roman Catholic priests before, at least until Henry VIII.'

His eyes twinkle. 'While I'm pretty sure we've never had a Methodist, I'm confident I can persuade him. After all, St Martin was French. He certainly wouldn't approve if I turned your Teddy down. Do you have a date in mind?'

'Yes, Saturday the 31st of October. This year,' I add, just in case there's any misunderstanding.

'Okay. The 31st of October, 1942 it is. I'm sure that will be alright,' he says, smiling at my adamant certainty of the date, guessing correctly that Teddy's had very little flexibility with his leave dates.

The vicar stands up and shakes my hand. 'I'm looking forward to it. That is if I'm invited?'

'Of course you will be, Revd Loveday.'

'Thank you. I look forward to meeting Nicholas. And please call me Eric,' he says.

***

'An Archbishop's Special Licence for marriage, please.'

The elderly clerk, well past retirement age, far too old for call up, does not blink. I'm irrationally panicked by his indifference. Maybe the licence has been suspended until the end of the war? Will he refuse to give me an application form? My face shows no alarm but inside my stomach muscles tense and my mouth dries.

The clerk shuffles slowly off through the gloomy Church of England office at No.1 The Sanctuary, close to Westminster Abbey.

Slivers of light, shining through the sandbagged windows, reflect off specks of dust, like tiny fireflies, wafting gently behind the clerk's back. He creeps off to a filing cabinet and checks two drawers before I hear him muttering to himself that he's found what he was looking for.

He returns to the service counter and, thank God, his wrinkled face, not unkindly, smiles as his knobbly, trembling fingers place an application form down in front of me.

'Here you are Miss,' he sighs.

I quickly read the form and its notes for guidance. The clerk draws my attention to the need for accompanying letters of reference as to my and Teddy's good character.

He coughs politely. 'And don't forget the cheque for ten pounds.'

Bloody hell, Archbishops don't come cheap, do they?

'And where are you getting married, Miss?'

'St Martin-in-the-Fields.'

He's impressed. 'Very nice too Miss, if I may say so.'

38.

Teddy

I'm *so* proud to be marrying Win.

And marrying her in one of London's most famous churches. I grin at how Win had fooled me in her letter, describing it as merely a simple church, conveniently situated in the centre of London.

Twisting around, near the altar, I see my friends and fellow SOE officers, Jacques de Guélis and Peter Harrat, doing a good job as my ushers, greeting and finding seats for guests.

There has been a bit of, how shall I say, intense discussion between Win and me about the differences between French and English traditional weddings. A French groom doesn't have a best man and the bride does not have bridesmaids. We've compromised on ushers to receive arriving guests. And receptions are less formal.

I hear a hushed buzz of excitement. It's time. I sneak a quick glance over my shoulder. My bride enters the church with the West Australian Agent-General, Frank Troy, on her arm. The grey, cold autumn day in Trafalgar Square is banished as the imposing figure of Jacques firmly closes the church's heavy, oak front door. The interior of St Martin-in-the-Fields is bathed in a warm, soft light from its candelabras, suspended from the high, gloriously gilded ceiling. Most pews are full and the church is chilly enough to require overcoats for our guests.

The organist starts my Babe's choice of Mendelssohn's *Wedding March*. Win sees me peeking down the aisle and grins, yes, a cheeky, confident grin, which says, 'Toots, I'm really having fun, isn't this great?'

Does nothing make her nervous?

Even though Win's white wedding dress and veil shimmer in the gentle church lights, I can still clearly see her bright eyes fixed firmly on my face. She has an arm linked with Frank Troy's. It's obvious from her almost military bearing, head proudly held high, shoulders back, a confident, measured pace that she is leading an awed-looking Frank down the aisle. I giggle internally. How typical of my Babe that she's taken charge. Why, it's almost as if the roles have been reversed and it is she, Win, giving Frank away. How lucky am I to be marrying such a wonderful woman who will be my equal partner as we face all the uncertain times ahead?

My father's Scottish family is well-represented by his siblings, including my Aunt Laura, a witness years ago at my parents' wedding in Paris, and their children, my cousins. My Uncle George had been flattered but reluctant when invited to give Win away – he had met her for the first time only recently. No matter. Frank gladly accepted the role.

I feel deep sadness that none of my French relatives can attend. I can't even let them know of my marriage, let alone invite them. Win too has shed a tear that nobody from her side is present but her many friends from Lexham Gardens, nurses and doctors, WVS, the newspaper world and Solomon are all here. The bright purple shirt of the Bishop of London, standing next to Eric, the church's vicar, provides a flash of colour.

I look at the overhead balconies and realise the church is packed. We've told Eric that any of his regular churchgoers would be welcome to watch from upstairs.

As Win gets closer, her veil picks up the rainbow colours from the stained-glass windows, despite their criss-cross sticky tape to withstand bomb blasts.

My face is strained but my Babe, her veil now brushed back, is, of course, grinning as we both stand in front of her old Methodist friend from Perth, the Revd. Nicholas Richardson.

Silence falls in the church as the congregation hangs on Eric's words. 'We come today to bless the joining of Edouard Albert Bisset and Winfred Wordsworth Marshall in marriage.'

Nicholas pauses. 'Who will give the bride away?'

'I will,' says Frank, his voice tremulous, looking sideways at Win.

Our rings are blessed before we exchange them. We then commit to one another with responses of, 'I do'.

Nicholas lights the unity candle. I had been puzzled when I first heard about this practice. He tells me this is what Methodists do to, 'represent the love shared between the two individuals.'

A wedding prayer, the Lord's Prayer, a blessing for the new couple, and then our first kiss as a married couple. We visit the registry where Eric checks the Archbishop's Licence and we sign the register. Legally and in the eyes of God we are now man and wife - it's all been a blur.

My SOE pals form a guard of honour and our guests shower us in pink confetti as we exit onto the terrace in front of the church, causing a traffic jam as drivers slow down to a crawl and press their horns in appreciation of fellow Londoners enjoying themselves in public, refusing to be depressed in the war-torn capital.

And then down the steps into a waiting taxi. The driver knows our destination. He's been paid in advance. It's only a five-minute drive and, at most, a ten-minute walk from Trafalgar Square to the Charing Cross hotel. I have obtained a good price for our reception, including a room for Win to change into her 'going-away' outfit – the hotel is bomb-damaged and keen to attract customers back.

39.

Win

I strip down to my bra, knickers and stockings. My bridal dress is folded neatly on the chair next to a dressing table.

Teddy creeps up behind me and softly puts his arms around me, kisses me on the side of my neck and nuzzles my hair. A hand caresses me down to my suspenders and gently flicks a buckle.

Why do men find suspenders so sexy?

'Mrs Bisset,' he whispers in my ear, nibbling its lobe.

I grab his hand before I get carried away by his passion.

'For God's sake, Toots, we can't. We've got all our guests waiting.' I turn around and give him a quick, affectionate kiss. 'You'll just have to wait, you silly man.'

I finish changing into my going-away outfit and freshen up in front of the mirror.

We re-enter the reception room to cheers and applause. There is a happy buzz of spoken French and a variety of English accents from Scottish to Australian.

Thank God, I can see people are enjoying themselves. Every hostess planning a party is nervous that the occasion might fall flat. Clever of Teddy to suggest the Charing Cross Hotel for our wedding reception, a short enjoyable stroll from the church for all our guests.

Sandwiches and *canapés* are being consumed at a fast rate by the hungry crowd and washed down with a plentiful supply of champagne.

There are several amusing speeches, many in French by his SOE colleagues, all complimentary about Teddy and me.

Major Whetmore gets a good laugh when he tells everyone about Teddy nearly missing the boat in France, so determined was he to retrieve the bottle of Jicky perfume for *his girl* - except, of course, I didn't know I was his girl then. And then wading out to the boat in shoulder-high water with the perfume bottle strapped down firmly under his cap.

Vera Atkins (Teddy says she's very important in the Firm) tells me Teddy is highly regarded and destined for important roles. I hope so because I know he's restless and keen to see active service in France.

Oh, if only my family could be here. I know Teddy feels the same about his French relatives.

I see my Methodist minister, Nicholas, chats amiably to Eric, the St Martin-in-the-Fields vicar and Geoffrey Fisher, the Bishop of London. I'm glad I've done my bit for inter-communal relations. In fact, the bishop takes me aside and offers to conduct the christening service for our first child, if Nicholas is unavailable.

I leave the priests and their theological discussion. I overhear the bishop saying to Nicholas what a great shame it was that Wesley's desire for Methodists to remain in the Church of England had resulted in unnecessary schism.

Old Sol tells everyone I have a great career as a concert pianist once I return to complete my studies with him.

After an hour I realise that I've had enough to drink and start to refuse top-ups. I'm relieved to spy Helen and Claude de Bernales' smart chauffeur, Simon, searching for me. Helen and Claude are not coming. Claude does not attend public functions anymore, particularly those where Australians might be present.

'The terrible newspaper publicity about Claude's business activities has made recluses out of us,' Helen tells me. 'Such lies,' she sniffs on the telephone.

But, as a wedding present, she insists that Simon will drive us to our honeymoon destination for which she will also pay.

Teddy is embarrassed by Helen's generosity, but I remind him that his Uncle George is paying for the drinks and canapes.

***

'Where are we going, Babe?' Teddy asks.

'You'll just have to wait and see,' I say, squeezing his knee.

Simon senses we are keen to get moving and speeds along, the big, powerful Buick smoothly taking corners and humming along the straight roads through the faded pastel greens and browns of England's autumnal countryside, russet leaves swirling behind us.

I don't let on to Teddy that I've never been to The Spread Eagle in Midhurst in the county of Sussex, south of London. Helen says that it's a lovely pub, more of a hotel, really.

'It's so historic and quite luxurious, darling,' she tells me. 'Just right for a couple of days to start your marriage in style. You'll love it.'

I hope she's right. I needn't have fretted. The pub's Queen's Suite confirms Helen's opinion.

'Thank you so much Mrs de Bernales,' shouts Teddy as he falls backwards, arms outstretched onto a huge four-poster bed.

'This place is so historic, Babe. The porter told me that Queen Elizabeth stayed in this very room.'

'She was known as the *Virgin* Queen,' I giggle, slurping my second glass of champagne which Helen has arranged to welcome us upon arrival.

'Queen by itself will do me,' Teddy replies, smirking. 'There's another extraordinary thing the receptionist told me,' he adds.

'What's that?'

'Apparently, in July, 1939 that ghastly, fat Nazi, Luftwaffe chief Goering, had dinner here with the German ambassador, von Ribbentrop, after they'd been to the Goodwood horse races.'

'You're joking, Teddy.'

'No, I'm not,' he retorts. 'He even showed me Ribbentrop's signature in the guest register.'

'What on earth was he doing here?'

'Meeting English Nazi sympathisers, I suppose.'

'You mean like Moseley?'

He shrugs his shoulders. 'Who knows?'

'Oh God, I hope he didn't sleep in this room,' I say, glancing around apprehensively.

40.

Teddy

Hélène and I have the downstairs of Arisaig House, yet another SOE-requisitioned country pile, to ourselves. This one is located miles away from anywhere in the north-west Scottish Highlands, close to the bracing shores of *Loch Nan Uanh*. A good place to teach people how to kill and survive in wild countryside.

We are sitting on a wide, well-worn sofa wrapped under a thick tartan rug, sipping whisky and absorbing the fading heat from charred logs in the baronial-sized fireplace.

Alcohol seems to have little effect on Hélène; she's already drunk her other team members, all of them men, almost under the table. Whereas I've been careful not to drink too much.

I feel guilty about having to mislead my team, kidding them it was an evening off to celebrate the end of five arduous weeks training in the Scottish Highlands.

In fact, the SOE instructors and I, their conducting officer, want to observe how our trainees take their drink and any tendency to shoot alcohol-fuelled mouths off. A couple did and might have to be weeded out. Most had enough common sense to realise that getting drunk in front of their instructors was not a good idea.

Hélène says in French (English is frowned upon except when asking the specialist instructors questions), 'What's next Teddy?'

'Parachute training.'

'Will you be coming with us?'

'Yes. I shall be your conducting officer all the way to, er, the end of finishing school.'

'Ah,' she smiles. 'You mean one of the houses on the Beaulieu estate, near Southampton, don't you?'

Hélène knows I won't respond, so ploughs on, 'I was down there for my preliminary training - you know, when you lot weed out the obviously unsuitable people. The house was called Vineyards. We called it the Madhouse. And there was definitely no wine.'

She pauses, trying to recall. And then, having dipped her finger lazily into her glass, she gently rubs some whisky onto her lips, as if it is some lip salve. She grins as she sees I'm watching her.

'But there was English bitter beer. Rather a lot of it, as I recall.' Her eyes crease in amusement. 'I had a good but unusual conducting officer. Very different to you.'

'Oh yes,' I say disinterestedly.

'Yes, his name was Denis Rake.'

My face gives me away.

'Ah, I can see you know Denis.' She grins. 'I got to know him quite well. He was having a furious row with someone when I first met him. I took his side and we became good friends.'

Hélène snuggles up closer.

'You know this is quite cosy, Teddy,' she says flirtatiously.

Careful Teddy. This woman is seriously attractive. So much so that some of us think her looks might be too dangerous. Won't German soldiers be drawn towards her?

She goes on, 'God knows how Denis managed to survive in France for so long with him being so obviously er,' she pauses, searching for the appropriate word.

'Queer,' I supply curtly.

'Yes,' she says slowly, registering my expression. 'He only managed to escape the Gestapo and get out because of an American called Virginia Hall. He said that she had a wooden

232

leg. And, you know what?' There's a big grin on her face, 'He said she called it Cuthbert.'

She laughs hilariously, drags on her cigarette and swirls her long hair, flashing red and gold from the glowing embers.

Hélène shakes her head. 'Tsk, tsk, Denis. Some of the tales he told.' She sees my stony face. 'Oh my God! He was telling the truth. Oh, come on, that can't be true?'

I pretend my pipe needs attention so I can look away. Yes, I'd heard plenty of gossip among us staffers in the local pub near our Baker Street HQ about an incredibly brave and resourceful American woman who was one of SOE's best agents. She did indeed have a wooden leg and, despite that, had unbelievably escaped across the snowy Pyrenees mountains to Spain.

Because of treachery and London's mistakes, she was for a while almost our sole active agent in France. Some say it was only because of her that SOE survived being culled by rivals, particularly the Secret Intelligence Service or MI6, who did not hide their opinion of us that we were a bunch of amateurs. Perhaps they had a point.

I'm not surprised at the flamboyant Denis Rake breaking the rules and telling tales about an agent. In my opinion, if we hadn't desperately needed *pianists* - wireless operators – and linguists, we would have kicked him out long ago. Still… his bravery was doubtless. Hélène looks at me quizzically. 'You really are more French than English, aren't you? I can tell by your accent - from Paris?'

I nod non-committedly.

'Do you know where I come from?'

'I think so.'

'Where?'

'Australia.'

'Ah, that's not fair. You've read my file.'

'Yes, but there's not much in it. I know your maiden name and your real first name, Nancy Wake, but that's just about all I know about you.'

I lie.

I don't add that I know she had stormed out of the SOE after having had a furious row with an examiner halfway through her previous training course. Buckmaster was keen to keep her because she'd already proved herself in France by helping numerous British escapees get over the border into Spain. The Gestapo nicknamed her the White Mouse because of her ability to evade capture. But eventually she too was forced to get out into Spain over the Pyrenees. Buckmaster had persuaded her to stay in the SOE and booked her into the next available training group - all men - with me as her conducting officer.

'How did you guess I was Australian then?'

'Your French is almost perfect but every now and then there's a hint in your pronunciation which is exactly the same as my Australian wife's.'

'Oh, Australian? Where from?'

'She's from Perth.'

'Perth?'

'Yes.'

'Oh,' she says. 'I hear it's a nice place. Nearly as beautiful as Sydney. I've never visited.' She takes another sip. 'Western Australia's a long way away from the rest of Australia, Teddy. Some of them don't like the Eastern States. In fact, not so long ago they had a referendum to secede. Most voted to leave.'

That's interesting. Something else I didn't know about Win's country.

We both sip our whisky. Our eyes meet over the rims of our glasses and look hastily away, surprised by the shock of a sudden *frisson* of strong mutual attraction.

Her eyes are extraordinary. One moment they seem blue, the next hazel.

Avoiding eye contact, we sit silently, both feeling uneasy - part guilt, part embarrassment.

Unspoken, but nonetheless shared between us, is the thought that perhaps our lives might have turned out differently had she and I met before we'd married other people.

Keen for us to return to safe ground, I ask, 'Tell me, what did you find was the best and worst part of the training here in the Highlands?'

My words relax us both.

'That's easy, Teddy.' She looks at the fire. 'The best part was learning how to kill Germans.'

Yes, she'd proved very good at killing with the knife and pistol. And even unarmed combat. And learning how to stalk deer. Our ghillie says if someone can get close to a stag, they will surely be able to creep up close to a German sentry.

'Why do you hate them so much? I mean you're not even French…'

Hélène draws her knees up to her chin, her boots peeping out from under the rug. Softly, she murmurs, 'I love France.' Then fiercely she adds, 'I love Paris and my home in Marseilles. The thought of Hitler in Paris makes me sick.'

She stares at me. 'Look, I first saw what the Nazis were doing in Vienna when I was a journalist. And then, later on, I drove an ambulance north of Paris after they'd invaded. I saw them deliberately dive-bombing crowds of refugees, innocent men, women and children. Their bodies were strewn all over the place. Blood and guts everywhere. I'll never forgive them for that.' She shakes her head in disgust. Throwing her cigarette butt into the fire she asks, 'And you?'

'I'm French,' I say simply, shrugging my shoulders. 'But, like you, I was up in the north. I saw plenty of terrible things on the roads.'

We sip our whiskies, careful to look only at the fire.

'And the worst part?' I remind her of the second part of my

question.

'Oh yes. Those bloody, damn ladders going on and on up that vertical, wet cliff face. How many feet was it? Fifty or sixty feet? My boots were slipping all over the rungs. Christ it was dangerous.

'Believe it or not, it was actually worse than escaping over the Pyrenees.' She drains her glass and grimaces. 'I've had enough of whisky and bitter beer. I can understand how Bonnie Prince Charlie must have felt holed up in that damn cave over there,' she gestures with her glass out of the window towards the loch. 'Like him, I can't wait to get back to France for some decent cognac and champagne.'

Hélène stands up and smiles. 'And kill some Germans, of course.' She yawns. '*Dormez bien*, Teddy.'

I watch her sashay away, her loose-fitting military uniform failing to hide her Jane Russell, Hollywood curves, and hear her boots treading softly on the wooden stairs heading upwards to her bedroom.

Oh, how I envy her. She'll be parachuting into France soon.

Apart from the few months' involvement in Operation Guillotine, to supply guns and ammunition to a French trawler, followed by the sickeningly, disastrous Dieppe raid, I've seen no active service since 1940.

But it's now 1943 and the war is at a tipping point.

I throw the rug off irritably, walk over to the fire and tap my pipe angrily on the grate.

I know Buckmaster and his *éminence grise*, Vera Atkins, value me as a popular and competent SOE staff officer and trainer. They don't want me to leave. But I've had enough of training others.

I must, *simply must,* get across to France again before it's all over.

41.

The Mater

'She's pregnant, John.'

'Oh, that's great news, Gladys,' my sweet husband replies, putting his latest book down on the sofa in our sitting room. His face beams in delight.

'We must have a drink to celebrate.'

I place the blue, flimsy paper of Win's latest aerogramme down on my lap.

I do not smile.

I try to imagine what it must be like for my daughter living alone on rations in her small, cold London flat, without a husband who seems to be away for most of the time, working all over the country. I know too that money is in short supply. She's just about coping solely on Teddy's officer pay now that she's resigned from her nurse's job. How will she manage with a baby as well?

Our ceiling fan spins slowly, keeping the hot evening air, but not my mood, tolerable.

I light a cigarette and take the gin and tonic offered by John, ice clinking against the glass with beads of moisture already forming on its outside.

'I wonder whether it's a boy or a girl,' John says, pouring himself a glass from a cold bottle of Swan lager.

He taps my glass. 'Cheers. Here's to Win and Teddy. I'm sure they'll make excellent parents. And we'll be good grandparents, of course,' he adds. 'What's the matter, Gladys?' he says, anxiously, noticing my worried face as he swallows his drink.

He tries to reassure me. 'I'm sure she'll be fine. The Blitz is over and London life is much safer now.

'Come on old girl, she's like you. She'll manage.'

I watch my cigarette smoke being wafted away by the ceiling fan, as my mind furiously focuses on how I can help Win. To calm my nerves, I take a swig of my drink.

John chuckles at my startled face. 'I made you a stiff one. I thought you'd need it.'

I ignore his feeble attempt at humour. 'I must go to her, John.'

The tone of my voice alarms him. 'Now hold on, Gladys. We went all through this before when you wanted to go to England to fetch her home after she met Teddy.'

I clench my glass.

Any harder, it would crack.

My mind is racing.

I check my watch. 'You said Jack was popping around for a drink at about six?'

Only about a quarter of an hour or so.

'Yes,' he nods at my innocent question. But then alarm spreads across his face. 'But come on, Gladys. You can't pester him for a favour like that.'

Oh yes, I can. And I damn well will!

The first sign that Jack is on his way is two tough-looking, young men walking around in front of our house, looking suspiciously up and down our quiet suburban street.

'I see Jack's bodyguards have arrived,' I say, knowing that our old friend won't be too long behind them.

Sure enough, the tall, athletic figure of Australia's prime minister, John Curtin - Jack to us - lopes through our front garden gate. Although his protectors disapprove, he always walks to our house – it's a ten-minute stroll. Because of the war, we see less of him. But he still insists on coming home for a bit of R&R, as he calls it, and to fulfil his duties as a member of parliament for the nearby port of Fremantle.

We embrace and I give him a warm peck on his cheek.

I feel a pang of guilt. He doesn't know the favour I'm going to corner him into granting.

Jack slips his jacket off and settles back into an armchair next to mine in our sitting room.

John hands him a cool glass of lemonade - a far cry from earlier days when he and other young Labor Party members would go on a bender and Jack would yell, slurring his words, how Marxism would cure all the ills of capitalism.

'How are Elsie and the children?' I ask.

'Grand, Gladys. Just grand,' he replies. 'She misses the singing and our Methodist church.' He sighs. 'It's not easy splitting our lives between Perth and Canberra.'

Our small talk finishes and the conversation drifts onto our prime minister's work.

'The war's not going very well. I have a cable fight with that bloody Churchill – excuse my language Gladys - almost every day. Britain never thought Japan would fight and made no plans to prepare for that.' He says vehemently, in a voice that John and I can imagine he uses in a cabinet meeting, 'We need our boys back here to defend Australia.'

Embarrassed by his outburst, Jack takes his glasses off and needlessly gives them a wipe on a shirt sleeve.

"How's Win getting on in London?' he asks smiling, expecting a return to pleasant small talk between good family friends.

Now's my chance. I remind him that our daughter married a Frenchman who's involved in secret operations in France.

'Oh yes, Frank Troy told me what a grand *fella* Teddy was and how proud he was to be asked to give Win away. He said it was a magnificent wedding. And our Nicholas Richardson conducted the service. Fancy that!' He shakes his head regret-fully. 'What a shame! Elsie and I would have loved to have been there.'

'We've just heard Win's expecting,' I say proudly, as Jack sips his drink.

His handsome face beams at John and me. 'Congratula-tions.' He chuckles. 'Grandparents, hey. Who would have thought it? It seems like yesterday when we were *tyro* reporters, doesn't it John?'

My dear John smiles warily. He knows that I'm spinning an ensnaring web.

I rest my hand on Jack's arm. 'The thing is Win's completely on her own. Teddy's work means he's away almost all the time. The thought of her by herself in a freezing London flat, ex-pecting a baby, with barely enough money for food and heating doesn't bear thinking about.' I ever so gently squeeze his arm. 'I'm her mother. I must go to her.'

Jack nods. 'Of course you must Gladys.'

He reflects, half to himself, 'But how are you going to get there? It's almost impossible. There are few flights and seats are restricted to mainly government people…'

The penny drops.

His voice tails off as he sees my determined eyes, staring straight at him. He grins ruefully at John who refuses to meet him in the eye.

Our prime minister shakes his head in mock admiration. 'Alright Gladys, I'll see what I can do. No promises, mind you!'

Poor Jack. He probably wished he had stayed in Canberra, rather than flying across the country for a quick holiday back home, only to be ambushed by Gladys Marshall.

***

A couple of weeks later, an official in Canberra tells me that I am booked on a Pan Am Clipper flying boat from Sydney to San Francisco. He also says that I am Mrs Marshall, a wool-merchant. His long-distance, tinny voice says dryly, 'I didn't know there were any major female wool-merchants in Australia. The prime minister suggests you keep conversation with your fellow passengers to a minimum, Mrs Marshall.'

I stick out like a sore thumb among the Australian government officials, diplomats and military officers - all of them men. I follow Jack's advice and keep myself to myself and hardly utter a word to anyone. To judge from the inquisitive looks cast in my direction they must think I'm a spy.

I fidget incessantly during the island stops the Clipper makes across the Pacific. Their idyllic beauty is wasted on me. I spend no time taking in the sights of America's west coast and fly as speedily as possible to New York. And then across the Atlantic to arrive at London's Croydon airport.

It has taken me less than four days. Kingsford Smith would have been proud of me.

***

The cab driver places my suitcase outside 18 Melbury Road near Holland Park, London. I'm relieved to see the road looks promising. A tree-lined avenue with elegant red brick buildings, their windows framed by sophisticated cream stonework.

It's a cold, autumn London morning, my misty breath floats in the air as I step gingerly out from the cab's warm passenger compartment down onto the pavement, greasy from dew.

I pay the fare and give a modest tip, clearly not enough because the cabbie's hand remains outstretched. I glare at him and his cheeky harassment vanishes.

In his best cockney, he grunts over his shoulder as he stomps back to his cab, 'Welcome to London, you old bag.'

'Rude, ungrateful man,' I mutter. The fare from the airport to the centre of London was already high. My tip was enough, surely?

I ring the bell.

After a couple of minutes my daughter opens the front door, still in her dressing gown.

'Hello Win,' I say matter-of-factly.

'Mater,' she shrieks.

I glance at her stomach. I guess she's already about three months gone. I hold my arms out and hug her, careful not to press too hard. Ignoring my reticence, Win grabs me tightly and plants several kisses on my cheeks.

When did she become so, er, demonstrative?

'How, when did you get here?' she splutters.

'I shall explain all in good time.' 'But let's get inside first, shall we? It's cold out here,' I recommend, shivering in an exaggerated manner.

I lift my suitcase and walk into the entrance hall - it's not much warmer than outside.

My favourable first impressions of Win's neighbourhood prove incorrect. Instead, my worst fears are realised. Win's flat is cramped, pokey and cold.

'I'll put the kettle on for a cup of tea,' she says, shuffling sideways into a tiny kitchen. I stand at the door and disapprovingly notice there is washing-up from last night's meal.

Win carefully measures a couple of small spoons of tea into a teapot, which she has warmed by sloshing around boiling water inside.

'We're rationed to only four ounces of tea a week,' she explains, tapping the spoon on top of the pot to get its last leaves.

We sit down together on a worn settee. She hands me a cup of brown liquid bearing a passing resemblance to tea. At least it's hot enough to warm my hands.

'Never mind how I got here,' I say firmly, raising a hand upwards to forestall her questions. 'What matters is that I came as quickly as I could to help you have your baby.'

'Oh, Mater, I'm so glad you're here.' Her voice strains with relief. 'I was beginning to feel a bit scared by myself with Teddy so often away.' She fiddles with her dressing gown. 'I find it difficult to sleep sometimes. That's why I overslept.'

Her voice cracks - she's on the point of sobbing.

I take her hand. 'Don't worry Win. I'm here now. Everything will be alright.'

She nods, gathering her composure.

'When's the due date, Win?'

'Late November.'

A telephone suddenly rings. Win jumps up and darts into the hallway to answer the call. Her muffled voice finishes the conversation by saying, 'that would be marvellous, darling.'

'That was Teddy,' she tells me beaming, as if I hadn't guessed. 'He's got to spend a couple of days in the Baker Street HQ. That usually means late nights but he's popping in for a spot of lunch.'

She shakes her head in disbelief. 'Like me, he can't believe you're here. He can hardly wait to meet you.'

'Did you have no inkling that he was coming?'

'No, it's often like that Mater. Sometimes Teddy says he is coming home for a week but then after a couple of days he gets a call, telling him he's needed somewhere else urgently.'

I pause and investigate the kitchen. 'I see, well, let's get the place tidied up a bit before he comes, shall we dear? And perhaps you should get washed and dressed too.'

'Oh God, in all the excitement I'd forgotten, Mater,' Win giggles girlishly. I have to remind myself that my daughter, although married and within months of becoming a mother, is still in her twenties.

I am feeling surprisingly nervous at the prospect of meeting Teddy for the first time. Of course, Win has sent Pop and me photographs and descriptions of Teddy's French upbringing and Scottish relatives in her gushing letters full of a new wife's pride in her husband. In one letter, she had said that all the girls had been 'swooning over him'. Nonetheless Teddy is still largely an unknown quantity. And I still harbour some resentment that Win has bypassed me in choosing her husband before I had a chance to inspect and approve him.

When Teddy arrives, I hear Win in the hallway whispering while she helps him take off his army greatcoat. Leading him by the hand she brings her husband into the little front room. Win is apprehensive, avoiding my eyes, desperate for me to like him.

I can see Teddy is certainly good looking but not uncommonly so. Yet, as he walks into the room and smiles at me, I detect something else, rather pleasing. His face and eyes express a strong masculine confidence and sincerity. Almost as if he's signalling, *This is me, I've got nothing to hide.* He walks gracefully, unlike the rude, clod-hopping cab driver who'd driven me here.

As he gets closer, I notice also that he has a lovely peach-like complexion. As a man, he would be unaware of his skin tone but it's something a woman would notice.

My son-in-law bows before me and gently takes my hand to his lips. He kisses it softly, his lips barely touching my skin. 'Mrs Marshall. It is a great honour.'

Well, that's the first time a man has kissed my hand. I confess to a matronly thrill.

I must admit too, even a middle-aged woman like me, who is well past swooning for a man, can completely understand Win's remark that young women find Teddy very attractive.

Perhaps my daughter didn't need me after all to vet her choice?

Over lunch I observe Win and Teddy. They are obviously soulmates and very much in love. Unabashed, they hold hands across the table as they catch up on gossip. It seems Win has met several of Teddy's work colleagues and his relatives. Teddy has the good manners to ask me about my journey, but I fend off his questions. As a man of secrets, he probably guesses I've pulled some sensitive strings to get here so quickly by plane.

After we've finished our lunch of bread and soup, they both light up. Teddy smokes a pipe. I approve – it seems manly.

I can tell they both smoke too much, but nearly everybody does these days. It must be the war.

I ask Win about Lloyd who arrived not long ago in April - which means both my children are now in England. He's been so busy training he hasn't had a chance to visit and meet Teddy yet. She tells me Lloyd phones frequently - she's half-expecting a call from him today.

In fact it's not long before Lloyd telephones. Win hands me the receiver with a big smile on her face. 'He can't believe you're here.'

Just like I did with Win, I brush off all Lloyd's questions about how I managed to get here. I know he's savvy enough to work it out eventually.

I tread carefully when I ask about his training. We all share his huge disappointment that his boyhood typhoid means he is ineligible for pilot training. To my surprise he sounds very cheerful.

'Mater,' he whispers quietly, to prevent him being over-heard - I can hardly hear him. 'I'm a Pathfinder, more important than the pilot.'

I know he trained to be a navigator but to my ears Path-finder sounds more like a character in a silly boy's game of cowboys and Indians.

'Where are you, Lloyd?'

'Somewhere in England,' he replies, annoyingly.

He says that he is due about a week's leave soon and will pop down to London for a couple of days and meet Teddy for the first time. I warn him it's a tiny flat and he can't have the sofa - that's my bed. But one of Teddy's French colleagues, Philippe someone or the other, has a tiny rabbit hole upstairs which is sometimes free.

'Don't worry, Mater, I'll sleep on some cushions on the floor if I have to. I'm used to roughing it.'

'Where else are you going on your leave?'

'Probably Dorothy's home.'

'Who?'

He sighs. 'I'll tell you more about Dorothy when I see you, Mater.'

Dear God! First Win chooses someone before I meet him and now Lloyd is getting involved with an English girl about whom I know nothing. All my carefully-laid plans for my children's futures have been rendered superfluous.

Teddy comes and goes. Like Lloyd, he refuses to inform us of his location. Sometimes he says he is at a 'finishing school.'

'Ridiculous,' I say. 'It sounds like you're teaching rich girls how to behave in society.'

He just grins and ignores my comment..

Other times, he lets slip that he has to go to Scotland to give a lecture. At least he returns from there with beef steak and fresh salmon mysteriously stashed in his kitbag.

He jokes that the salmon has been poached by throwing dynamite into a loch.

I like Teddy. And I can tell he likes me. There appears to be no ill-feeling caused by Pop and my original refusal to their marriage. He tells me repeatedly how grateful he is that I've arrived to help look after his wife.

Although less than previously, the number of Luftwaffe bombs continues to increase. Londoners shrug their shoulders and tell newcomers like me sanguinely that it's not as bad as the Blitz. Occasionally bombs fall near us.

Meanwhile Win gets bigger and bigger. It won't be long now before I'm a grandmother.

Christmas 1943 is no longer on the far horizon. It's only weeks away.

41.

Win

'Two fingers dilation,' says the trainee nurse enthusiastically, keen to impress her instructing midwife. Her head pops up from under a white sheet, which looks like a big tent supported by the poles of my raised knees, a couple of fingers held up to confirm her measurement.

The midwife, holding my hand, nods. 'So far plain sailing, Mrs Bisset. I can't see any cause for concern. It shouldn't be too long dear, maybe an hour or so. Nurse will call me when I'm needed. She'll time your contractions.'

The midwife says reassuringly, 'I'm only just down the corridor. I've got two other young women in labour.'

The midwife looks across my huge bulging stomach at the Mater, who's holding my hand on the other side of my bed in the delivery room. 'Bit like our London buses, Mrs Marshall. You wait for hours then three come along at once.'

The conversation is interrupted by the noise of bomb explosions. That's four days in a row the Luftwaffe has increased their number of raids. Some people are beginning to call it the baby Blitz.

Time passes slowly. I hear every single tick-tock of the seconds on the wall clock.

Even though the delivery room is cold, sweat is dribbling off my forehead down my cheeks. The Mater wipes my forehead with a damp cloth and encourages me to be brave.

Although it seems like several hours to me, I can tell from glancing at the clock that it's really only about an hour before the Nurse says, looking down at the watch pinned to her chest, 'That's three minutes between contractions. I shall get the midwife.'

'No, I *shall* get the midwife,' the Mater says determinedly, marching off down the corridor.

'Bear down Miss Bisset,' the midwife commands after she hurriedly returns, with a stern-faced Mater escorting her, and takes a brief look in the tent.

The pain of the contractions is now intense and becoming almost continuous but the midwife's prediction is correct; my baby eventually slides out as smoothly as a bar of soap. I can't see anything but, by God, it really hurt, if only for an hour.

The midwife announces cheerfully that I have a baby daughter and that she is in good health, slaps her bottom, smiles at my baby's cry, cuts the cord and disappears quickly to attend to the other expecting mothers.

Or was it to get away from the Mater?

My new-born daughter, wrapped in muslin cloth and a blanket, is placed by the nurse in my arms.

'Is she alright?' I ask the nurse, seeking reassurance, as I anxiously inspect the pinky-blue face of my baby.

'Yes, she's perfect,' she assures me.

The Mater bends over and kisses me on my forehead. 'Well done, Win. Everything's going to be alright now.'

***

Our tiny baby lies on her back, grips my little finger and smiles. Mater tickles her tummy and makes baby goo-goo noises. She tells me that she and her mother did the same to me.

She looks up at me and says seriously, 'It's funny how life goes on Win. It sounds trite but it's something that a grand-mother feels much more strongly than a parent of a new-born child. You'll probably be exhausted over the coming months and won't have time to think about anything else except your child.'

She squeezes my hand. 'But for me it's like a relay runner handing over the baton to the next member of the team. It's your turn now to bring up a child.' She stops for a second. 'And it's scary how quickly the race is run. Twenty-six years ago, *you* arrived and the midwife put you into *my* arms. It now feels like the blink of an eye.'

She adds, purposefully, 'One day you'll experience the same feeling as me. Satisfaction and pride that I've done my duty in raising a girl, who is now a woman, capable of being a good mother.'

Our baby has a name. Teddy and I agree on Laura Ann Wordsworth Bisset. Laura is Teddy's aunt who has been very kind and helpful to me. Wordsworth, because we are his descendants and Ann, just because we like the name.

I choose my moment carefully. Feeding Laura, while the Mater sips a cup of tea, I steer our conversation towards the christening.

'I've chosen St Mary Abbots,' I say casually. 'It's our local church, only about a quarter of an hour's walk from here. And I've got the Bishop of London to christen Laura. He made the offer at our wedding.'

'Hmm… Church of England?' sniffs the Mater.

I know what she's thinking - why didn't I ask the Reverend Nicholas Richardson in his south London Methodist church? After all, he married Teddy and me.

I tell her truthfully that it's just too far from our flat. Also, I cannot tell a lie, I'm snobbishly proud that a bishop will be christening my daughter.

But a week before the christening our area is rocked by bomb explosions and the sky is lit up by fires near the church. Sure enough, a very distressed vicar calls around to say Jerry has dropped firebombs on his church. He's convinced the very tall steeple was the target. Most of the interior woodwork has been badly burnt but, by some miracle, the stone building is intact and safe.

'Those Victorians certainly built things to last,' he says. He beams and clasps his hands as if offering a prayer. 'Thank God, the bishop is delighted that we can clear the mess inside in time for your christening to go ahead,' he adds, sounding as if pleasing the bishop has more priority than Laura's christening.

A few days later our little procession of Laura in Teddy's arms, the Mater, Lloyd and I, leave our flat and walk down Kensington High Street towards the church where a large congregation of our friends await us.

With the still smouldering timber around us, we gather near the font where the bishop takes Laura into his arms, I feel that somehow it is God's will that a new innocent life should be launched in a church so nearly destroyed but surviving against the odds.

At the pub after Laura's christening service, Lloyd's Pathfinder badge attracts attention. I notice people treat him as a sort of hero. Teddy tells me that Lloyd's job is difficult and dangerous. I can tell from his voice that he's worried about Lloyd's chances of survival. Apparently, my brother's plane flies first and, quite literally, lights the path for the bombers to make sure their bombs are on target. Unsurprisingly Pathfinders are prime targets for the Germans.

Moving around with the Mater, offering trays of savoury eats we catch a snippet of a conversation between Teddy and Lloyd who are talking about Lloyd's RAF base. Teddy says something like, 'Ah yes, Graveley, near Huntingdon. We used it for a while…'

Ah, I think to myself, Lloyd's, 'somewhere in England' is Graveley. The Mater's ears prick up too.

By chance, chatting to the bishop, the Mater and I learn he is a graduate in theology from Cambridge. Oh yes, he says that he knows Graveley well, not far from his college. There are some nice country walks there. Cheerful little pub called the Three Horseshoes.

The bishop features two months later in a poignant letter which the Mater receives a few months later from Pop, enclosing a cutting about Laura's christening from Perth's *Daily News*.

I read it aloud to Teddy:

The blackened, roofless wreck of what had been, until a week before, the oldest church in Kensington, was the scene for the recent christening of the baby of a former well-known Perth girl and her British Army husband.

The bishop walked through the ashes - some embers were still burning - to what was left of the font of St Mary Abbots, built in the 12th century, to conduct the ceremony.

The Germans had dropped fire bombs on it, leaving only the walls enclosing the charred remnants of the woodwork.

'This child should be blessed. It is named surely in the sight of God in every sense,' said the bishop.

Baby is Laura Ann Wordsworth Bisset, daughter of Captain and Mrs EG Bisset. Mrs Bisset was formerly Win Marshall of Cottesloe.

Scene was described in an airgraph letter from a former West Australian girl now in London, received in Perth during the weekend.

'It was a strange, almost eerie, sight to see the bishop in full canonicals, baptising in the sunlight under a bright blue sky a little child of Australian extraction,' she wrote.

'Its eyes were as blue as the sky which she must have been looking at in wonder. Its smile was the only one there. All other faces looked gravely at the ruin all around them.'

The baby wore a long, priceless lace christening robe which had been in the father's family for so many generations that any count had long been lost of the number of times it had been used.

In addition to the young mother and father, the mother's brother, also in uniform, and her mother and relatives of the father were present.

On the way to the church the party passed the ruins of a dance hall where four hundred people had recently lost their lives thanks to a German bomb. A freshly-made wreath had been placed in the midst of the ruins.

I pocket the cutting amongst my things and forget about it. Events overtake me so I never remember to find out the identity of the girl who was quoted in the article.

42.

Teddy

'Lunch, dear boy?' Jacques de Guelis' voice booms down the phone, his avuncular drawl aping his upper-class English colleagues who dominate the top ranks of SOE.

Dining with Jacques - a famous *bon viveur* - is always a pleasure; the conversation sparkles, sometimes outrageously, there is always good wine and the food is tasty by wartime London standards.

He interrupts my reply. 'I want you to join a junket I'm planning in France. I know you're keen to get back to France and fight Jerry.'

Can it be true that at last I'll see some action? That the frustrating month after month of being a staff officer in SOE's HQ, helping with our agents' final training, taking them for a last good meal, seeing them off on their night flights to France, and subsequently writing disingenuous replies to relatives anxious for news of their offspring, is coming to an end?

Jacque eases into his pure, exquisite French and purrs, 'I'm assembling a team. I am allowed to choose whom I like.'

I hear him puff on his cigar. 'Shall we say, 11.30 at *Chez Victor?* It's early I know but I need to brief you before we are joined by another guest whom you have not met before.'

He adds, 'Teddy, this is meant to be an interview. Your appointment to my team is conditional on my guest's approval. Don't let me down, I've told him I value you highly.'

I put the telephone down, excited by Jacques' invitation but puzzled by his choice of restaurant. I have avoided *Chez Victor* above the York Minster pub, after my unpleasant brush there with de Gaulle over a year ago. Since then, it has become even more popular with his followers, who regard it as their Officers' Mess where they loudly echo their leader's fury that he is being side-lined by Churchill and Roosevelt in the plans to invade France. It is also a favourite haunt of the Gaullist security service, nominally a sister organisation of SOE. Relations between the two groups in London can be strained, sometimes vitriolic.

It is May 1944 and southern England is awash with American troops and equipment. Fevered final exercises of allied troops storming ashore on beaches is taking place at numerous locations along England's south coast. We all realise the invasion will be in northern France, but the actual landing place is known to only a few senior American and British planners and kept from de Gaulle. The tittle-tattle on the grapevine is that the French leader cannot be trusted to keep even this a secret. Jacque chuckles at the French leader's anger because he's an ardent royalist and loathes de Gaulle - he's had a nasty run-in with the touchy French leader before.

The allied armies are ready. Keeping trained troops waiting for too long risks damage to their morale and a fall-off in military standards. Everyone is convinced the invasion must be soon. If not this summer, then when?

The stress I feel is the mirror image of the one I experienced down in Wareham four years ago when, fed up with being scared, I just wished Hitler to get the dreaded invasion over with. Now, my emotion is, for Christ's sake let's just get going and invade France.

In the quiet hours between breakfast and lunch only a few *Chez Victor* tables are occupied when Jacques and I sit down in the restaurant. Nonetheless, our British Army uniforms attract some inquisitive stares, including from the owner, Victor Berlemont, as he approaches our table. His huge handlebar moustache twitches in pleasant surprise when he realises that we are French. Jacques orders two over-priced *apéritifs* from the owner's famous *absinthe*-making machine. Everyone ignores the government's 5 shillings a head limit for restaurant meals by paying over the odds for wine and drinks. In fact, London restaurants and night clubs have never had it so good. Business is booming. Pre-war supplies of fine wine and brandy are holding up surprisingly well.

Surely they can't be smuggled in from France?

'*Santé*, Teddy.'

'*Santé*, Jacques,' I smile.

Jacques leans back, sips his cloudy drink and starts his ritual of rolling and sniffing his cigar. Satisfied, he lights up and ostentatiously blows out his match with cigar smoke, leans back and checks we can't be overheard.

He glances jovially at me and chuckles. 'So Teddy, we are soldiers now, not saboteurs.'

Another puff of smoke wafts contentedly upwards. 'Even though they desperately refuse to admit it, *les Boches* are losing the war. And the invasion is imminent.'

Jacques shakes his head in disbelief at Nazi stubbornness and, although we both hate to admit, bravery.

He pauses to take another sip to emphasise what he now says, 'Once the invasion starts SOE's role will reverse. We will no longer be training and equipping the Resistance to sabotage factories, trains and bridges. Instead, our SOE will come out of the shadows and help them become soldiers to prevent Jerry rushing reinforcements to the front line.'

He laughs at the delicious irony of what he now adds, 'And preventing them sabotaging railways and power stations as they retreat.' He adds despondently, 'Much as I dislike conceding it, there is another consequence of the invasion. All resistance organisations in France, including this mission, will come under the command of de Gaulle.'

Now, that *is* news to me.

Jacques pushes on. 'Part of our new strategy is to parachute teams of five or six people from the Allies to help our French resistance colleagues. Each team will have experts in identifying suitable dropping zones for equipment or landing light planes. They will have radio operators, trainers in small arms and explosives, and advisers on tactics. Everything that a large group of the resistance needs to enable it to start fighting Jerry as soon as possible.'

Jacques takes a short break and blows smoke upwards and then grins at me. 'You would be our small arms and explosives expert and tactical adviser, Teddy.'

'Does that mean we will be in British Army uniforms?' I ask hopefully, remembering my promise to myself that I'd never return to France in civvies and risk being shot as a spy.

'Yes, it does. And our colleagues will wear the uniforms of their countries, or in our case, adopted countries, be they British, French, American or Canadian. Which is why they will be called Inter-Allied missions.'

Jacques inhales deeply.

'Even though the SOE is best suited to manage this type of operation, we must respect the sensitivities of our compatriots and allies.'

My genial giant of a friend sighs. 'In our case, I will be sharing command with one of de Gaulle's acolytes, Commandant Thomas, who will be joining us shortly.'

So that's why we are eating at Chez Victor. I note the expediency that a French Commandant is the same rank as a British major.

I raise my eyebrows. 'A joint command, Jacques?'

'Yes, I agree it could be difficult. But it *has* to work. It *must* work.' He looks sadly at me. 'We've had reports that the disagreements between communist and Gaullist Resistance factions have led to bloodshed and even deaths.

'I shall gladly allow Thomas to take responsibility for the delicate politics of the situation while I concentrate on military matters.'

He swallows the last of his drink and waves an arm in invitation to an austere-looking French Commandant who, right on time, is striding into the restaurant, looking around for his luncheon companions.

As a junior to a more senior officer, I stand and salute our new arrival.

Looking up at me, Commandant Thomas nods curtly. 'Sit down, Captain.'

Jacques introduces the Commandant as the joint commander of the Inter-Allied mission we are about to discuss. Thomas's face is as stiff as the creases in his well-ironed trousers. He places his spotlessly clean *képi* down on the spare chair at our table and opens his leather briefcase, the bright buckle reflecting the overhead lights.

Thomas takes a sheet of paper out - obviously my *curriculum vitae* - regards me sternly and, looking up and down from my resumé, starts to question me - interrogate might be a better word. I confirm I have been brought up in Paris and have three years' experience in training a wide variety of men and women, many like me, of French and British parentage. I am an expert in small-arms and explosives. And yes, I have been on the front line during the disastrous British Army retreat from the German *Blitzkrieg*.

Of course, I am French, not English.

I do not add the nuance that I sometimes oddly feel English in France and vice versa in England.

'Excellent,' says Thomas.

'That means, despite your uniforms,' he sniffs in disapproval, 'all the officers will be French, except for our doctor,' he adds, satisfied.

The Commandant glances at Jacques and nods at me. 'Thank you, Captain. You'll understand that I have to be rigorous in checking your credentials.'

The implication of his words is clear. A recommendation by the arch royalist, de Gaulle-hating, Major Jacques Theodore Paul Marie Vaillant de Guélis would not be taken at face value by any Free French organisation.

Jacques smiles. 'An *aperitif* Commandant?'

'Yes please, Major. But something sparkling would be my preference.'

Our restaurateur is waved across to our table and compliments Jacques on his choice of Krug. An aproned waiter appears rapidly with an ice bucket and Champagne bottle which he opens expertly. Jacques tastes and approves. Our three glasses are filled.

Looking around at the room's décor, the wooden bar and the waiters' aprons, Jacques sighs contentedly. 'We could be in Paris.' He smiles at me. 'Welcome to *Mission Tilleul*, Teddy.'

***

I spend weeks of training in the latest weapons, explosives and guerrilla tactics. Then the allies land in Normandy on June 6th. We are desperate to start our mission but we experience exasperating, bureaucratic delay while our fellow security services check and confirm that none of the *Mission Tilleul* team has information about other secret operations which might be useful to the Germans, if we are captured. Finally, permission is obtained and now frantic preparation follows to parachute us into France. We are allowed two days' leave to say goodbye to our families.

To mark the occasion, I book a table for me and Win at our favourite haunt, Oddenino's.

The nightclub is heaving with its usual younger and less well-off crowd - people like us - than in the more swanky, expensive London venues. As usual at Oddenino's, once it becomes late enough, singers and performers from West End shows, which have closed for the night, appear and let their hair down. Another band arrives. The successful Normandy landings encourage raucous celebration. An impromptu, saucy cabaret starts. There is a sprinkling of young women of easy virtue who pair off with young officers and disappear into the hotel next door. Hedonistic revelry reigns because, 'It'll soon be over, won't it?'

It's two a clock when we get back to our flat. Although tipsy and tired, we manage to creep into our bedroom without waking the Mater or Laura.

Our lovemaking has a rough edge of desperation. My fault. I haven't seen Win for weeks and am inconsiderate.

I lie awake next to a sleeping Win and think about my departure late tomorrow night and realise it will actually be tonight when I fly off on a great adventure.

I can't wait.

***

We are approaching our *Mission Tilleul* dropping zone in the Corrèze region of south west France's Massif Central.

I shiver as a sharp, unexpected premonition of death grips me. I gaze out, as if mesmerised, through the pitching and rolling aeroplane's open door into the dark night sky. My temple throbs with a hangover from Oddenino's over-indulgence.

I am struggling to suppress panic as vivid, flashing images fill my memory of one of my trainees whose parachute failed to open and who plunged to his death. I recall helping to pick up the limp, soggy mess of broken, splintered bones protruding through torn, blood-stained clothes. A face frozen in terror is imprinted in my memory.

The United States Air Force dispatcher, laconically chewing gum, sees my fear. Talk is impossible over the roar of the engines. Instead, he asks, using a thumbs up or down gesture accompanied by raised eyebrows, whether I still wish to jump.

I grimace a smile, twist my wrist and reply with a thumb's up.

A light above the door to the cockpit flashes green.

The young American grabs my arm and pulls me to the edge of the abyss and shoves me out. A few seconds later I am jerked upwards, like a puppet on a string, as my parachute cracks open.

I gaze up at the aircraft, already fading in the dim, moonlit sky, and immediately see the next parachute open above me. That will be James Edgar, one of our team's wireless operators.

The ground is rushing upwards in the dim moonlight. I brace for landing.

My training takes over as I break my fall by rolling across the ground. I feel soft grass, damp with dew.

'Bienvenue en France,' a twangy regional accent says peering down at me.

It is the early morning of 8th July 1944, about a month after D-Day or *Le Jour J* in French.

43.

The Mater

I hear the first one. A noise like a flatulating balloon deliberately let loose by a giggling child.

Win is bouncing Laura up and down on her knee.

'What was that?' she asks, as puzzled as me.

The noise passes not far over our heads in the sky and stops a mile or so away. We hold our breath, sensing something dreadful is about to happen.

Our trepidation is confirmed. The silence is broken by the loud boom of a major explosion. Our windows rattle but do not crack.

We quickly find out over the coming days that Hitler is bombarding London with rocket bombs as revenge for the terrible death and destruction the British and American air forces are inflicting on Germany's major cities, day and night.

Isn't that what my son Lloyd is doing?

The Nazi's V1 rockets bombs are nicknamed Doodlebugs by everyone, as if the innocuous, silly name, somehow diminishes their deadly effect. Hundreds start to arrive every week and London's defences seem powerless against this new, terrible weapon.

The news soon spreads that the rockets hit the capital haphazardly with no clear targets. This adds to the fear of the London population that death can strike willy-nilly, at any time in any place. Droves of people head for the relative safety of country villages and small towns. I'm told it's becoming like the Blitz evacuation all over again.

I can see the situation is making Win on edge, worried more about Laura than herself.

'Didn't you say you had a friend who had invited you to stay if things ever got bad in London again?' I ask as Win lights up another cigarette, her third of the morning.

She gives me short shrift when I casually hint she is smoking too much.

'Yes, Mater: Hope Munday. She married one of Teddy's trainees. A very young man called Tony Brooks. They became very good friends. I think she said she lived in a place called – what was it? – ah yes, Leverington Hall. Somewhere in Cambridgeshire.'

Remembering the occasion, Win smiles. 'Hope is still a kid herself, about seventeen, I think. Teddy was going to be the best man but *as usual* was called away on urgent SOE business.'

Win takes a moment to collect her thoughts while stroking Laura's hair with her spare hand.

'She lives with her parents so I'm not sure if they would welcome three strangers into their home.'

But it transpires that Hope, now Mrs Brooks, says her parents would be very happy to put some Australians up for a month or so until the Doodlebug situation hopefully improves. Please come as soon as you can, tomorrow even, there's bags of room, Hope entreats Win excitedly.

'She's thrilled at the prospect of chatting to someone about her husband Tony's secret job,' Win tells me.

It doesn't take long to pack our suitcases. A few days later we buy railway tickets and call a cab for the station.

'Don't blame you luv' says the cabbie to Win.

'Them Doodlebugs are a bleedin' menace. My sister's taken her nipper off to our parents in the country.'

Timely confirmation comes of our driver's words with the muffled sound of an explosion and a cloud of smoke rising above the rooftops somewhere towards the city centre.

Kings Cross station is packed and sweltering under the summer sun, shining through its grimy glass roof. The long sweating queues wait patiently to buy their tickets. Despite an undercurrent of fear, there is no panic. Londoners have long become fatalistic about being blown to bits by bombs.

'If your number's up, your number's up,' usually accompanied by a shrug of the shoulders is the typical response.

We finally squeeze on board a crowded train and the conductor, seeing Laura, orders two soldiers out of their seats for a 'mother and little baby'. Sitting opposite us is a family group of two children and what looks like their young mother and grandmother.

The station guard blows his whistle and waves his green flag. Our heavily laden train jerks and groans slowly away. With a polite nod to Win and me, the grandmother stands up and slides the compartment window shut to seal out the soot-specked smoke and steam billowing along the platform. Moving more quickly now through the streaky brown suburbs of north London, I reflect that we are not much different from the millions of refugees around Europe fleeing the Nazi menace.

I see the young woman is trying to fight back tears. Eventually she succumbs and starts to sob quietly. I try to hand her my clean, cotton handkerchief but one of her two children, a girl who looks about ten, smiles her thanks, takes it from me and gently dabs her mother's eyes. Her younger brother sits wide-eyed and still. He utters not a single word for the entire journey.

The grandmother offers a quiet, sorrowful explanation, 'My son-in-law was killed two days ago. He'd just come out of hospital after being slightly wounded. He popped out for a pint with some of his mates. But the pub,' her voice falters, 'got a direct hit from a Doodlebug. There was nothing left of them. Not a trace. We couldn't even bury him.'

She shakes her head, distraught at the unfairness of it all and says bitterly, 'It would have been better if he'd stayed in France fighting the Germans and hadn't come home.'

Win and I are silent, guilty that we can't say anything to make things easier for this bereaving little family. We part company with them on the platform at King's Lynn, near enough to the North Sea for screeching seagulls circling overhead on the lookout for scraps of food. As consoling relatives lead the small, grieving family away I wish the grandmother the best of luck.

She returns a wan smile and says, 'You too. Who knows what's round the corner with this war?'

Running along the platform towards us, waving an arm, is a pretty young girl with blonde hair and a peaches and cream English complexion who shouts excitedly, 'Win, Win.'

My daughter hands me Laura, hugs the girl and pulls her hand towards me.

'Mater, this is Hope.'

To my eyes Hope looks about fifteen. But she authoritatively summons a porter to carry our luggage into the station carpark and put it into the boot of a large car. Looking around, I can't see a driver. My face registers surprise that this young slip of a girl is allowed to drive this shiny saloon by herself.

'Don't worry Mrs Marshall, I've been driving tractors since I was thirteen,' she waves a hand gaily. I tell myself not to be silly and scared. After all, I remind myself, I was the first woman to be flown across Australia. And that was in a rickety biplane.

We drive for about half an hour and then stop by a field for Win to change Laura who has become too smelly for the car and definitely not in a suitable condition to be introduced to Hope's parents.

Letting Win change Laura's nappy on a picnic blanket placed over the grass verge, Hope and I indulge in small talk. She confides in me that her husband, Tony, thinks the world of Teddy.

'And that's good enough for my parents, Mrs Marshall. They love Tony,' she adds pugnaciously.

I help Win and Laura back into the car and Hope accelerates onto the road with a reassuring, 'Not long to go Win. Only about ten minutes.'

Leverington Hall lives up to its name; it's a large, historic country pile. I breathe an inward sigh of relief. My fears of us three refugees being squeezed together into one room are dispelled.

Our host, Major George Munday, awarded a Military Cross in WWI, and his charming wife, Pamela, greet us in the large entrance hall. 'Pam' shows us to our rooms, invites us to freshen up and then to join them downstairs in the drawing room for pre-dinner drinks.

There's even a cot for Laura; placing a hand on its well-worn wooden rails, Pam says, 'Would you believe it, Win, this was Hope's. It seems like yesterday when she was sleeping in it. I kept it for any grandchildren who might come our way. I'm glad it may prove useful now.' She laughs kindly. 'A bit earlier than I expected, of course.'

We wash, change and spruce ourselves up before we descend the grand staircase, down to the chequered stone entrance hall. I hold one of Win's hands steady as she carries Laura with the other.

The portraits on the walls observe our progress downstairs – do they approve, I wonder?

George and Pam are kindness personified. They come across as the best sort of genuine country folk. Even though money does not seem to be a problem, there are no airs and graces. The champagne flows to celebrate the landings in Normandy and conversation over the dinner table is animated as we speculate on how much longer the war will last.

'It'll be over by Christmas, won't it Daddy?' Hope asks excitedly.

Her father smiles in ostensible agreement.

Hope's parents are keen to know about Western Australia. I know enough about my state's farming to answer their questions. I steer the conversation away from politics. My Australian Labor Party loyalties might not be viewed favourably by the Mundays, whom I deduce from various comments are prosperous country Tories.

The next day, leaving Win and Laura behind with Hope to spend their hours chatting and gossiping, as wives of men working in an organisation about which they cannot talk in public, I announce I will catch a bus to Peterborough. I profess a great interest in its cathedral, one of the most important 12th-century buildings in England. I turn down George's offer of a lift. I wish to travel by bus and experience the countryside at leisure.

I lie.

I wish to visit Peterborough to see if I can travel further on to Gravely. From the moment I overhear at Laura's christening where Lloyd is stationed, I have been planning to visit him. Knowing how dangerous his job is, I am desperate to see him again, fearing that my son could be killed at any moment.

And I want to know about his English girlfriend, Dorothy. Although he telephones regularly, it is not the same as seeing him in person. I have a mother's need to hug and kiss her little boy. But I must tread carefully. Lloyd could be in serious trouble if he is suspected of telling his mother where he is stationed. *Careless Talk Costs Lives* posters are everywhere in public places.

A friendly Peterborough postmaster directs me to the bus stop for Graveley. Yes, he confirms, the bus stops right outside the Three Horseshoes pub which the bishop told me about at Laura's christening.

The bus soon fills up with a group of cheery, sun-tanned Land Army girls off to work in farm fields, dairies and chicken coops. Their brightly coloured turbans nodding like a flock of gossiping parrots as they giggle over last night's escapades. Here and there grey-haired women hold their grandchildren close, protecting them from unforeseen danger. I wonder if they have sad stories to relate like the tragic family who were sitting opposite us in the train from London to King's Lynn?

There are middle-aged women too, holding shopping baskets steady on their laps, nattering with friends about the meagre rations, shortages and lack of news from their sons and husbands. While they show an air of quiet determination, underneath I sense exhaustion and resigned weariness. The news from France is encouraging, but how long is this awful, awful war going to go on for?

Apart from young grandsons everyone on the bus, including the driver, is female.

Is this a sign of how society will change after the war?

Two hours after leaving Leverington, travelling up and down the gentle slopes of Cambridgeshire, I arrive in Graveley. I alight from the bus conveniently close to the Three Horseshoes. Typically, an English village has a pub near the parish church, but I can't see a place of worship nearby. Graveley is too small perhaps? A hamlet really.

Lounging on benches outside The Three Horseshoes, enjoying their beer in the late afternoon sun, are three or four RAF servicemen. None of them are officers, so I ignore them.

Although the only bar is not crowded, a middle-aged woman by herself in a pub, especially a stranger, attracts some

268

inquisitive looks. I march determinedly to the bar and wait to be served.

The barman soon arrives. 'Good afternoon, Madam. What can I get you?'

I order half a pint of lemon squash.

'How can I help you?' he asks, taking my money. 'I saw you get off the bus. You're not from around here so you must be looking for somewhere or someone,' he explains.

I decide to take a risk and play my cards immediately. 'I'm looking for a Lloyd Marshall, who's serving with 35 Squadron.'

I explain that I'm his landlady from his last posting and have some personal possessions he forgot to take with him.

'Why don't you sit down over there,' he suggests politely to me. I am, after all, a woman standing at a bar by herself.

Pointing with his chin at a group of officers grouped around a table he says, 'While I bring you your drink, I'll ask those lads if they know, er, your son. I've never met an Australian landlady before,' he smiles sympathetically, as my face registers concern.

'There's quite a few Aussies in the squadron. I picked your accent up straight away. Don't worry, I won't report you to the RAF police,' he whispers. 'We get quite a few local girls in here, going out with aircrew. Sometimes things get a bit rowdy and I get the occasional parent, fathers mainly, coming in to complain. I'll tell those lads you're one of their mothers.'

As I correctly half expect, he's supposed to inform the air force base of any strangers nosing around the place.

There are barely suppressed chuckles and amused sly glances thrown my way from the group of young men when the publican chats to them, carrying me my drink.

'Well, you're in luck,' he says. 'They do know your son,' he whispers. 'One of them said he's a clever clog. Said your Lloyd is one of the best navigators. Called him a master bomber.'

That would be Lloyd of course.

'Tell you what, I'll call the base and ask him to come here, pronto. His former landlady needs to see him urgently.'

I thank him and he disappears from the bar, returning after a few minutes to confirm that Lloyd has got the message.

Sure enough, I soon hear a motorbike, its brakes squealing, screeching to a stop outside.

My Lloyd strides into the pub and looks enquiringly at the publican who raises a dishcloth-covered hand towards me, sitting by myself at window table. My son's face is stunned white with shock and then turns red in anger and embarrassment.

'Mater, what the hell are you doing here?' he hisses, bending down, his two hands gripping tightly the sides of the small round table.

He refrains from kissing me, noticing that the group of colleagues are watching us in amusement.

'Why don't we go outside?' I suggest coolly. 'There's a couple of spare benches. We can talk more privately.'

He stomps through the door. Normally he would wait for me to go first. Not this time; anger has smothered his manners.

I sit next to him with my hands folded on my lap. I jump in with an explanation. 'Win, Laura and I are staying with one of your sister's friends in Leverington.'

He shakes his head. He's never heard of the place. No surprise; it's about fifty miles from here.

'We've come to escape the flying bombs in London,' I say softly. 'I just had to see you again,' I add weakly.

'But how did you know I was in Graveley?'

'I overheard you talking to Teddy at Laura's christening.'

'Oh Christ,' he swears.

I crumble and start to sob. 'I'm so sorry, Lloyd.'

Lloyd is shocked. He's never seen me cry before.

I wipe a tear away. 'I was terrified I might never see you again.'

He gently squeezes my hands and remains silent for a moment or two. Roles reversed, like a father to a daughter he gently admonishes me.

'Mater, it was very silly, you could have got me into a lot of trouble. Family visitors are not allowed here.' He smiles. 'But trust you! You've probably managed to get away with it.'

Now he chuckles. 'The publican tells me that you're a furious Mum, angry that I've misbehaved with her daughter?'

I nod, a fleeting grin across my face. 'Yes, I must thank him. He came up with that ploy.'

Relieved that there was no rancour between us, I turn to another issue that is occupying my mind. I pat his hand. 'Now, please tell me more about Dorothy.'

Win may have got away with marrying somebody I hadn't met but - although I approve of Teddy - I am determined not to allow Lloyd the same latitude.

His face softens and his eyes widen, gazing brightly into the distance. Oh God, I see instantly he's head over heels in love with this unknown girl.

But is she suitable, I scream silently?

Dorothy, it seems, is the daughter of a respectable farming family who live near the training base where he'd been stationed for months. He refuses to tell me where. That bloody frustrating phrase 'somewhere in England' is chucked at me once again by my adamant, obstinate boy.

'Don't worry Mater, you'll meet her soon enough,' he says attempting to mollify me.

But it's clear that there are plans afoot to cement their relationship into something more serious before I have a chance to meet her.

What's more concerning, Lloyd is talking about not return-ing to Australia as soon as this blasted war is over.

He lets slip, 'One of my English friends has suggested I try for his old college.' He pauses. 'Balliol, Mater.'

My face is blank.

'That's Oxford University, Mater. He was a Fellow at Bal-liol and says he'll recommend me.'

My practical mind asks the obvious question, 'But how will you support yourself? Your father and I haven't enough money.' I see a shadow of worry on his face. I press on. 'Would Dorothy's parents oblige?'

His expression suggests not.

Lloyd frowns. 'I have some savings, Mater. I sort of hoped you and Pop would help out.'

My raised eyebrows signal the answer from his parents would be, 'No.'

He sighs. 'I understand.'

We turn to safer topics of conversation and the time flies. He tells me about his Pathfinder colleagues and the bits of his flying he feels comfortable enough to describe. Even that's enough to underline my worst fears. Lloyd will be lucky to sur-vive this war.

I conceal my terror and glance at my watch. I've already noted the bus timetable. It'll take me at least two hours to get back to Win - even though it's midsummer it will be almost dark. Lloyd escorts me to the bus stop and promises to visit us in Leverington as soon as he's got some leave.

He hugs me close and kisses me on my cheek as he helps me up the stairs into the bus.

I wave goodbye, biting my trembling lip so hard that I taste a drop of blood. Out of sight, I dissolve into silent tears. 'Will I ever see my boy again?'

Lloyd never gets the opportunity to come to Leverington. London's defences improve and the Doodlebug menace becomes bearable enough for Win, Laura and me not to overstay our welcome.

'Come again, please Win,' entreats Hope. Her parents politely repeat the invitation but not so enthusiastically. Understandable. Laura is not the best sleeper and being kept awake at night by someone else's baby soon becomes tiresome.

***

But come September, our hopes of a much safer London are dashed. Not long after our return, Win is feeding Laura when we hear the boom of an enormous explosion – much bigger than a Doodlebug. The window next to me in the front room rattles in its frame, as if a big thunderstorm is approaching. A quick glance upwards confirms the summer sky is clear. Win hugs Laura closer to her breast.

It's definitely an explosion, not close, but somewhere else in the centre of London. It can't be a Jerry bombing raid or Doodlebug rocket attack because there's been no air raid warning.

The BBC news tells us later there's been a large gas explosion.

The government explanation quickly becomes untenable over the coming days as more huge explosions occur without warning. Some are closer to us and windows are shattered in Melbury Road.

London doesn't panic but there's an air of quiet, weary desperation. The capital survived the Blitz and is coping with the Doodlebugs, but it seems clear that Hitler now has another secret, deadly weapon. A rocket which nobody can hear, which drops out of the sky without warning, and destroys whole streets and can kill hundreds. We learn its name: V2. But fortunately, there are fewer V2s than Doodlebugs.

We decide to stick it out in London.

44.

Teddy

'For God's sake James, where are the fucking guns? It's been almost two weeks now since you signalled our order.'

Poor James Edgar is getting the rough edge of our commander's tongue - in English, just to make sure there's no misunderstanding.

'Are you sure you've sent the messages correctly?' Major Jacques de Guélis fumes, towering over our diminutive wireless operator, crouched over his wireless set on the big kitchen table in the small home of the Sauviat family who have been helping the Resistance and Allied servicemen, on the run, for years.

Brave people.

Their small house nestles isolated in dark woods not far from a tiny village called Chadebec in the Corrèze region of the *Massif Central*. Now the Allies have landed in Normandy, the chances of the Germans prioritising their resources to locate our wireless signals and raid the house are slim, nonetheless we are constantly on guard to slip away into the trees at a moment's notice.

'He has definitely sent the messages correctly,' I interrupt, placing a supportive hand on James' shoulder. I glare at Jacques, warning him to lay off James. 'You know my Morse is pretty good. I've watched him, just to be certain there's no fault at our end,' I add firmly.

I tap my pipe out in an ashtray on the table and say, while still watching our wireless operator as he puts his headphones on again, and repeats the message, appealing for weapons, 'And, I've checked the damn set to see that it's working okay.'

I pause.

'You know, I'm beginning to think there's a problem in London. Could it be just a simple explanation? You know, the left hand not knowing what the right hand is doing?'

We're all on edge. The credibility of Mission Tilleul is at stake. We promise weapons and ammunition to the mutually hostile Gaullist Free French and communist factions to reinforce De Gaulle's command that all French resistance groups must now cooperate with each other.

Jacques reminds us, despair in his voice, that our compatriots are sometimes prepared to kill each other, rather just than the common enemy. 'The communists shot four or five Gaullists about a month ago, not long before we arrived. Apparently it was a tit-for-tat killing,' he continues sadly. 'If we can't get those weapons and ammunition soon, they'll lose faith in us and we will fail.' Jacques takes a deep breath and orders. 'Sort it out Teddy. If necessary, signal bloody Buckmaster and Vera Atkins direct to ask them what the hell is going on.'

He stomps outside, chewing angrily on his cigar.

'Thank you, Teddy,' James says softly, glad to see the back of Jacques for a while.

Thank God, in early August the weapons eventually start to arrive, parachutes dropping like glistening mushrooms in the moonlight. We try to distribute them as evenly as possible, careful not to favour one side or the other. Inevitably there are complaints we are not being even-handed.

The enthusiastic groups of young men in the Resistance learn quickly from my training in the use of automatic weapons and hand grenades.

I suggest improvements in ambush tactics and participate successfully in attacking German patrols, gaining respect among the Resistance leaders, as the unusual Parisian in British Army uniform, for my high standards in teaching and a willingness to fight alongside them in combat.

At least the military objective has been agreed by all the Resistance groups in our region; to prevent the Germans from using the main road, the RN 89, which cuts diagonally through the *Massif Central*. For the Germans this road is the critical route north to send men and equipment to Normandy. Guarding the RN 89, like a line of *bastide* towns, are German garrisons in Brive la Galliard, Tulle, Égletons and Ussel.

The town of Égletons is our target.

We are joined by a group of French SAS from London. They are as poorly briefed as we were about the wide extent of the Resistance in the region. They are surprised and disappointed to learn there is no longer any requirement for sabotage. In fact, part of our job now in this part of France is to prevent harmful sabotage by retreating Germans.

Don't the SOE and Free French talk to each other in London?

Although the SAS refuse to put themselves under the command of Mission Tilleul, they are happy to join us and our Resistance comrades in attacking Égletons, whose garrison is based in a newly reinforced concrete school building.

The German commander refuses to surrender, confident his strong building is like a giant bunker.

He is correct.

We fail to take the school at our first attempt and it becomes a tough, bloody siege. Although we get close and even inside its courtyard, we fail to crack its tough walls and suffer several casualties.

What's more, our positions are repeatedly bombed by the Luftwaffe. Running on adrenaline, I scuttle from one Bren gun emplacement to another, ignoring explosions and machine gun bullets, showing my younger, inexperienced comrades how best to shoot at the dive bombers - a difficult task for experienced gunners and one requiring great courage from beginners.

Jacques repeatedly requests air support from the RAF but to no avail - we are not a priority.

During another attack on the school by us, I notice that one of our Bren gunners is firing inaccurately and take over his gun. I creep forwards, as close to the school as I dare, and start shooting at a window where a German machine gun is positioned. Puffs of dust explode from the concrete around the window showing my aim is on target.

But my pent-up anger at the months of being prevented from fighting in France spills out and I lose my self-control. Sweat drips into my eyes and my knuckles turn white with the effort of holding my jerking weapon. I begin to shoot wildly without stopping, without aiming.

I scarcely feel a tap on my shoulder. This is followed by a hard pull, dragging me backwards. I twist around, panting and wide-eyed and see the extended arm of James Edgar, crawling towards me.

He bellows at me, 'Teddy, for God's sake man! Pull yourself together!' He takes a deep breath, spits out dust and shouts, 'Jacques has ordered us to retreat.'

Jacques tells us a heavily-armed German column from Clermont-Ferrand is on its way to reinforce the garrison in the school. Faced by a far superior force, we know we have to suspend the siege.

Not long afterwards, watching through my binoculars from a safe distance, I see the garrison's commanding officer greeting the column's leader. It is 19th August. Although difficult to discern against the grey bullet-scarred school, I sense from their decisive arm signals, ordering their troops, both commanders look like veterans to me.

The column takes up defensive positions around the school. Furiously, we witness its soldiers pillage the remaining, undamaged homes in Égletons.

Our feeling of helplessness turns to loud cheers and we wave our weapons above our heads, as we urge on a dozen low-flying RAF Mosquitoes, which suddenly appear from nowhere to swoop down on the school. Their accurate bombing severely damages the column and inflicts many casualties, so much so that all the Germans in Égletons withdraw south along the RN 89, and smaller country roads, towards Tulle.

Jacques beams in pleasure that his repeated requests for RAF support suddenly bear fruit.

Harried and ambushed all the way, the column commander threatens to take reprisals from Tulle's inhabitants. He withdraws his threat after a warning there will be reciprocal action against German prisoners of the Resistance, of whom there are currently thousands.

Onlookers are now amazed by the sight of a solitary German aircraft, which drops a message for the column, or what remains of it. The Germans make an about turn and start heading back to Égletons.

They do not get far.

Attacked from all sides, including mines laid in the roads by the French SAS, the remnants of the column are soon defeated.

And all along the RN 89 the Germans are surrendering to successful Resistance attacks.

Brive la Galliarde, Tulle, Egletons and Ussel are swiftly liberated.

On 22nd August 1944 the war is effectively over in the *Massif Central.*

We are victorious and spend the next few weeks recuperating and celebrating.

Jacque's emotions are mixed. 'Yes, Teddy, I know our mission was a success.' He groans in exasperation. 'But imagine how much more effective we could have been if London had got us here quicker and our weapons had been more swiftly delivered.'

On the 17th September there is a military parade and award of medals in Limoges for the Allied soldiers who have fought alongside the Resistance in the Massif Central. My part in the Égletons siege is recognised by the award of a *Croix de Guerre*.

Arrangements are made to fly the Mission Tilleul team back to England. But there is no room on the small plane for me. I say goodbye to the lucky Commandant Thomas and James Edgar and am ordered to drive to the new SOE headquarters in Paris. Jacques has already left, seconded to another mission.

I hitch a ride from an American Army Captain, Ted Fraser, who, like me, is wearing a newly presented French medal. We head off to Vichy *en route* to Paris in a US Army jeep laden with several jerrycans of fuel.

I am at the end of an exhilarating two month's whirlwind of fighting and am proud to have played a role, however small, in driving the Germans out of France.

And I can't wait to see Win and Laura again.

45.

Teddy

Vichy is in an orgy of celebration after the Germans had pulled out a few days ago. Our jeep is plied with flowers; it's not long before our cheeks are covered with lipstick from girls keen to kiss English and American officers. We drive slowly through the crowded city-centre streets, looking for a hotel. We stop on the cobbled street outside the *Hotel des Ambassadeurs,* a smart, imposing building. It shouts luxury.

Why not? I have forty thousand *francs* in my pocket to pay for war expenses. The mission's over and there won't be too many questions asked about hotel bills.

Feverish celebration is spilling out from the hotel onto the warm afternoon street. The foyer looks full of happy people. A warm welcome seems assured.

'This will do,' I say.

A bell-boy appears and takes our luggage. But not our guns.

We trudge up the steps into the hotel. The people immediately in front of us step nervously aside as they see our dusty uniforms and guns over our shoulders. But then they smile and crowd around us when they see each of us is wearing the Croix de Guerre.

'Catch you later,' Ted says apologetically as he is dragged away by a bunch of US Army uniforms.

At the same time a woman shrieks, 'Teddy, Teddy,' and waves across the *melée.*

Before I can see who's shouting at me, she elbows her way through the swirling scrum and throws her arms around me and squeezes me as tightly as a lover, a bottle of brandy in one hand, cigarette in the other. I feel her breasts against my chest, hips pressing close to mine. She kisses me on my lips. I taste her tongue, fresh lipstick, tobacco and cognac.

'Bloody hell,' she exclaims, pushing me away in mock outrage at my instinctive reaction. 'You're the first man I've kissed in France for ages.' She chuckles and stands back, her seductive eyes summing me up. Of course. Nancy Wake.

Christ, I'd forgotten how sexy she was. I smile looking at her. The loose-fitting *Resistant* top and trousers still fail to hide those Hollywood, Jane Russell curves. She flicks her hair back over her shoulder and links an arm through mine.

'Come on sweetie. We're going to paint the town red.'

I laugh, holding up my sub-machine gun. 'Let me lock this in my room first.'

'Don't be long,' she purrs in exaggerated flirtation.

Once more linked together in the lobby, on the way out, she grabs a man out of the heaving scrum. He simpers and smiles at me. Oh God - I recognise the short, jovial face of Denis Rake. I'd forgotten he'd volunteered to go back to France and had jumped at the chance to become Nancy's radio operator.

We start to push our way through the crowds to the front door but are stopped by a tall, impeccably-dressed man. He introduces himself as the Swiss Ambassador and invites Nancy and 'her friends' to a cocktail party. He brushes aside Nancy's protestations that she looks too scruffy.

'Shall we say six o'clock?' he insists, pointing to a reception room on the other side of the lobby.

Nancy uses the next couple of hours to make herself presentable.

'You scrub up well, darling,' Denis simpers when she returns after a couple of hours.

'So do you two ruffians,' she says noticing we have shaved and washed.

Nancy is the star turn at the ambassador's party. Denis and I become wallflowers, bemused by the attention she attracts from diplomats, French resistance leaders, Vichy city officials and Allied officers.

'The Resistance love her, Teddy. She's brave and beautiful,' Dennis says.

'Looks like she's famous.'

Nancy glances across the room every now and then and smiles at us. She eventually manages to break free.

'C'mon you two,' she orders as we link arms and trot out into the street teaming with celebrating people.

Anyone associated with the Resistance or wearing an Allied uniform is grabbed and plied with wine and food.

La Marseillaise and *Le Chant Des Partisans* are belted out in drunken ecstasy and fury at what the Germans did to France by the maquis, civilians, and the few British and Americans. There is an undercurrent of shame too among the *Vichysoises*, fuelled by the association of their city with the collaborationist Pétain regime.

Nancy drinks and drinks. While she has gone to the loo, Denis grins and winks at me. 'Watch out Teddy. Nancy's taken a shine to you. She wouldn't let the *Résistants* touch her.' He arches his eyebrows and looks at me. 'But now? The war's over for us. Who knows? You could be a lucky man tonight.'

'I'm married with a baby daughter,' I stammer, my guilty red cheeks betraying my thoughts.

He smirks lewdly and winks again.

God, he's awful.

The evening continues from bar to bar, bistro to bistro.

My Croix de Guerre is spotted again and again and I am hoisted repeatedly up onto shoulders in swirling crowds who embrace us as we surge from bar to bistro. A conga starts.

Eventually we manage to break free and collapse, laughing onto a bench in a nearby riverside park.

Nancy leans back, savouring the warm late-summer evening, sips her cognac and shakes her head in exaggerated disbelief. She looks at Denis and smiles. 'Good God, Den Den, we're speaking English.'

'I know, luv. Strange innit?'

'And thinking in English too,' she adds softly. 'Teddy,' she grins, turning to me, 'this is the first time I've heard you speak English. All that time in that Scottish hellhole, we only spoke French. And you know what?' She places her hand on my arm and gently squeezes, her eyes flirting with mine. 'You have a faint but charming French accent.'

'And you, dear Nancy, as I told you in that Scottish hellhole, have a faint but charming Australian accent in English *and* French,' I retort in mock anger, trying to avoid her eyes, conscious I'm slurring my words.

Her lips form a *moue* and she blows a kiss at me.

Denis swirls his wine around. 'Well, who gives a damn?' he pouts, interrogating his glass sulkily. 'I know the French snigger at my Belgian accent. And I certainly don't speak Oxford English.' He puts on a mock lah-di-dah accent. 'And I don't give a damn, don't you know.'

We chuckle in unison, strengthening our warm feeling of camaraderie which has been building through the evening.

We saunter over to the promenade, standing close together looking down at the slow-moving River Allier, handing Nancy's cognac bottle around.

Nancy hums a melody and I supply the famous line from the Song of the Partisans… *Nous on marche et nous on tue, nous on crève* - we march and we kill, we die.'

Denis improvises by adding at the end the SOE agents' standard, eccentric farewell, '*A Bientôt. Merde!*'

We lean on the balustrade gently humming and singing, with Denis bellowing at the end of each line the agents' good-bye.

'I hate the water,' Denis suddenly says, elbows on the balustrade, hunched forward, glaring at the river. He takes a swig and spits the words, 'I was on a ship which was bombed and sank. A fucking bomb went down the funnel, right in front of me. Thousands drowned or were machine gunned in the sea by the bloody Germans. I was covered in oil as black as the ace of spades.' He just manages to stop himself sobbing. 'Christ, I was lucky and got picked up.'

'Thousands Den Den?' Nancy smiles. 'Come on, even for you that's quite a claim.'

'Yes thousands, Duckie. Maybe six or seven thousand,' Denis says fiercely. 'It was called the *Lancastria*. We weren't allowed to talk about it afterwards - Churchill didn't want the shine taken off Dunkirk.'

Nancy sips from the bottle to hide her disbelief.

I break the silence. 'He's right, Nancy. I was there too.' I forestall Denis' surprise. 'On the shore, not the ship. The worst thing I ever saw,' I add. 'I had to check officers' bodies washed up on the beach for anything which might help the Germans. Bloody oil affected my skin.'

I take a long drink.

Nancy breaks our maudlin silence. 'You know, in a funny way we represent the best of SOE.'

'How so'? I ask, surprised by her sudden serious tone.

'We're not average people – we're mongrels really. Look at us. Teddy, you're French and Scottish; I'm Australian married to a Frenchman, although, the French call me English; and you, Den-Den, you're a real mongrel, a Pommy Belgian queer!'

'Watch it *dahling*, I've kissed plenty of Aussie queers in my time,' retorts Denis.

We all laugh at his words, which in normal peace time would be considered scandalous in polite company.

Nancy continues, 'We all love France and hate the Germans. Despite how different we were from most people, or maybe because of that,' Nancy shrugs her shoulders, 'the SOE believed that we had it in us to gain the trust of the Resistance. They turned out to be right. And London knew when it fouled things up – and by God they did - we could be trusted to sort it out.'

It's getting late – well past midnight and the noise of the revellers is beginning to die down. I feel a faint, cool breeze caressing my cheeks, whispering summer is drawing to a close.

'*Fin de la saison,*' I announce, slurring my words badly.

'Yes, in many, many ways,' Nancy replies sadly.

Very dark now, the silent sky bears down, smothering our gaiety, replacing it with a sombre collective memory of what we and our SOE comrades have gone through in the last five years.

From a few miles away, we hear the crackle of a machine gun.

'*Épuration sauvage* - settling scores,' sighs Dennis.

Nancy grimaces and shrugs her shoulders. 'It's not so long ago that I ordered a traitor to be executed.' She shakes her head. 'And my French Resistance comrades refused to carry out my order.'

'Why was that?' I ask.

'She was a woman.' Nancy pauses. 'I told them that if they didn't do it, then I damn well would.' She smiles. 'You trained me well, Teddy.'

'Didn't he just,' says Denis.

I begin to stumble. I must get back to my room. Drink seems to have no effect on Nancy.

My last memory is being laid down on a bed by her and Denis.

I hear him say, 'Bad luck, duckie.'

Nancy kisses me on the forehead and sighs, 'Sweet dreams, Teddy.'

46.

Teddy

The next morning Ted Fraser and I are outside the hotel loading our jeep.

The bell boy, unused to handling weapons, nervously hands up to me in the jeep my American Marlin sub-machine gun.

'Merde,' I swear as it slips from my grasp and falls onto the hard cobbled road. The gun goes off. A flash reflects off the hotel windows and the report echoes down the narrow street, rattling bottles and bouncing off upturned tables - the detritus of last night's revelries.

Something punches me agonisingly hard in the guts and the pain sears upwards.

Stunned, my mind freezes at first before I realise what's happened - I've shot myself.

'Je suis touché,' I gasp and collapse onto a seat, my head jerking backwards.

I look up and see a valet on a hotel balcony staring down at me. His hands are pressed hard against his cheeks, moulding his mouth into a perfect O. He screams. Odd, I hear nothing.

In English I shout, 'Win'. And then, 'Laura'. But no sound comes out of my mouth. I sense only a frothy dribble of blood.

Everything is quiet in the street as I topple forwards and bang my head on the hard metal seat opposite.

Out of the corner of an eye I see Ted bending down and lifting my shoulders. He raises a hand and jabs a morphine syringe swiftly into my arm.

But I feel nothing.

Ted turns into a grey, fuzzy shadow and then disappears into an all-enveloping darkness.

I recall last night's singing. '...*nous, on marche, nous, on tue et nous, on crève...*'

The irony is not lost on me as I die.

My brain orders a smile.

But my lips remain closed.

Somewhere deep in my being I hear myself sob silently, 'Goodbye Babe darling, *plus douces caresses et tendre braises.*'

Stillness seeps into my soul and gently soothes my life away.

Teddy's body is taken to the Hopital Radio close by. After the formality of a post-mortem, he is laid in a coffin and taken into a nearby Protestant church. Later that morning two mourners, a man and a woman holding arms, place a carefully wrapped bunch of flowers on the coffin.

The woman is softly weeping. The man gently helps her take a step back. They salute in unison and murmur softly, 'A Bientôt Teddy. Merde!'

47.

Win

I pick up the small, burgundy-coloured notebook which I am using as my diary and read my entry from *Thursday Sept 28th 1944:*

Dear love, I never expected to have to make this entry.

Jean Le H came home tonight, very white in the face, and told me you had been killed.

I couldn't believe it for a while, and I still can't believe it.

You my dearest, brave Teddy. I felt sick with shock and didn't know what to do with myself...

I must wait patiently for my life to finish so that I can meet you in a greater and happier world.

We were so happy my dear. The gods are jealous gods.

I'm going to keep on with my diary - it'll be like speaking to you.

Little Laura was having her bath when Jean Le H. told me. I looked at her, and the first great sadness filled me.

The Mater has been a great comfort to me - she was so upset. I feel now I have paid my debts to my parents.

Lloyd will be upset, poor kid. He told the Mater you were a man with a capital M.

Monday October 2nd

Dear love, I'm writing with your pen and the ink that you used is still in it. I am wearing the watch that was last on your wrist when the bullet passed clean through your heart that always beat so faithfully for me. How many times have I not lain on your breast and heard it beat?

Your comb is there, and the old pipe, your good old friend, and the Croix de Guerre and your ring which I am wearing next to my wedding ring as a symbol of our new marriage in the spiritual world.

Yes, dearest, I've read your diary too. Yes, I know that you needed me. My body is yours as I told you the night before you left. You were rather ashamed of yourself the next day but I wasn't. I was gloriously happy and attempted to bring my personal habits into line with the overflowing intimacy you accorded me on that wonderful night.

My soul is yours too, dear. I do want to die soon, so that I can meet you in that other place. However, I know that such good fortune will not be mine for a long time, and I must just make the best of this long time on earth and perhaps help to fight for the cause to which you gave your life.

Oh, mon âme, I love you. There is no strength in my body to rail against this fate.

Thursday October 5th

Dear Love, you're helping me now. I now feel your influence calming and sweetening me.

There is a story of Churchill and his reactions when he heard of France's preparation to sign an armistice. In front of a shocked cabinet, he stood up and said, 'We now stand isolated and alone in the world.' Then with a lift of his chin he said, 'I find it rather inspiring.'

And that's how I'm finding it now, dearest. I want to lift my chin and face these coming years of loneliness with fearlessness and courage. Whatever talents I have at my disposal I want to use in fighting for the cause for which you died. I don't want to be hard and bitter, but kindly and tolerant and the sort of person you always declared I was whilst you lived.

I look into little Laura's face and find your features there. Her nature is already apparent - a sweet soft nature that reacts to kindness and love. (Although I regret to say she's shrieking her head off at the moment.)

There is a small mark on a page where a tear falls from my cheeks. I am cross with myself and hastily dab it off with my hankie - I know you would want me to be brave.

Laura gurgles happily on my knee.

Poor lamb. She will grow up not knowing her father and will have to make do with her mother's memories.

Teddy, I will move your body from Vichy, the headquarters of that ghastly traitor-regime, to your Normandy home. I hear that the Duc de Namur assisted with your funeral. I will appeal to him for help.

I am determined to go and live in France. I want our daughter to be French as well as Australian. But the Mater is ordering me to return to Perth with her. We have furious arguments - I don't want to go. She is pulling strings with her contacts to get us a ship's passage as soon as possible.

If Laura and I are forced by the Mater to go with her we will come back, I promise.

I promise Teddy.

Epilogue

The middle-aged man loosens his collar and slumps wearily back in his chair, grateful for the cooling, afternoon sea-breeze which is just beginning to flutter the neatly stacked piles of papers on his desk, carrying with it the faintest sound of softly-breaking surf.

He is desperate for a drink. But he often feels like that. He'd promised his supporters years ago that he'd give up. And he's kept his word.

A train puffs past the open window of the modest, Californian-style bungalow, heading through the sun-bleached, sandy suburbs from the city to the port. An empty glass clinks against a full bottle of rainbow-coloured Jameson - he always keeps whiskey in his study for visitors. And to test his mettle.

He sighs sympathetically as he looks across at the faint, sighing crease left by his visitor in a well-worn, leather chair.

'Jack, I've got another huge favour to ask,' his old journalist friend and neighbour, John Marshall, had said in a voice cracked with paternal despair. 'This time I need to get the Mater back. Together with Win and Laura, as quick as I can. They're stranded.'

Australia's prime minister is glad to help. A cablegram would be sent immediately, he promises.

Now he has to find the right words. He wipes his bad eye and begins to chew gently on the end of a pencil, as he considers his intended recipient.

He's never liked the privileged, upper-class English. His chippy Irish, publican father had seen to that. Although he still quarrels bitterly about the war with the man in London - relations are still frosty - he admits grudgingly that their leader has a soaring gift of oratory that he can never emulate. Still, he is proud of his own record of achievement and knows most in his own country hold him in great affection.

He starts to write:

Dear Prime Minister,'

No.

The unnecessary formality annoys him - it might harm the chances of success.

He crosses the words out, flecks of black lead streaking across his old reporter's pad.

He begins again. This time the headline is:

Personal

And the message starts:

Dear Winston,

Letter to Win from the author

Dear Win

Wherever you are, whatever your state, I hope you and Teddy are reunited and have the chance to read my book.

I know you tried to write your own story but found it impossible - you were just too close to each other.

Your book, I'm sure, would have been autobiographical. Whereas I had no choice other than to write a historical novel because I had to imagine the dialogue and fill in parts of the story which remained unknown to me. I apologise if any of my assumptions are inaccurate and I have inadvertently offended you and Teddy.

You'll see that, at the end, I quoted *verbatim* from your diary. My moderate talent as a writer meant I couldn't possibly improve upon your own words.

I would like to end by saying thank you to you and Teddy. For me it's been a privilege and pleasure getting to know you both so well through my research and writing. I have learnt so much, including a better appreciation of the deep pain you must have felt when Teddy failed to return from France.

At the beginning of this book, I quoted Dylan Thomas. Please forgive me for repeating his beautiful words again whose sentiment seems particularly apt to, *A Remarkable Stillness*:

> *'Though lovers be lost, love shall not;*
> *And death shall have no dominion.'*

Yours sincerely
Jonathan

The Cast

Leading roles

'Win' - Winfred Bisset (née Marshall) gifted young West Australian pianist, twice winner of the Australasian Schools Pianoforte Competition – the second within five points of a perfect score.

'Teddy' - Captain Edouard Bisset, Croix de Guerre, courageous and popular young Scottish-French officer in the British Army Intelligence Corps, seconded to the Special Operations Executive (SOE).

Supporting roles

'Sol' - Solomon Cutner MBE, famous child prodigy, later one of the world's greatest pianists and teacher of Win as a young woman.

'The Mater' - Mrs Gladys Marshall, a strong personality and mother of Win.

'Pop' - John Marshall, journalist, and father of Win. Well-connected among Australian Labor Party circles.

Cameo roles

Mrs Hope Brooks (née Munday) - wife of Tony Brooks (see SOE cameo roles following).

Rt Hon John Curtin – Prime Minister of Australia

Grahame Deans – Win's first boyfriend.

Squadron Leader Lloyd Marshall DFC, RAAF, member of an RAF Pathfinder squadron, talented polymath, and brother of Win.

Cameo roles - the Musicians

Lazare Lévy, a world-leading French pianist and teacher of Sol as a young man.

Miss Ida Roberts, Win's first piano teacher.

Dr Simon Rumshisky, the elusive 'world's best' piano teacher who rehabilitated a teenage Sol.

Mathilde Verne, the harsh manager and teacher of Sol as a child prodigy.

Sir Henry Wood, conductor, 'father' of London's Proms.

Cameo roles - Special Operations Executive (SOE)

Major Anthony (Tony) Brooks DSO, MC, Croix de guerre, Légion d'honneur, the SOE's youngest (20) and one of its most successful agents in France.

Colonel Maurice Buckmaster OBE, Croix de Guerre, the head of SOE's F (French) Section.

Sergeant James Edgar Chevalier de L'Ordre de la Legion d'Honneur, Croix de Guerre, citoyen d'honneur de la commune de Sussac, wireless operator for Mission Tilleul.

Major Jacques de Guélis, MBE, MC, three times awarded Croix de Guerre, one with silver star, a 'genial giant' of a man, co-commander of Mission Tilleul.

Jean Le Harivel, Croix de Guerre.

Percy (Peter) Harratt DSO, MC & Bar.

Denis Rake, DSO, Croix de Guerre avec Palme and Nancy Wake's 'pianist' - radio operator.

Nancy Wake, Companion of the Order of Australia, GM, Officier de la Légion d'honneur, Médaille de la Resistance Française, Medal of Freedom (USA), RSA Badge in Gold (NZ), famous agent, aka the *White Mouse* by the Gestapo.

Major Edwin Whetmore, Senior Field Security Officer.

Cameo role- U.S. Office of Strategic Services (OSS)

Captain Ted Fraser – An OSS officer

Cameo role - Bureau Central de Renseignements et d'Action (BCRA)

Commandant Thomas – Free French intelligence agency co-commander with SOE's Major Jacques de Guélis of Mission Tilleul

Cameo role - Royal Navy Inshore Patrol Flotilla

Lieutenant Richard Townsend DSC

There are also minor roles too numerous to list played by mostly real and occasionally, to suit the story, imagined persons.

Author's notes

Win Bisset (née **Marshall**)

Although most of my formative years were spent in Perth, Western Australia, as far as I can remember I first met Win Bisset in 1966 at the wedding of my brother, Jeremy, to her daughter, Laura, at St Martins-in-the-Fields, overlooking London's Trafalgar Square. I was told that Win had married her husband, a Frenchman called Teddy, at the same church during WWII. Laura was given away at her wedding by someone called Colonel Buckmaster who had been Teddy's commanding officer during WWII.

After the service on the way to the wedding reception, I recall clearly my father hailing a taxi and the cabbie responding to the address my father gave with the puzzling words, 'Oh, you mean the Spies' club?'

At the reception I learnt that Teddy Bisset had sadly been killed, fighting with the Resistance in France, leaving Win and Laura by themselves in London. I remember being shown a photograph of Teddy on the club walls.

Many years later I met Win regularly in Perth, Western Australia when I was either on holiday or working there. She gave my daughter, Jackie, piano lessons for a brief period. Jackie still has a tape recording of one of her lessons with Win.

In her old age, Win used to reminisce about periods of her earlier life - you can get a flavour by watching the video clip and her interview by the Grove Library, both on the Facebook public group: *A Remarkable Stillness*.

Win often repeated that she had not wanted to return to Perth after Teddy's death but had been forced to, presumably by her parents. I assumed at first she'd wanted to remain in

London, but I was wrong. In fact, as I read her diaries, it became clear she had wanted to live in France where she hoped to bring up Laura as both French and Australian. She tried unsuccessfully for some time to be posted to Paris by her employer, the *Australian Women's Weekly*.

My abiding memory of Win was her strong character and bright-eyed, attractive personality.

Teddy Bisset

Readers will notice the gap in my knowledge about Teddy's French family. I tried many times to contact them using addresses in Win's letters. Regrettably I got no response.

Mrs Gladys Marshall (The Mater)

Before I started writing this book, I had heard that The Mater was a forceful figure in Win's life. And so, it proved as I read Win's diaries. No one can doubt the reciprocal love these two, as mother and daughter, had for each other, but equally it is clear from Win's diary entries that these strong characters did not always see eye-to-eye.

In this book I write of the time when Win, The Mater and baby Laura leave London to stay at one of Win's friends at Leverington Hall, Cambridgeshire, in order to escape the V1 (Doodlebug) rocket bombardment of the English capital. Win wrote in her diary that The Mater disappeared for several hours to an unknown destination. In an example of my novelist's privilege, I imagined The Mater went off to visit her son, Lloyd Marshall, who was in an RAF Pathfinder squadron based in Graveley, Cambridgeshire – where else would she go off so secretly? Pathfinders were the aeroplanes which flew at the front of the RAF bombing raids and dropped flares to highlight the targets for the following bombers. As such they were, in turn, the prime targets for German air defences and suffered high casualties. The chances of Lloyd surviving WWII would have been low. The Pathfinder crews were rightly regarded as heroes. It is easy to imagine The Mater, as a frantic mother, nonetheless a tough, strong-willed woman, risking a strictly forbidden visit to Lloyd's high security RAF base, desperate to see her courageous son, perhaps for the last time.

I had no knowledge that the Mater was the first woman to be flown (by Kingsford Smith) across Australia. And that, helped by John Curtin, she posed as a wool merchant to fly to England to be with Win at the birth of her daughter. What an incredible woman!

SOE

Hundreds of books have been written about the history of the SOE and its agents. This book is not one of them. It is a historical novel. Although I have tried to keep as far as possible to the true story of Win and Teddy, I have used my author's privilege to imagine events, conversations and background colour. I hope the hundreds of SOE *aficionados* will bear this in mind if they feel I have occasionally overstepped the mark in describing the SOE and its activities.

Acknowledgements

I must start first by thanking Dr Peter Dixon who was of immense help to me in the initial stages of my research for *A Remarkable Stillness*. Peter's book, *Guardians of Churchill's Secret Army* about the role of Intelligence Corps' personnel in SOE, summarises Teddy and Win Bisset's story in its first chapter. This provided me with a roadmap for my own book. In an act of great generosity, Peter also gave me, in electronic form, the results of his research at London's Imperial War Museum, saving me a great deal of work. Much of the material is in the form of the numerous letters between Win and Teddy which had been donated by Win, delivered by her granddaughter, Julia Rush (see below) to the museum where they were gratefully received by Mark Seaman (see Bibliography). They provide a valuable resource for anyone researching the effect of WWII on everyday life in the UK.

Next, I must thank Win Bisset's granddaughter and my niece, Julia Rush, who kindly lent me Win's diaries which she started writing immediately after Teddy's death. Win's diary entries, written nearly every day were, in reality, letters to Teddy expressing her love, relaying news, and asking for his advice on everything from work problems to boyfriends. She regularly looked back to the couple's life together and helped me really understand their feelings as brave young people (like millions of others) confronting the horrors thrown up by WWII, resonating for me, while I wrote this book, with Putin's invasion of Ukraine.

Julia also lent me Win's short notebook on Solomon's idiosyncratic piano teaching methods. This, coupled with Bryan Crimp's *Solo*, the definitive biography of Solomon, enabled me to see how Solomon must have replicated the methods used by his saviour, the elusive Simon Rumshisky.

Teddy's first cousin, once removed, Jon Wilson, brought to life members of the Bisset clan who lived in London. Jon also solved a puzzle; a location by the name of Northfields was referred to by Teddy and Win in their letters. It turned out to be the name of Teddy's Uncle George's house in Valence Road, Muswell Hill. Win diaries some years later referred to Uncle George as being very generous to her in his will. She had no idea he was so well off.

I am very grateful to Kaye Love who was a friend of Win and Teddy's daughter, Laura, later my sister-in-law. Kaye's father was Grahame Deans – Win's first boyfriend. Kaye sent me the photographs of Win and Grahame enjoying themselves on his father's boat, *The Victory*. I've included these in the Facebook public group, *A Remarkable Stillness*.

Janet Churchouse gave me her views on piano teaching and proved a helpful sounding-board.

The memories of Solomon's great niece, Professor Dame Hazel Genn, provided me with colourful background to the great pianist's personality. What a tragedy it is Solomon seems largely forgotten today.

Delphine Isaaman's biography of her mother's cousin, *Jacques de Guelis, SOE's Genial Giant*, is a fascinating account of an ebullient, larger than life SOE character, who was an usher at Teddy and Win's wedding and his co-commanding officer on Mission Tilleul. What a tragedy his life was also ended prematurely in 1945 when his car was rammed in suspicious circumstances in Germany, about a week after Germany's surrender.

Dominique Seaux is the *guru* of information on Mission Tilleul and helped me greatly to corroborate Teddy's final military operation.

My thanks are due to our friends, Martin and Philippa Stanley, for taking my wife, Jenny, and me for the lovely walk at

Selsey along the English south coast to St Wilfred's church where I came across Kipling's poignant poem, *Eddi's Service*, which is recited in this book.

Also in Selsey, Ruth Mariner kindly sent me an aerial photograph which enabled me to identify the location of The White House where Win once was a guest.

I am grateful to my friend and author of gripping Italian detective stories set in southern Italy, Richard Walmsley, who read an early draft of this book and corrected my many grammatical errors. My West Australian publisher, Ian Hooper of Leschenault Press, deserves great credit and my thanks for his skilful editing which, combined with his erudite comments and suggestions, ensured that my book got over the finishing line in a good condition. A big thank you is also due to Brittany Wilson for her eye-catching book cover design.

Finally, I must express my immense gratitude to my wife, Jenny, without whose patience, advice and encouragement I would never have finished, *A Remarkable Stillness*.

Bibliography

In addition to Peter Dixon, Delphine Isaaman and Brian Crimp's books referred to in my 'Acknowledgements', I found the following interesting and very useful:

Mark Seaman's *Saboteur* is, in my view, the best account of an SOE agent's work, in this case the very young Tony Brooks who went on to become one of SOE's most successful operators.

He was one of the few who went on to work for MI6 after WWII. As his conducting officer, Teddy oversaw Tony's SOE training, and they became firm friends. Although Teddy accepted Tony's invitation to be the best man at his wedding to Hope Munday, he was called away on urgent SOE business. During the initial blizzard of Doodlebug (V1) attacks in 1944, Win, her mother (the Mater) and baby Laura stayed with Hope and her parents at Leverington Hall in Cambridgeshire.

A Woman of No Importance by Sonia Purnell recounts the incredible story of Virginia Hall, the American woman who, despite a prosthetic leg, became one of SOE's most effective agents. After WWII, she worked for the nascent CIA.

Sarah Hall's *A Life of Secrets* is a biography of Vera Atkins, assistant to Maurice Buckmaster, the head of SOE's F Section. Teddy worked closely with Vera Atkins while serving as an SOE staff officer, leading up to his involvement in Mission Tilleul. After the war, Atkins, to her great credit, made it her job to find out what happened to the female SOE agents in France who never returned. I found the descriptions of their torture, implicit sexual assault, and brutal murders deeply distressing.

Paddy Ashdown's *Game of Spies* is an absorbing account of a true, triangular story of betrayal, cunning and heroism among the SOE, the French Resistance and the Gestapo in Bordeaux.

David O'Keefe's *One Day In August* convinced me that the main reason for the disastrous Dieppe raid was to 'pinch' the latest version of Enigma, the German encryption machine.

I drew on Jonathan Fenby's impressively researched book, *The Sinking of the Lancastria*, for a fascinating account of the UK's greatest maritime disaster.

Printed in Great Britain
by Amazon

45043510R00179